LONEN'S WAR

SORCEROUS MOONS – BOOK 1

BY

JEFFE KENNEDY

This book was previously published with a different cover

An Unquiet Heart

Alone in her tower, Princess Oria has spent too long studying her people's barbarian enemies, the Destrye—and neglected the search for calm that will control her magic and release her to society. Her restlessness makes meditation hopeless and her fragility renders human companionship unbearable. Oria is near giving up. Then the Destrye attack, and her people's lives depend on her handling of their prince...

A Fight Without Hope

When the cornered Destrye decided to strike back, Lonen never thought he'd live through the battle, let alone demand justice as a conqueror. And yet he must keep up his guard against the sorceress who speaks for the city. Oria's people are devious, her claims of ignorance absurd. The frank honesty her eyes promise could be just one more layer of deception.

A Savage Bargain

Fighting for time and trust, Oria and Lonen have one final sacrifice to choose... before an even greater threat consumes them all.

Dedication

To Sassy Outwater,
who wanted a fire-breathing guide dog.
Close enough?

~ **1** ~

ORIA SQUINTED INTO the heat shimmer rising in the distance beyond the high walls of the city. Maybe if she looked long and hard enough, the weapons of the clashing armies would give off a telltale glitter or the shouts of the men would echo back. But, even though her high tower gave her one of the longest views in Bára, she remained blind and deaf, stuck in her chambers, remote from the battle underway.

Just as she'd lived most of her life isolated from the rest of the world.

Despite the lack of other evidence of war, the hot wind seemed to carry an unfamiliar smell to her rooftop garden. Layered among the scents of sand, the brackish bay, and distant ocean came something new. Something like roasting meat, redolent of rage, despair, and determination. An unsettling combination unlike anything she'd ever experienced. But until this, no one had attempted to attack Bára in her lifetime. Not for a long time before that either, according to the histories.

She paced the gilded balcony as Chuffta, perched on the rail, watched her without moving, green eyes sliding back and forth as if he were watching a xola match.

"You realize you walk much and get nowhere," he said in her head.

"Yes, yes—the story of my life," she snapped at her Familiar. "Besides, it's not as if I need to conserve my energy just to hide in my rooms while the city falls."

"Bára will not fall," Queen Rhianna said in a mild tone. Her nimble fingers never faltered as they wove seven needles threaded with different colors in an intricate embroidery, a casually powerful exhibition of her magical skill, her the golden metal mask that covered her face without eye holes demonstrating her ability to see in other ways. "It has not these many years and there's no reason to believe it will now. Don't put attention on a result you do not want. You know better than to articulate such thoughts, lest they manifest in truth."

Oria frowned at her mother. "I don't know any such thing, but let's try it out. Everything is fine! The Destrye army has vanished into thin air and we're no longer under attack."

Queen Rhianna sighed, leaking the barest hint of exasperation through her carefully cultivated calm. "Your casual attitude toward powerful forces beyond your ken will be your undoing, daughter. You should know better than that, too, by now."

"If they're beyond my ken, how can I respect them?" she grumbled.

"You've never met a Destrye and you fear them, so your logic is faulty," Chuffta pointed out.

She did—and fear of their ancient barbarian enemy drove her to rudeness, as Chuffta obliquely noted. Sometimes her Familiar's wisdom grated on her. Okay, a lot of the time, but he offered sincere advice and helped her when no one else could. *True growth is uncomfortable, even painful,* the temple taught. She made herself stop and stroke the winged lizard's soft white scales between his eyes. "You're right. I apologize, to both of you," she added to her mother.

"What is Chuffta right about?" her mother asked.

"That I'm afraid of the Destrye without knowing any, so my logic is bad. Though there are plenty of stories and illustrations to inform *that* opinion." Oria's longtime morbid fascination with the warrior race that shared their continent had led her to ignore the texts she was meant to study in order to linger over the vivid drawings of the Destrye with their big bodies, darkly gnarled hair, black-furred garments, eyes wild in their cruel faces. So unlike the Bárans.

"As there are similarly many stories, diagrams, demonstrations, and *lessons* on how magic works," her mother was saying in a placid yet pointed tone. "You may not yet have access to all of the temple's knowledge, but you know the basic laws. If you paid as much attention to those as to the gory histories, you might be making more progress than you are."

"Yes, but they never really *explain* anything. Like 'you'll understand *hwil* only when you master *hwil*.' How in Sgatha is that remotely helpful?"

"Some things may only be understood through experience. You know that we would tell you if it could be put into words."

Oria did know that, not that it helped. "None of this has anything to do with my original question. How can you sit and *sew* not knowing what's going on out there?" She flung an impotent hand at the desert beyond the city walls.

Her mother raised her featureless mask toward Oria. "Is pacing about like a wild thing giving you information on how the battle goes?"

"Maybe not, but it makes me feel better than sitting still does."

"I know it's difficult for you now, but once you master *hwil*, all will become clear. You'll understand that there's infinite motion in stillness, and you'll be able to channel the energy that makes you so restless into its intended purpose. You will find great relief in channeling your sgath to the common pool And, following that, you can begin to seek your perfect partner and perhaps find a temple-blessed marriage. Once connected to him, you will be able to express your magic to its greatest extent, as Sgatha intended."

Oria turned to stare into the distance again, choking back her impatience. Queen Rhianna, like the other sorcerers and sorceresses of Bára who wore the masks of their office, exemplified *hwil*, the art of peacefulness under duress. *Sgath only flows through a calm mind*, Oria's teachers explained again and again. Though they never said it out loud, in the last years their featureless golden masks seemed to hold disapproval— and the resignation of those who'd given up on her.

Oria could never sit through a full meditation session. Her body unfailingly thrummed with restlessness to get up, to do something. Her mind dashed from thought to thought, like the jewelbirds in the garden, pausing in its mad flight only to hover over the worry that she'd never find the key, never qualify to receive a mask of her own. Never realize her mother's patient hopes.

If course, the possibility that she ever would grew less likely with each passing day since she'd never even glimpsed this perfect state of *hwil* where all became clear. Of them all, only her mother remained confident that she could.

Would it be so terrible if she didn't, beyond disappointing her mother's unshakeable belief? Her three brothers had all passed the final testing, each possessing enough power and control to succeed their father, needing only marriages to solidify their positions as heirs. They'd all taken their masks before they were twenty—including her baby brother Yar the year before, a prodigy at sixteen—while Oria trailed miserably far behind, facing her twenty-second birthday within weeks.

Truly, the blow to her pride rankled. And in her secret heart, more than a little unbecoming jealousy, nursed all those years as her brothers practiced the showy battle magics below her tower, so she could at least watch. They'd meant to entertain her, not deepen her envy.

Oh, her teachers could go on about how the male grien magic was easier to learn; that it burgeoned in young men, pushing up from the ground below Bára like the sap in the trees in springtime. How they only had to practice restraint, focus, and release, and that such things came naturally to men, while women's magic worked in the reverse. Instead of exploding outward, sgath drew in and received.

Thus the emphasis on meditation, calmness, and peacefulness. A woman should be like a serene lake, always refilling from those deep wells, so she could nurture with her magic. The sacred blessing of creation belonged to women, a divine obligation that provided Bára and her sister cities with the blessing of fruits, greens, and grains in the desert.

In the most exalted partnership, a sgath sorceress and a grien sorcerer married with temple blessing, their magics complementing and enhancing each other in a perfectly balanced flow. She to receive and grow magical energy, he to focus and release it. For this reason, the temple frowned on same-sex partnerships as not ideal, though they weren't strictly forbidden. Many settled for lesser marriages, not temple-blessed, and every person regardless of gender possessed some sgath and some grien, in different measures. Even the purest and strongest sgath carried a seed of grien, just as their parent moons, Sgatha and Grienon, waxed and waned, one around the other's orbit. Diligent study led a sorcerer or sorceress to develop his or her best self, all the better to serve Bára.

And that best self would be reflected in a temple-blessed marriage, such as her parents enjoyed. An ideal none of Oria's brothers had yet achieved. Something she could be first in, if only she could find a way to be still long enough to grasp the essence of *hwil*.

If only.

As the partnered sorceresses of the city did their half of the work of defense, the halcyon shimmer of women's magic pooled below Oria's tower, radiating from their stations on the walls, flowing out like a reverse bore tide. Queen Rhianna would have been with them if she hadn't elected to keep her daughter company. As it was, between the immense power of her sgath and her temple-blessed marriage with the king, she could be anywhere and feed him magic, a constant vital flow Oria sensed but could no more access than she could the battle taking place leagues away.

Thus it remained the sorceresses' job to stay within the protective circle of Bára while the men went forth to battle the Destrye with their powerful grien, fueled by sgath.

"This system has worked for centuries," Chuffta told her. *"In this way the cities have survived many onslaughts."*

"Like you've been around for any more of them than I have," Oria retorted in a dry tone, but scratched Chuffta's wing joints where he couldn't easily reach them. He arched his neck, purring as she relieved an itch.

Her mother had no trouble following that thought. "Chuffta may be young, as you are, but the derkesthai have stood by and advised many a queen and princess of our line while our armies fought in the distance. I know you'd fret less if you could be directing your energy to feeding power to our sorcerers, but your time will come. The women in our family are like—"

"Like the fruit that ripens in the dry season, long after the rains have passed," Oria chimed along with the familiar adage. "I know, I know. Unless they don't bloom at all." Like her various aunts, exiled to live in other walled cities, far from the temple and the source of all magic.

Queen Rhianna tilted her face up, as if looking at her daughter, though she wouldn't be literally. The smooth golden mask of the sorceress gazed at her with eyeless serenity. "Or all the more powerful for the slow ripening. I would not have made the journey to invite Chuffta to be your Familiar and guide for when you take your mask unless I believed you would find your magic. Nor would you be able to hear him if you were mind-dead."

"Nor would I have agreed to put up with you for any other reason," Chuffta teased in his dry mind-voice.

"I know you love me. You think I'm charming, brilliant—and funny." She stroked the winged lizard's softly scaled hide, always soothing with its sueded texture. Of all her fears, the possibility of losing Chuffta worried her most. They'd been together since her seventh birthday. He was the greatest gift she'd ever received. If she failed to take her mask, he'd have no reason to stay with her. She could deal with a life without being a sorceress, even with a mind-dead half-marriage without magical completion—though what an unhappy life that would be—but living without the rustle of Chuffta's thoughts in her head? A desolate prospect, indeed.

"What people believe becomes real." Chuffta echoed her mother's advice.

If only it were that easy. Like a jewelbird going to the wrong blossoms, Oria's thoughts seemed to forever return to the worst-case scenario. The dreadful potential outcomes of any situation filled her head far more readily than any other. Unbidden, they sprang to life in her mind. So much so that she diligently hid the extent of them from Chuffta, her teachers, and especially her mother. A woman's sgath magic could turn toxic, undermining as easily as it nurtured. If they knew how poisonous her thoughts could be, they'd stop training her altogether. The techniques they taught were far too potent to chance in irresponsible hands.

Another warning repeated far too often for comfort.

It all came down to this: She must learn to calm and quiet her mind. To be like her mother and live serenely behind the mask of a priestess, with no desire to pace in restless agitation, only happy thoughts running through her mind, not dread of the future.

Focusing on positive images, she determinedly rehearsed them in her head. The Destrye would go back to their sterile and magicless land. The battle would be won, perhaps so soundly that the fierce warrior people would never come after hers again. Bára would be safe and her father would peacefully hold his throne for many joyful years to come. Her brothers would continue the elaborate courtship and testing rituals to find their ideal wives among the priestesses of the temple, which she wanted for them with all her heart. (Never mind that little corner blackened with jealousy—she'd excise it.) *Focus on the result you want.* And she, herself, a paragon of peaceful maturity with vast powers of concentration, would find her *hwil* and receive her mask. Somewhere out there, her perfect match awaited, too. Perhaps she already knew him, and he only needed her to grow just a bit more so they could join in a blissful, eternal union.

A fine hope. Though more unlikely with every passing day. Especially with the Destrye attacking.

"When will they send news?" she muttered at the horizon.

This time, no one answered her.

~ 2 ~

Lonen swung his iron axe with grim determination, ignoring the sweat dripping from his soaked hair into his eyes. This land of burning sun roasted a man as surely as a slow fire tenderized a haunch of meat. The golem dropped, halved by his axe, and three more took its place while Alby, Lonen's first lieutenant, followed to chop apart the fallen one. Emotionless, thoughtless, the monster creatures advanced in relentless, silent waves, tearing with long, saber-sharp claws, rending Destrye flesh with crystalline-fanged mouths if they got near enough.

For too many years his people had superstitiously feared engaging the golems in battle, terrified by the things that felt no weapon, that kept coming with implacable strength, shredding every living creature between them and their goal. Until Ayden the Great had discovered by happenstance—and via the dire necessity of being trapped and alone when golems attacked his camp—that iron affected the creatures as nothing else did. The legend of Ayden, all on his own, killing a squad of the invincible golems with only the iron pick he used to clean his horse's hooves was told and retold among all the Destrye.

The epic tale replaced despair with hope—and had been the turning point in the war, just as Lonen had been old enough to shoulder his iron axe and help with his peoples' defense.

With the discovery that iron could take out the lifeless puppets the Bárans employed, King Archimago had implemented new strategies. But despite their early exultation at being able to fight back, the end of the conflict remained a distant dream and, unfortunately, plenty of despair remained. The hope wore thin quickly enough under the grind of what turned out to be the beginning of actual war, with the Destrye fighting back instead of hiding from the golems' raids and eerily quiet rampages.

They'd reduced the incursions for a time, but the enemy rallied, sending more golems until there seemed to be two for every one that fell. And forcing the Destrye to abandon Dru's lakes, one after another to be drained by the golems' unquenchable thirst and the endless chain of wagons taking the water away in barrels that held far more than seemed possible.

Finally, it became clear that all of Dru would wither and die, and the Destrye people would erode to nothing under the relentless onslaught. For every step they took forward, the enemy set them back two. So the king had sent his best trackers to follow the supply chains and find the source of the monsters. By dint of years of effort and many lives lost, they'd located the puppet masters, those who stole the Destrye's most precious and lamentably finite resource. The scouts had brought back the first descriptions of the crimson-robed men who wore smooth metal masks and commanded tremendous—and impossible—magics.

Getting within reach of them had taken more months of slow effort.

Alby cut apart two of the golems Lonen had cleaved with his axe, while Lonen hacked up the other. No more immediately surged into the space, not with the way his men had moved their perimeter. Lonen took advantage of the momentary lull to study the flow of the battle, beyond the center section under his command.

They'd come farther than the Destrye ever had before, reaching the apparently placid shallow brackish bay where a once mighty river had once emptied to the sea. The sudden treacherous bore tides had drowned a number of Destrye and their mounts, too entrenched in the silt to escape the onrushing surf that arrived with a roar like thunder. Finally, though, they'd learned to time their crossing to the moons, then found this strangely hot and barren land on the other side.

The plain of battle might be teeming with the featureless, waxy, pale golems as always, but for the first time their troops had cleaved through enough of them to come within sight of the golden-masked sorcerers who directed the monsters, and the towers of the walled city of Bára beyond.

King Archimago had thrown everything into this conflict, and the battlefield showed it, teeming with bold Destrye warriors. He'd even committed his sons, Lonen fighting shoulder-to-shoulder with his three brothers. After all, of what use were a king's heirs if all their people died?

They'd done well, pressing the enemy ever back, drawing within sight of the distant walled city that spawned the foul magic users. But then they stalled against the bulwark of those cursed sorcerers, who'd turned out to wield even more devastating magics than the scouts had reported.

To the right, a legion of Destrye surged, making swift inroads. Too swift, it turned out, as they drew the attention of one of the sorcerers. A tall man in a golden mask raised his hands and fire flew from them, forming a blazing ball that shot into the merciless blue sky, then rained down on the Destrye troops. The men screamed, hair and clothing catching fire, then disappeared from view as they fell.

The battle mages only seemed able to send the fireballs within a certain distance, not unlike an archer's range. They also avoided singeing their golems, which had a distressing tendency to melt into a viscous substance that clung and singed Destrye flesh if a fighter remained too close. It became a tricky proposition as more golems fell before the Destrye's iron, opening a gap between the front line of assault and the long phalanx of golden-masked men on their platforms—and creating a clear path for the fireballs.

Taking heed of the lesson, Lonen gave orders to draw his men back. "Keep it tight and steady!" he shouted.

Under Lonen's feet, the earth rumbled and shifted, making him stumble to catch his balance. Relieved of the incessant need to hack through the golems, Lonen observed what he could as they withdrew. He scanned the Báran mages and, sure enough, another had his arms upraised, his faceless mask pointed off to the left, where Lonen's older brother Nolan led his forces. Another rumble, like thunder from below, and the ground cracked open, a jagged black lightning bolt of doom. Destrye and golems alike spilled over the crumbling edges like precious water through the bottom of a broken bucket, plunging into the great crevasse.

The despairing cries of falling Destrye added to the screams of those burning, though the golems remained, as ever, eerily silent. Lonen fought a similar plunge of his heart. Not Nolan, his laughing dreamer of a brother. Surely he'd stayed well back and remained safe.

His older brother Ion forged his way through Lonen's line of sight from the other direction, a line of blood dripping from a score down his temple and cheek. Lonen set his own men against the wedge of Ion's battalion to hold a perimeter against the golems surging from the fore, and to cleave a larger path for Ion's men. Lonen himself took down five more of the things, chopping them with his axe like so much firewood, ignoring how the pieces feebly plucked at his boots as he stepped on them.

Spiking the warriors' boots with iron nails to further decimate the golems had been another of King Archimago's strokes of genius.

"We have to take out the mages or we'll be entirely lost," Ion gritted once he got close enough. "Father says pull back. The closer we get, the more easily they employ those greater magics."

Lonen bit down on an argument. To come so near and withdraw felt very much like defeat. But of course they were right. It made no sense to destroy the golem army only to dash themselves against the implacable forces the battle mages wielded.

Nodding, he set his men to creating a new perimeter, fitting them against the forces on his other flank, directed by his brother Arnon. Ion moved on with his battalion, taking over those between Lonen and the great crack in the earth, all that remained of Nolan's section of the battlefield.

Was Nolan even now clinging to a crumbling lip—or writhing broken at the bottom of the chasm? He couldn't bear to contemplate it.

Fortunately, the press of battle, of staging their retreat while holding a firm line at their backs, required all Lonen's attention. If his brother had indeed died, there would be time enough later to mourn.

If Lonen even survived that long.

THEY GATHERED HOURS later, wearied, covered in smeared ash and blood, in King Archimago's tent: Lonen, Ion, and Arnon, and their father.

Nolan had not been found. He was lost, along with an entire regiment of brave Destrye.

Their father leaned his head in his hands, visibly aged since they'd engaged in battle that morning, on top of the years he'd already piled on in the past months of fighting to get within striking distance of their faceless enemy. Ion dismissed the retainers, the captains of other regiments. This moment was for family.

Stepping around the table, he put a hand on their father's shoulder. "We don't know he's dead."

The king laughed without humor, a sharp crack like the one that had rent the earth. "Would you wish him alive and trapped below ground with those monsters? Perhaps captured and tortured by those sorcerers?"

A dismal thought that hadn't occurred to Lonen. Nor to his two remaining brothers, by the expressions on their faces.

"It could be I was wrong to bring us all here," Archimago said into his palms, his voice weak, nothing like the robust warrior who'd taught Lonen everything he knew.

"We couldn't know their powers would be so enormous." Ion gripped their father's shoulder. "There was no way to know, short of this battle."

Lonen leaned his axe against the table, shoulders tired and aching now that he'd stepped away from the fight. His men would be exhausted, too, and they'd soon have to rotate out the ones holding the defensive line around the encampment. Two hours of rest at a time, no more. So far the sorcerers hadn't pursued their forces, which made no sense. True, the golems continued to attack, but why not open the earth beneath the Destrye tents and rain fire and storms on them from above? Had Lonen been in their position, he would have pressed the advantage, eliminating his enemies from under the sun forever. If only.

"There wasn't any way for the scouts to assess a thing that never showed until now," Arnon added, catching Lonen's eye. "We had to walk this path to discover what we now know."

"Besides"—Lonen took his cue from his younger brother— "you made the only choice you could. We were forced into the offensive. Had we stuck to the old ways, the Destrye would have surely perished."

Their father raised his head, eyes dark in his weathered face. "And now we will be decimated in one fell swoop, immediately instead of through slow erosion."

"Even if we all die on this battlefield," put in Arnon, always the philosophical one, "the Destrye are not destroyed. This assault has at least provided a diversion for the rest of our people to escape to a new place. A land where they can live in peace."

"A caravan of women guarded by boys and old men." The king shook his head wearily, staring at his hands on the scarred wooden table covered with maps of all the territory they'd crossed. "If only I'd sent Nolan with them. He would be still alive and the Destrye not scattered to the tides."

Lonen and his brothers exchanged looks over their father's head. It wasn't like him to second-guess his decisions. None of the choices had been easy ones—even though they'd seemed simple, forced on them by their ruthless enemy. But now the king seemed already defeated, as if they'd lost the war instead of the day's battle.

In truth, they'd lost a great deal that day. Perhaps more than they could recover from, and yet—

"Why haven't they come after us?" Lonen found himself saying aloud.

Arnon frowned at the change of subject, but Ion, their father's heir, nodded in approval. "It's a good question, and we should take that into account in planning our next strategy."

"Our next strategy?" Their father looked from one of them to the next, his blank black eyes seeming to see only the grief-filled images that haunted them. "There is nothing more we can do except attempt to flee. They've destroyed half our forces."

"But why only half?" Lonen persisted.

"*Only* half?" Arnon echoed incredulously. "That's ten thousand men who died in our service that you're dismissing."

"They died to protect our people," Lonen growled, "for the very same reason you and I fought today. Not for a throne but for their wives and children who were forced to flee even as they marched away from them. And yes, I say 'only' because they could have killed us all. The fireballs, the earthquakes, the thunderstorms—you saw the power of their magic. Why aren't we *all* dead?"

"Because we pulled back," Ion said, looking thoughtful. "We're out of range now."

"Exactly," Lonen replied. "And something is keeping them from pursuing and keeping us within range. What?"

The king sat up straighter. "We need to find out. That could be the key to emerging from this debacle victorious after all."

In the silence of his skull, Lonen thought victory might be a little much to hope for. Forestalling total destruction of the Destrye, however, remained a hope, however slim. With his mother, his sisters, and his beloved Natly on their way to who knows where, he'd resigned himself to never seeing them again, never feeling the kiss of Natly's lovely lips, the silk of her darkly oiled hair. If he could buy them a better life with his death, then it would be well worth paying.

"Yes." Ion sat at the table, nodding at his brothers to follow suit. "Call in the captains and every scout we can recall. We need to pool our information and plan our strategy."

~ 3 ~

At long last, the next morning, the Báran army returned.

Oria held vigil from her tower as always, Chuffta beside
her, though Queen Rhianna had long since descended to greet
her victorious husband and sons. Somewhere in the cheering
throngs below, beneath the shredded flowers tossed from high
towers all around, they'd be embracing and celebrating the
joyous day.

*"You'll see them soon enough, and it would be difficult for you to
withstand that level of energy."*

"Yes, yes—I know." Yet another drawback of not yet mas-
tering *hwil*. Oria, like all those gifted with sgath, tended to
absorb any and all energy around her. She'd always been
excessively fragile. Without the skill to ground the sgath and
feed it to another, she overfilled, which resulted in shameful
meltdowns. Chuffta served as a buffer for her, but he could do
only so much. Living within the walls of Bára helped, of
course, and being up in her tower made a huge difference,
something her mother had known and insisted on since Oria
was very young. She couldn't remember any other life.

Mostly Oria had played alone or with perfectly *hwil* nurse-
priestesses, and even as an adult she descended from her tower
only on the most tranquil days for brief appearances as the sole

royal princess or to attend critical temple ceremonies. Otherwise, only those with perfect control of their emotional output were allowed to visit or wait on her. Thus she spent most of her days on the sunny terrace with a nearly complete view of Bára, biding her time to suddenly understand *hwil*, watching real lives from above.

"Princess." Alva, her lady-in-waiting, came out and curtsied, no whisper of emotion emanating from behind her smooth mask. "Her royal highness Queen Rhianna asks me to tell you that the family will convene for the midday meal in the second-level salon so that you may join them."

"Thank you, Alva. Tell her I look forward to hearing the news." Oria had already bathed and dressed for the day, so she had nothing to do but wait. And pace around her small perimeter, observing the jubilation of the city. Hours yet to kill. If only she could fly like Chuffta, she could zoom into the sky and circle above everyone, at least able to see the victory parade.

"*Perhaps use this time to practice meditation?*" Chuffta suggested in a gentle tone.

Oria sighed. The last thing she wanted to do was sit and attempt to calm her mind. But as always, her Familiar offered good advice. Her family showed thoughtfulness in coming to her; they all had excellent control, and naturally, all were masters of *hwil*. Energy would likely still run high in the room—particularly as a meal of the royal family required more than her few servants—and she'd handle it better if she at least attempted to ground herself beforehand.

She plopped herself down onto the sun-heated tiles, folding her legs and arranging her skirts around her so the raw silk wouldn't wrinkle, forcing a change of clothes.

"*Would you like me to guide you?*"

"Yes, please." With Chuffta's help, she could go deeper, get closer to mental stillness than she could without. Not that it was enough to come anywhere near the state of *hwil* others described, something she failed to do, over and over.

"Shh. Let go of those thoughts. You are who you are. I love you as you are. Forget the expectations. Hwil is different for everyone, and you'll find your path to yours. Now, imagine a deep blue lake. Lovely, pure, and warm. You're standing on the shore, warm water lapping your toes. It is peaceful, restful. You step in, the water lapping around your ankles. You go deeper, the water surrounding, embracing, accepting you. With each step, you count backwards from one-hundred. Ninety-nine. Ninety-eight. Ninety-seven…"

Oria followed along, seeing and feeling as Chuffta suggested. Absorbing the directions from his mind-voice was easier than when her teachers guided aloud. Mostly because they always seemed to have that *tone*. Though they offered her the deference due her rank, they still condescended to her untutored ways. Especially High Priestess Febe.

"With each step, your thoughts dissipate into the water. The cool, deep blue water fills your being, giving you peace, joy, calm."

Chuffta didn't judge her, and she calmed, sinking into the deep waters. Still, part of her stood aside, wondering if there might be fish in the lake. If so, what kind would they be? She'd never seen a lake, of course, but she'd read descriptions and pored over the illustrations. Bigger lakes and oceans had fish that lived in them, apparently. So there could be many of them, schools of fish brightly darting about. Flashing here and there. Then scattering at the approach of a predator. Large and sharp toothed, it arose from the depths of the water, an immense shadow that resolved into the hard face of an axe-wielding Destrye warrior. What had happened at the battle? Had the Bárans vanquished the enemy entirely, banished them back to whatever wilderness they'd emerged out of? Impatience to know rippled through her. How much time had passed—would lunch be soon?

"Nearly," Chuffta said. *"And that's enough for now."*

Abruptly Oria recalled that she was meant to be meditating. The same thing happened every time. She always started out with the best of intentions, then got distracted along the way, her thoughts turning to more interesting ideas than a pure, deep lake, enticing as that image might be. "Sorry," she said, chagrined. Sometimes it seemed she'd spent her life apologizing for the same failure, over and over.

"Then don't apologize. This is not a failure. The window will open for you when you're ready."

"I'm ready! I don't know how to make myself be more ready than this."

Chuffta laughed in her mind. *"You cannot force this. It must come in its own time."*

"Wonderful. Just like lunch." She stood and offered her forearm for Chuffta to hop onto. "We might as well go down and wait for them."

The lizard spread his wings for the short flight from the balustrade to her, his claws sinking into the leather padding of her sleeve, his sinuous tail winding around her wrist. All her gowns were made with thick shields on her left forearm and shoulder, so he could accompany her everywhere. Ironic, as she so seldom left her tower, but it spoke to the eternal optimism that she'd take her mask at any moment and be free to walk about Bára like everyone else.

Alva fell in beside her, then opened the double doors to her rooms that always remained closed, though the buffer they provided was primarily symbolic. Guards kept watch over the tower at the base and at several intermediary levels between, but almost never ventured to the top three floors. And any priest or battle mage who'd achieved enough *hwil* for Oria to tolerate his nearness could be better used elsewhere in the city, for the many magical feats that kept Bára running with such beauty and efficiency. Or, more recently, for defending Bára against the Destrye.

Chuffta, too, acted as a formidable bodyguard.

They wended down the wide circular stairs to the next level. Large windows let in light and air, keeping the interior fresh and breezy. She wasn't the first princess of her line to spend a good twenty years sequestered in the tower—her mother had done the same—and generations before had gone to considerable lengths to make it a pleasant place to live, if one could get over the seething restlessness. Sometimes Oria fancied she sensed the fidgety energy of past residents in the stone walls, radiating out like the residual heat of day lingering long after sunset.

"The victory is most welcome news, Princess," Alva offered in a smooth tone.

Oria gave her a speculative glance. "Is that verifiable information, or assumption?"

"Assumption. Would there be cheering and a parade without victory? And no enemy is pouring through our gates."

"You were on the walls for the battle yesterday—couldn't you sense how things went?"

Alva shook her head, smooth mask gleaming. "Without a husband, I only feed sgath into the common pool. It feels much like being a vessel that knows not who drinks the water it pours."

Suppressing a shudder—something about that image crawled under her skin in an unpleasant way—Oria didn't reply. She had no good reason to think it, but something told her the return of the army signaled only a pause in the conflict. The breeze coming in the wide windows carried that scent, of something carnal, full of rage. It hadn't gone away. Not far enough.

"Trust that intuition."

"Do you sense it, too?" she murmured to Chuffta.

"No, silly. You are the sorceress in this relationship. I don't sense exactly what you do—I only taste some of it through you. Being sensitive is a gift as well as a curse. Of course you sense what others do not."

Of course. From meat-filled scents to the echoes of restive ancestresses in the very stones of the tower, all very reasonable and rational to pay attention to.

Chuffta mentally snorted. *"I never called you rational."*

"Gee, thanks."

Alva, long accustomed to Oria's one-sided conversations, remained quiet, pausing to open the doors to the salon with a studied sweep of her graceful arms. Shouts broke through, slapping Oria like a physical blow. She gasped, clutching the doorframe lest the energy knock her backward.

"Steady." Chuffta hopped up to her shoulder, only the tip of his tail remaining around her wrist, the rest winding down her arm like a decorative band, and stroked her cheek with his angled head. *"Let it pass through."*

"Calm down, please." Queen Rhianna's voice remained mellifluous, but nevertheless carried the tone of maternal command they all responded to without thought. Even though the reprimand had been directed at Oria's brothers, it worked on her, too, steadying her as much as Chuffta's stabilizing presence in her mind.

If only her mother could follow her around all her life, chiming gentle reminders.

Oria smothered a grimace at the thought and cooled her expression into a facsimile of serenity. *Hwil* might remain out of her reach for the moment, but she'd mastered the appearance of it. The smooth golden masks of her family all turned to face her.

"Forgive us for startling you, Oria. We arrived earlier than expected," her father said, holding out his hands. "You look lovely and peaceful today, flower of my heart."

She took his hands and let him draw her into his strong embrace, inhaling the feel of him. With her parents, being flesh of their flesh, born of their magical energy, she could enjoy physical contact without reserve. Always so welcome. He'd bathed and changed into fresh clothes for their meal, out of the crimson priest's robes he and her brothers would have worn into battle, and into the light, beige ones that better forgave the midday heat.

In turn, each of her brothers embraced her; some of their young male excitement buzzing through their *hwil* like a displaced swarm from a broken hive even though they carefully touched her only over her gown, so she kept the contact brief. They all treated her as if she might break apart, which irritated even as she appreciated the consideration her parents had drummed into them regarding their delicate sister. Still, there was nothing wrong with her physical body. The healer-priestesses pronounced her strong as a desert pony.

It was inside that she remained as fragile as a blown-glass figurine.

"Let us sit." Queen Rhianna spread her hands at the table, the waxed wood gleaming gold. They arranged themselves around it, her father at the head, her mother at the foot, her eldest brother, Nat, at their father's right hand, the second eldest, Ben, at his left. Oria sat at her mother's right hand, her younger brother, Yar, across from her. Her mother linked hands with her, but Ben hovered his palm over hers, symbolically sparing her the stress of skin-to-skin contact. It impacted her less from her siblings, but they were different enough from her not to be in as perfect harmony as her parents.

"We give thanks for the gift of *hwil*," the king intoned. "Which both protects us from the power of grien and sgath and allows us to draw from their blessings, to share with all the world. Here, in this safe place, we remove our masks and take the sustenance of food and drink with those we love best."

Oria folded her hands in her lap while servants stepped forward with dainty silver knives, one for each royal, and cut the knotted ribbons of their masks. Her family held the masks in place, then removed them as one, setting them reverently on the mats to their left, placed there for that express purpose. They accepted damp cloths, perfumed with menthol herbs, to cool their flushed faces. Alva gave a cloth to Oria also, a long-established courtesy to include the royal children who'd not yet taken their masks.

They meant well, but the rest of her family actually *needed* the cloths. So instead of playing the game of wiping away nonexistent sweat in exaggerated gestures as she had growing up, Oria set hers aside, making a deliberate effort to let go of the feeling of being excluded. Chuffta sent her an affectionate thought. Giving back the cloths, her family relaxed and smiled at one another, her favorite part of the ritual. Though she knew their faces well, it warmed her heart to see them again. The king accepted a flask of wine and poured for them all, the servants bringing them first to the queen, then to Oria, and then to her brothers in reverse age order.

She held her glass until her father raised his. "To my beautiful family."

Not to victory, as she'd anticipated. The wine, kept chilled on ice in the cellars even through the hottest season, tasted lightly sweet as the fragrance of day-blooming flowers, but the faint scent of roasting meat drifted through her head nonetheless. Her father and brothers all smelled on the surface like the honeyed soap the men preferred, and yet it seemed the smell of carnage clung to them, tingeing the flavor of the wine with the bitterness of char. Oria swallowed back against it.

"What news of the battle then?" she asked as the servants brought out the first course, a cold berry cream soup.

Her brothers all glanced at their father, though Yar gave her a cheeky grin first, clearly pleased with himself. King Tav's expression remained calm, revealing nothing. "Always so impatient, my gifted daughter."

A mild reproof, but one that stung. Yes, yes—if she had *hwil*, she wouldn't have prompted them for information. Still, they all knew she struggled with impatience, so it didn't need reiterating. Oria blew out a retort without speaking it and focused on her soup. Delicious, a perfect complement to the wine. But not enough to distract her from the undercurrents beneath the apparently peaceful meal. Her brothers might have silenced their voices, but their emotions ran high. Their bright energy tugged at her, eroding her hard-won calm like a receding tide dragging at the sandy shore.

Her father let the silence stretch out and finally Oria set down her glass spoon so carefully that it made no sound. "I can feel that things aren't right and it's getting to me. Would you please tell me what happened before I have to excuse myself?"

Her mother gave her an approving smile. Much as Oria hated confessing to crumbling control, she'd finally agreed that was better than melting down because she wouldn't admit to it.

"Tav," Rhianna said, "there's no need to push her. Not today."

Her father's eyes rested on his wife with burning warmth, a slight smile breaking the calm of his visage. He gestured to his man to remove the soup. "As always, you are wise. This, then, is what occurred. The Destrye had indeed made their way to within leagues of the city and seemed determined to storm the walls."

"*Unfortunate,*" Chuffta commented, the irony settling her thrill of fear. Her mother, naturally, showed no reaction, but it seemed not all the dismay belonged to Oria.

"But we were victorious!" Yar burst through, that cocky grin cracking his unfortunately still-pimpled cheeks. "We halved their numbers and sent them scrambling. They were still retreating this morning. Let the cowardly barbarians run with their tails between their legs!"

"And us harrying them with golems all the way," Ben added with a thin smile of triumph. Of all her brothers, Ben had been the oldest when he took the mask. Not as old as Oria was now, but they'd at least shared the struggle to find *hwil* that Nat and Yar had escaped. Privately Oria thought the trial had tempered him, made him less impetuous than her other brothers—and that he'd be a better heir than Nat because of it.

Nat…he had a meanness to him. She'd stopped mentioning it because everyone told her that older brothers always give grief to their little sisters. Chuffta didn't like him either, which validated her unease.

"*I don't have a good reason, though,*" Chuffta mused. "*He reminds me of those sand mites that get under the scales.*"

She smiled a little at that and found Nat watching her with cold eyes, as if he somehow knew she discussed him. "Don't be afraid, baby sister," he said. "Unfortunate that you're too fragile to leave your tower more often than a few times a year, but we're here to protect you. Those meat-headed warriors ran away, squealing like little girls."

"They did!" Yar crowed, clearly delighted. "And now we'll be able to return to the business of finding our ideal wives. I bet I find mine first. Pretty Priestess Jania seems likely."

"You don't even know what she looks like under her mask," Nat scoffed.

"I can see the shape of her body well enough. Besides, her face doesn't matter. It's the matching of sgath and grien that does." Yar rubbed his palms together. "So far we match."

"You wish you could find a temple-blessed marriage," Ben muttered, a bitterness to it. From what Oria gathered, his testing and courtship went as slowly as his qualifying for the mask had. Though he didn't discuss such things with her. "You'll be beyond lucky to find a priestess who can barely tolerate your touch."

"He does, because he wants to tup someone besides—"

"And if the Destrye don't continue to retreat?" Queen Rhianna interrupted Nat.

"Well, they will," Nat replied, with a confident nod. "Why wouldn't they? We decimated them."

Their father waved off his half-eaten salad, leaned his elbows on the table in its place, steepled his fingers, and met his wife's gaze. Their magical connection clicked into place, the cycle of their regard flowed between them, warming Oria like the rising sun on a frosty morning. Like her father's embrace and the cool calm of her mother's presence, the perfectly balanced partnership between her parents grounded Oria more than all the meditation and mental discipline lessons.

"If they don't, we will have to take other steps," the king said slowly, speaking only to the queen. "Tell the priestesses to build all the sgath possible. We may need it."

~ 4 ~

L ONEN LED HIS men across the sand, which swirled like so much soft shadow with Sgatha not yet risen to shed her rosy light and Grienon—in the sky as he nearly always was—falling into his darkest phase, then to slowly wax to full white in the next few hours.

The sleeping city loomed ahead, shrouded in dim lights and traces of fog rolling off the ocean in the chill night air. How it could be so cold at night when the days blazed so hot made no sense. Thankful for his black fur cloak, both for the warmth and the way it helped him blend into the night, Lonen pulled the hood closer around his face, paying close attention to his footing.

They'd waited for this night, this hour, charting the moons for the best shrouding darkness. The golems moved by night as well as by day—as Ayden the Great had discovered to his sorrow and Dru's triumph—but low light confused their vision. It had been a considered gamble, waiting so long, giving the Báran sorcerers time to replenish the golem ranks the Destrye had painstakingly hacked their way through. Of course, the entire war had been a calculated risk, betting the potential future of their people against their certain destruction. Not much of a choice in the end, put in those terms.

So far events had played as predicted. The Destrye had

fully decamped and marched away from Bára for days at a time, allowing just enough golems to pursue unharmed to convey back to their masters that the rout continued in full force. The army withdrew to the far hills, which at least held enough game to replenish their food supplies, though far less than even Dru's declining forests.

When the moons' phases allowed, Lonen and Arnon had peeled off with small troops, seeing them through the silent lines of their pursuers, then releasing the men under trusted lieutenants to creep back to Bára's environs in secret. Lonen and Arnon then returned to the main force to ostentatiously march again the next day.

None of their scholars could be sure how intelligent the golems were, if they could recognize the faces or scents of the human leaders, but it didn't pay to be careless. Lonen's hunting dogs knew him from his brothers—why wouldn't the golem hounds belonging to the Báran sorcerers?

In this way they left behind pieces of the Destrye forces, like the goddess Arill scattering seeds across the land, orchards growing in her wake. Except the Destrye seeded the Bárans' destruction, carefully building over days and weeks.

Finally, Lonen rejoined all those men he'd scattered to the winds, taking several days to travel at night and hide himself during daylight, timing his crossing to avoid the blazingly fast and lethal bore tides of the bay before Bára. Somewhere out there Ion, Arnon, the king, and their best captains did likewise. They'd form a net around the desert city and draw the sorcerers away from the walls. Scattered thinly enough by attack on all sides, the defense would have to fail at one point or another—allowing the crack Destrye squads into the city with a single mission in mind.

Destroy the source of the sorcerers' power.

Another gamble there, that the sorcerers had not pursued beyond a fixed range because they dared not go too far from the source of their magic. In a perfect world, the Destrye would have spent time on feints, testing the theory, determining the range.

But the world had stopped being perfect the first time the golems raided.

As Lonen and his men slipped through the wandering golems who milled about, ghostly white in the darkness, in a loose defense around the city, he prayed that his squad would make it through the walls. Not for glory—there would be no glory this night—but to spare himself the grief of losing another of his brothers. Or his father. There'd been no word from Natly or his mother and sisters. No message from any of their dispersed people on the Trail of New Hope. They hadn't truly expected any. King Archimago thought it best to leave no connection between the refugees and the warriors who went after their enemy. The other half of their people were as safe as any could make them.

Still, Lonen's mind insisted on imagining their gruesome deaths at the fangs and claws of pursuing golems. Defended by only a few, the women, children, and elderly would be easy pickings. They carried little water with them, relying on the old maps to guide them to oases, so the golems should have no reason to pursue, but there was always a chance…

Too many gambles, too much reliance on luck: a fickle goddess at best and a vengeful bitch at worst.

In the distance, shouts went up. Ion's men, judging by the direction. They'd engaged the enemy and as agreed, upon running afoul of the golem net first, were sending up as much noise as possible. The battle mages, inevitably alerted, should focus their defensive efforts there.

Time to move quickly, before their enemy realized they'd been stealthily surrounded—as much as a walled city with rock spires at her back could be. Signaling to his men, Lonen broke into a ground-eating lope. They fanned out, iron axes and knives swinging in a pattern to intercept the golems that loomed up out of the dark. Lonen's axe bit, his momentum taking him into a sickening collision with the creature's slick, resilient body, a foul parody of a lover's embrace. Claws raked his back before Lonen yanked back the axe to slice through the golem from the other direction. Gritting his teeth against the pain, he finished the thing, then ran to catch up with his men.

He passed a few, wrestling their own monsters here and there, but kept going. That was the rule of this engagement— any man who could get to the wall, should. No stopping to help anyone. They weren't out to survive the night. At least not past getting into the city and destroying the source of the sorcerers' power.

Whatever it might be.

Fireballs flew through the night, heralding the arrival of the mages. The magic fire lit the sky to nearly daylight brilliance; illuminating Lonen, his men, and the entire area. A miscalculation there, as the golems, upon seeing them so clearly, gave chase from all directions. Fortunately for Lonen's chances, unfortunately for Arnon's, most of the golems moved toward the brightest light, leaving Lonen and his men relatively unfettered by the mindless creatures.

Lights also flared into life on the city walls, moving in a progressive wave, voices carrying through the thin desert air. This time there would be no retreat. They'd committed utterly. King Archimago had left some forces in reserve, to send after the refugees on the Trail of New Hope should this attempt fail, but otherwise he'd bring the remainder of the army up behind them with the intent of slaughtering first the golems then the hopefully incapacitated battle mages.

If they all died, they'd do it knowing they'd given everything to the effort.

Lonen and his men reached the shadow of the wall after a long slog through the soft, still-hot sand dunes massed against it. Destrye scouts had noted during the previous disastrous battle that various gates studded the walls. A large main gate faced the road, big enough to admit wagons and other conveyances. As it had in the previous battle, that gate opened, vomiting out a torrent of battle mages on wagons pulled by golems, the sorcerers' golden masks shining as brightly as the torches they reflected as they moved into position. No going that route.

Though that had never been the plan. Instead Lonen and his squad ran for the smaller gates. The first they came to was, of course, tightly closed and barred. That was fine. They didn't intend to go *through* it. Lonen would use it as a platform to lever up. Gripping his knife between his teeth, his axe secured to his back, he clambered along the bars of the gate. He reached the lintel above, hauling himself up.

Pausing there, he set a spike between the stones, pounding it in with a hammer from his belt and looping a rope through it. He dropped the free end, waiting for Alby's tug to confirm he'd grasped it.

Then Lonen climbed.

The towering wall wasn't the trees and cliffs of home, but it offered a similar set of chinks and handholds. Back in the deep shadow cast by the wall, Lonen felt his way, the old habits from boyhood kicking in. The adage advised not to look down, but really, for climbing like this, it was often better not to look at all.

Fix the feet. Reach, fingers smoothing along the stones. Seek. Find. Grasp.

Then set another spike, connect the rope, wait for the tug. Repeat.

Fix. Reach. Seek. Find. Grasp.

Fix. Reach. Seek. Find. Grasp.

His world narrowed to only that. No thinking about the explosions, the spike of lightning and roar of thunder, the rumble of earth and the harrowing screams of men. All that dimmed as the trancelike focus on the climb took over. Later he'd notice the trembling muscle fatigue, the scraped hands and broken skin bearing testimony to the all-consuming attention to survival, to gaining the victory of the summit. But in this moment he might be in the forest, bark rough against his cheek, the rustle of green leaves above and the chortle of the creek below.

He was suspended there, peaceful again. Carefree.

Fix. Reach. Seek. Find. Grasp.

Fix. Reach. Seek. Find. Grasp.

Fix. Reach. See—

His scrambling hand hit something wrong, bright bruising pain in his knuckles. A limb? No, no—the parapet overhang at the top of the wall. He'd made it.

Inching up his footholds, he gathered himself into a crouch. The next bit would have to go fast. He found a grip with one hand, then another as high as he dared. It felt like it could be the flat surface of the top, but who could be sure? Tensing his thighs, he sprang, praying he wouldn't launch himself directly into a swarm of the enemy.

His hands caught, held.

Slipped.

And he fell in a sickening arc, hands flailing for purchase.

The rope around his waist grabbed hard, catching all his weight, vising the air out of his lungs, and slamming him into the wall with a brain-rattling thud.

At least the knife between his teeth helped silence his grunt of pain.

"Prince Lonen!" Alby hissed from several lengths below. "Are you all right?"

They'd climbed together enough times for Alby to know to stay back. Lonen waited to be sure the spike would hold, then tugged the rope below three times in their all-clear signal.

Resolute, he made himself climb again, forcing himself to go as slowly as before. *Don't assume the handholds will be the same.* That made for careless mistakes.

He didn't count the fall as a mistake—it had let him glimpse the top of the parapet. Plus, he hadn't been spotted. The flat top had been a false perception. Next time he needed to reach higher and deeper. Now that he had it in his head, he could do it.

And he would be ready to take out the crimson-robed sorcerer standing a short distance down the wall, golden mask facing the tumult in the distance. That priest had been still, no upraised arms spewing battle magic, so perhaps he channeled it from whatever foul source they tapped.

Lonen found his final spike again, checked its stability, then reached for the top once more. Not there. Just past it. There.

He sprang. Caught. Slipped. Held.

With a mighty kick, he launched himself over the top. The priest turned in surprise and Lonen knew his gazed fixed on him even though the golden mask had no eyeholes. No time for the shudder of revulsion, the instinctive fear. Every moment he hesitated the priest could raise his hands and end Lonen's life, along with the hopes of all the Destrye.

No time to pull his axe. Yanking the knife from his teeth, he charged, fast and silent as a golem.

The blade sank deep into the priest's heart, the slight body falling back, a woman's gasp of shock rattling from behind the smooth metal. Her hood fell away and her hair, a mass of blond silk, spilled over his hands along with the hot blood pumping from her rent chest. He pulled the knife away and lowered her body to the walkway below the parapet. Putting her out of easy sight of her people, yes, but also…

He'd never killed a woman before.

Lucky for him and the Destrye, he hadn't known before he dealt the lethal blow, as he might have hesitated. The woman gasped, lungs frantic for air that would do her no good, with her life's blood pooling around her, but he found and cut the ribbons holding the mask on her face anyway. Dull eyes in a once lovely face, already going slack with death.

"I'm sorry," he told her. The words echoed in his memory. Back to the forest of his youth and a doe he'd brought down with his bow. The arrow had been enough to drop her, but fell short of a clean kill. He'd found her in the soft leaves, glistening eyes dimming exactly like this as her life soaked into the forest loam, instead of pooling on hard rock, running in black streams in the cracks of the stones. "I'm sorry," he said again, as he had then.

And cut her throat to finish it.

"Their women fight?" Alby breathed next to him, a world of astonished horror in his voice.

"I don't know, but they're complicit." Lonen pointed his blade at another crimson-robed priest stationed farther down, also facing the battle. Still and rapt, unaware of them as if focused out of her body. "Kill as many as you can."

"I can't kill a woman," Alby said, horrified gaze still fixed on the dead woman's face.

Deliberately callous, Lonen wiped his blade on the priestess's robes. "They came after us and have killed *our* women, our children, even our hound dogs and house cats. Forget your sympathy. They're the monsters. This is a sorceress, not a woman. Pass the word to the men who reach the top. Kill as many as they can find who focus on the battle, then get back."

Alby swallowed back a retort, one that gave him a look of quiet agony as it went down, then went to obey.

Lonen steeled his gut and went to kill more sorceresses.

~ 5 ~

"*ORIA, WAKE UP.*"

"Hmm?" Oria stretched, then frowned up at the flickering shadows playing over the high ceiling. The city walls must be ablaze with torches. Was it that early in the night still? No, because she'd gone to sleep well after they'd been doused to night levels. She'd sat out in the terrace garden to savor the fragrance of the night-blooming flowers and the sight of the white bats that came in like ghosts to drink from them.

"*Wake up. Bára is under attack.*"

Chuffta peered at her from beside her pillow, eyes catching the orange gleam of flame, turning the calm green mad.

"The Destrye?" She sat up, threw off the down comforter, and shivered at the sudden chill. Yanking off her sleeping gown, she pulled on underthings and a casual gown of sturdy cotton. "Where's Alva?"

"*On the walls. All the high-level sorceresses are on the walls.*"

Chuffta's mind-voice dripped with sorrow and an unusual blankness behind which something else wailed with grief.

Oh no. *Mother.*

"Tell me what's going on," she demanded, striding out to the terrace and the balcony overlooking the city. The walls blazed, as did the plain beyond. Thunder boomed through the sky as lightning forked through it, her father's magic, alive and well, which meant her mother should be also. One of Nat's fireballs raced out, then fizzled into shivers of descending flame that quickly winked out.

"I think some of the Destrye have climbed the walls and are killing the sorceresses." Chuffta gave it to her fast.

"But why would—" She cut off her own foolish question. Somehow they knew. The Destrye had discovered the battle magics would sputter and die without the priestesses feeding it to the men. Even now the mages were exhausting themselves, only her father's storm magic still going strong. Because her mother would be somewhere near Oria, and not on the walls.

"Where are you going?"

"To find my mother. She must be nearby."

"The city is in chaos. People dying and grieving the dead. You cannot go down there—it will be too much for you."

No news there—her head already pounded with the overload, even this high up, from the miasma of emotion rising like heat off the desert floor. It would be worse lower down, among them. But not worse than being slaughtered by the cruel Destrye on the walls of their own home. Why wouldn't they just go back where they came from and leave Bára alone?

"I can't stay up here while my people, my own family, are suffering and dying."

"What can you do that others cannot?"

She flinched at the sting of his caustic, but accurate point. "Maybe nothing, but if I stay here then I'm certainly contributing nothing. It's bad enough that I can't fight. Don't ask me to be more helpless and useless than I am." Due to her own failure to learn. If she'd exercised some simple self-discipline, she might not have been slumbering in peace while others died.

"You can't blame yourself. And if you'd been on the walls with

the others, you might be dead as well."

A harrowing thought. She didn't argue with Chuffta, simply held out her forearm for him. With a sigh that sliced disapprovingly through her mind, he flew to her and dug in his talons. They pierced through the padding to her skin, demonstrating the displeasure that seeped from him. Deserved, no doubt, and yet…

"Don't punish me," she gritted through her teeth. "I can't bear for you to be angry with me on top of all the other emotion."

"*I apologize, Princess.*" His mental tone layered contrition over the cuts he'd made, soothing and steadying. He hopped up to her shoulder and rubbed his soft-scaled cheek against hers. "*I am upset also.*"

"The great guru Chuffta, ever placid and master of all things *hwil?*" She ran down the steps, only then realizing she'd forgotten to put on shoes. She so rarely wore them, only donning slippers for the few court occasions and city celebrations she all-too-briefly attended. As she passed each window on the spiraling downward journey, she looked out, searching for signs of priestesses on the walls and battle magic in the sky.

"*Watch your step or you'll break both our necks,*" Chuffta chided, spreading his wings for balance, catching one in her hair.

"Like you couldn't simply take wing instead of tumbling." But she slowed and kept her eyes on the stairs. She couldn't see much through the windows, regardless.

"*I'd never abandon you to save myself.*"

She nearly threw some of his oft-repeated advice back at him, not to make promises he couldn't keep, but the possibility of separation from him loomed too close, edged too sharp with blood-drenched Destrye blades. Pausing on a landing to catch her breath—had she ever run so fast for so long?—she stroked the long tail he'd wrapped around her waist for extra stability. "Promise me you will. If the Destrye get to me, you must fly away and warn the other cities, the other temples. Tell them what happened here. That the enemy knows to kill our priestesses to disable the mages. That Bára is in enemy hands."

"I pledged my loyalty to you and—"

"Exactly," she interrupted him. Something that surprised them both, as she never had done so before. "Consider this a last service to me. If I fall, fly away. Warn them or not, but save yourself."

With an unhappy mental mutter he agreed and she continued down the endless stairs, going more slowly to stave off at least physical exhaustion. Outside, the night had gone quiet. No more rumble of the earth or crash of thunder. Silence had never been so ominous.

She reached the ground floor without encountering any of the usual guardsmen. They'd all been called away, apparently. Good that they'd gone to help, but daunting to contemplate that if the Destrye made it to her tower, there'd be no one to stop them from killing her. Or worse. The history books held tales both dire and vague of what happened to women who fell into enemy hands. She'd gone through a phase in adolescence of gruesome fascination with those sorts of tales. None related *exactly* what befell the women, only that they suffered terribly and it had to do with sex; sorceresses tormented by intimate flesh-to-flesh contact with men not only incompatible, but entirely without magical sensitivity.

The heavy bar on the door gave her some trouble, Chuffta regretfully unable to help. While he could grasp things well enough with his prehensile tail and feet, being aloft gave him no leverage to help lift something that weighty. On his somewhat helpful advice, Oria bent her knees and wedged a shoulder under the bar, pushing up with her legs as Chuffta flew circles over her head, admonishing her to try harder.

Apparently, now that he'd agreed to this plan, he was all in.

The bar lifted out of the slats by slow degrees, then tilted and fell with an alarming clatter, Oria barely scooting her bare toes out of the way in time. At the noise, the door flew open and Renzo, one of her usual guards, crashed through, sword drawn and eyes wild. At least they hadn't left her entirely alone.

"Princess Oria!" He pulled back several feet, visibly calming himself, which she greatly appreciated as his battle-ready aggression, anxiety and frustration swamped her with a wave of frenetic energy. Chuffta landed again on her shoulder, touching her skin with his, which helped dampen the overload considerably. "What are you doing down here?" Renzo demanded, all normal protocol discarded. "It's not safe. You don't know—"

"I do know," she snapped, and his eyes widened at her brusque tone. Normally Oria remained subdued and quietly withdrawn when he escorted her. On those occasions she'd been working on her balanced calm, not soaking in the bristling emotions of a city under attack. "Do you know where Queen Rhianna is?"

"Ah…" He shook his head, then nodded. "Yes, Princess."

"Take me to her."

At least he adjusted to the changed reality quickly, saluting smartly and taking the lead—sword still drawn, eyes scanning the shadows—to guide her through the echoing empty hallways of the palace.

"Have the Destrye penetrated inside the city, do you know?"

Renzo shook his head, light brown curls shifting with the

vigorous movement. "I don't know for sure, but I don't think so. The enemy attacked an hour after midnight. The king called for the princes, emptied the temple of the most powerful priests and priestesses, and mustered every guard who could be spared. The priestesses took to the walls and the rest went to meet the Destrye. Only the queen and her personal guard remained behind—and me, to guard your tower."

And they hadn't even bothered to wake her. The only person in all of Bára who'd slept through it all.

"Not all of it," Chuffta reminded her.

She sent him an affectionate thought, envisioning a hug that was impractical in reality, in gratitude that he'd awakened her, but didn't speak it aloud. The nonmagical tended to be disconcerted by her one-sided conversations with her Familiar. They did much better in her presence if they all pretended Chuffta was a pet, nothing more. No one else in Bára had an ivory-scaled winged lizard for a pet, though derkesthai populated Báran children's tales. Amazing what the ordinary person would accept in order to cope with the existence of magical gifts they didn't possess.

They reached her mother's favored salon quickly, as it lay not far from Oria's tower. The queen's guards bristled, then gave way as they recognized Renzo and snapped to attention at the sight of Oria. They didn't attempt to stop her, but opened the doors for Renzo to pass through first, speaking to the guards inside the doors. Renzo's tall frame blocked the narrow opening and Oria chafed to push him aside, craning to see past him. Chuffta simply took off and flew over his head.

"She is in a deep trance," he reported. *"She does not look well."*

Renzo and the queen's guards were arguing about whether Queen Rhianna could be disturbed, the discord jangling through Oria's skull, all that much worse without Chuffta's buffering contact. She balled her fists by her sides, reaching for some measure of calm, and failed worse than usual.

"Enough!" she screeched, the sound grating to her own ears. The men all fell silent, Renzo spinning to gape at her. In his astonishment he allowed the door to swing wide, so Oria plowed through them all, slamming through the interior door before any of them recovered enough to prevent her.

Lit by a few candles that burned low, her mother sat in a chair by a window that looked out on the city wall a short distance across the chasm. The way the palace ranged over the steep hillside, the ground floor of Oria's tower stood stories high over the sheer drop to the wall's base on this side. The parapet of the wall stood nearly level with the window's view, though a significant distance separated them.

"Mother!" Oria cried, rushing to her and taking her hands. Cold and limp. Such a deep trance. "Should I remove her mask?" she asked Chuffta, who perched on the window ledge. Temple law and custom of privacy strictly forbade removing anyone else's mask, except in dire emergencies. Surely this counted? Still, Oria hesitated, looking to Chuffta for his advice, since he hadn't yet answered. His sinuous neck curved so his head reversed from his body, he sat motionless, staring with reptilian interest at the view out the window.

At a man running along the parapet, illuminated by the blazing torches.

Destrye. Wearing a dark fur cloak that swirled heavily around him, he loped in a half-crouch, a dully gleaming knife in one hand, an enormous axe strapped to his back. Furred boots rose to his knees, crossed with leather, his muscular thighs bare except for black curls that matched the thick locks of his wildly tangled hair and beard. He melded from one shadow to the next, and Oria might not have seen him if

Chuffta hadn't spotted him.

As if feeling their attention, however, he froze mid-step at the rim of a pool of light. Still but for the swivel of his wolfish head, he scanned his surroundings, thorough and unhurried.

Then locked gazes with Oria.

~ 6 ~

L ONEN HAD SEEN many strange things in the past weeks. Impossible magic and horrific deaths that would take him years to purge from his nightmares, if he ever could.

If he lived that long.

The sight of the woman in the window hit him with enough force to unbalance him. Through the blood-drenched night, he'd kept focus on one kill after the next and only on that, much the way he'd climbed the wall, except that he slit the throats of defenseless women, one after another, instead of reaching for holds. They died so easily, seeming oblivious to his approach, focusing their placid attention outward to the battle where the booming assault of the sorcerers diminished and ceased as their sisters succumbed to the blades of Lonen and his men.

The fact that they didn't fight back, that they remained so vulnerable, sickened him, each death layering on unclean guilt that he'd ignored until the vision of the woman in the window knifed into him like an unseen blade. Maybe it was because her fair coloring was so much like the first woman he'd killed. After that one, he hadn't looked at their faces, taking the dispensation offered by their featureless masks.

For whatever reason, the sight of her gripped him, standing in the open window, illuminated by candlelight in an otherwise dark tower that rose from a deep abyss. Her hair shone a copper color he'd never seen on a living being, like a hammered metal cloak that shifted with her startled movements. She put a hand to her throat, eyes dark in her fine-boned face. A creature from children's tales perched beside her, staring at him intently. He would have thought it a statue carved from alabaster, but it swiveled its head on its neck to look at the woman, then back to him.

Lonen had seen illustrations of dragons in his boyhood books, but they'd been huge and…fictional. This thing looked very like those, only smaller—maybe as long as his forearm, not counting the tail. All white, it shimmered in the bright torchlight from the walls much as the woman's hair did. It sat on its haunches, taloned feet clutching the stone windowsill, bat-winged forearms mantled. Large eyes with bright green shine dominated a wedge-shaped head with a narrow jaw and large ears. It lashed its long, sinuous tail against the stone, as a cat watching birds would.

Beautiful, both of them, and as fantastical as if they'd stepped out of one of those storybooks. The wonder of the sight swept away all the bloody horror. She was the bright face of the terrible magics—something lovely, pure and other-worldly. Something in him lunged at the prospect of such beauty in the world, a part of him he hadn't known existed. Or rather, a part he hadn't thought survived from childhood. That sense of wonder he'd felt looking at those storybook illustrations, long since lost to the grind of the Golem Wars. He lifted a hand, not sure what he meant to do. A salute? A greeting?

"Prince Lonen!" Alby ran up, bow in hand. "Why do you— a sorceress!" He reached for an arrow and notched it, a smooth, practiced movement that Lonen barely stopped in time.

"No," he commanded. "Stand down. She wears no mask. She isn't one of them."

"They're all the enemy," Alby insisted through gritted teeth, resisting Lonen's grip. "She's seen us."

"It doesn't matter." Abruptly weariness swamped Lonen. Far too soon for him to wear out, as much remained to be done. That bright bubble of the fantastic had distracted him, the shattering of that brief moment of childlike wonder more painful for the sudden loss of it. He'd have been better off not feeling it at all. "Her people are largely dead, their defenses falling around them. Look out at the plain."

Alby followed his nod. Grienon, enormous and low in the sky, waxed toward full, shedding silvery light on the quiet field. None of the magical fireballs or earthquakes thundered through the night. The golems had dropped like corn stalks after harvest. The Destrye forces moved in a familiar cleanup pattern, groups of warriors methodically searching the field for the dying, to either save or dispatch, depending on which side they'd fought for—and if they *could* be saved. Other groups remained in pitched battle, but the Destrye had the upper hand. Without their magic, the Bárans would eventually fall.

For as many years as they'd worked towards this day, Lonen had expected to feel jubilation, triumph, the roar of victory. Not the drag of exhaustion and regret. Their plan had worked far better than any of them had dared to hope—and yet only bleakness filled his heart.

The copper-haired woman's fault, for showing him a glimpse of a dream of something more than monstrous death and destruction. He'd been better off hoping simply to live to the next moment, or not to die in vain.

Hope and the promise of wonder could destroy a man's spirit more surely than a well-wielded blade.

With one last look at the woman in the window, he turned his back on her and her false promise. "Come, Alby. Let's find a ladder or stairway down to the city inside the walls, so we can open the gates." One that wouldn't plunge him into that dark abyss. "There must be stairs or ladders that the sorceresses climbed. By sunrise, Bára will be ours."

Soon he would be done with this evil place.

"STUPID TO STAND *in the window like that. You made a perfect target.*"

"Advice that might have been useful in the past and is irrelevant to the present is best not offered," Oria replied with one of Chuffta's favored adages, the oft-repeated words all her shattered mind could pull together. The impact of the Destrye's energy and high emotional state had pushed her even closer to the edge of control. He had no mental discipline, not even a shred of control over his raging feelings. They'd doused her with a bewildering range—wonder, hate blended with an odd joyfulness, horror, despair, soaring hope, and surprising regret. Not at all how she had expected a barbarian warrior to feel, but then she'd never encountered one before.

Yet despite their scope and potency—especially at such a short distance—his emotions hadn't overloaded her. Just left her a bit battered.

She sank to her knees, both because her weakened legs wouldn't hold her and to better chafe her mother's cold hands.

Blood pulsed weakly in her wrists, a faint flutter of butterfly wings. The two warriors had been speaking to each other, though she'd heard them as clearly as if they'd stood in the same room, the thin cool air transmitting their words. Had the Destyre been speaking the truth? Everyone dead, Bára fallen. The night had gone ominously silent, so it seemed so.

"It doesn't matter," the Destrye warrior had said of her, of whether she lived or died. The other man had called him *prince* and he'd taken her measure and declared her not worth killing, a strange tinge of betrayal to the bitter emotion. She should be grateful for the reprieve from imminent death, though the old anger burned at her worthlessness. Something even a Destrye prince could recognize across the gap of a chasm.

Enough thinking about that rough man who'd so strangely grabbed all her attention.

"Mother!" She spoke sharply to penetrate the trance. Deeper than Oria had ever seen. If all the sorceresses on the walls had gone so far into sgath, no wonder they'd all died. Still no response from the queen. Enough of this, too. "Chuffta— use your talons to cut the mask ribbons."

"The temple forbids—"

"I think all bets are off tonight. It's not as if Priestess Febe will be looking for trespasses against holy law to punish in the next few hours." If the high priestess of Bára's temple had even survived. She might have been on the walls, too.

"Lift me then."

Oria held up her left forearm for Chuffta to land on, his feet gripping as he used his thumb talons to carefully slice the ribbons at Rhianna's temple. Holding the mask with her right hand in a numb parody of the usual ritual, Oria kept it in place while her Familiar sliced the other two sets of ribbons at cheek and jaw.

When the mask loosened, she drew it gently away, then tossed it on the floor. Not proper treatment for the sacred relic, but the sight of her mother's wide open eyes, dull and spiritless in her deathly pale face, sent a fresh rill of terror through her and Oria forgot all else.

"Oh, Mother," she moaned, patting the queen's cold cheeks. "Come back to me, please. I need you. Don't leave me alone."

"You're not alone. I'm always with you." Chuffta, on her shoulder again, stroked her cheek with his own, his tail looped around down around her arm to her wrist in reassuring affection. *"Don't cry, Oria."*

She brushed impatiently at her tears. "It's not all mine."

"Yes, you're overloading. We should go back up the tower."

"You heard the Destrye. There's no one left in charge. I might not be a priestess, but I can't be so fragile that I leave Bára without direction. My father and mother would expect that much." Her mother, who still stared without moving or blinking. Perhaps dead inside a body that yet lived. "I'll get through somehow."

"And if you break?"

"Then I break."

"You won't do Bára any good if you're broken."

She wrenched her gaze from her mother's blank eyes to Chuffta's worried ones. "Look—either I do no good because I break doing my best to serve Bára in her hour of greatest need, or I do no good because I'm sitting in my tower preserving a potential, something that may never manifest. The choice seems clear. If I can just wake up the queen, she can take over."

"Oria, she may be…"

"Don't say it," she replied fiercely, taking her mother's face in her hands. Wishing for *hwil* more than ever before, she tried to calm her mind, then she deliberately reached for any glimmer of emotional energy. Strange and awkward to go in a totally different direction—to move outward, to attempt to receive instead of vigilantly defending herself. It opened her to the crashing terrors, angers, and sorrows around her, but she focused on her mother, letting Chuffta do his best to screen the rest of it.

And there. A thread of soul-killing grief, dark but potent. Oria fastened on it, pulling it up and out.

"Oria," her mother breathed.

"Oh, thank all the stars!" Oria gripped her mother's still-limp hands. "Are you all right?"

Rhianna's eyes filled, then overflowed, a waterfall of tears flowing down her face. "He's gone. Tav is dead. There's a hole where he was. Oh no, no, no. Why did you bring me back?" She collapsed into sobs, not seeming to hear or feel Oria's reassurances.

Oria's heart bottomed out. Her father dead, her mother beyond reason. Likely her brothers dead, too. This wasn't how it should be. Oria wasn't the strong one. Of them all, she had the least ability to cope, much less to lead. She wanted more than anything to crawl into her mother's lap and be comforted, but that wouldn't happen. Maybe never again.

Not many made temple-blessed marriages, so the nature of such relationships were long on myth and romance, but short on facts. The ballads and tales always told of the sorcerer and sorceress dying together—either in sweet old age, in each other's arms, or, tragically, battling some dire foe. Never did one survive the other.

Maybe her mother's total and shocking loss of *hwil* hinted at why. The world quivered under Oria, spinning into a new pattern. One where her unshakeable parents were no longer the fixed points in her life, her mother no longer the single person who believed in Oria. Her father was gone forever and her mother this sobbing, hysterical wreck of a person.

Feeling sorry for herself accomplished nothing, however. Though it felt as if the world had ended, it no doubt continued hurtling headlong into disaster.

"Stay with her, Chuffta."

"No, you need me more."

Too tired to argue, she pulled herself to her feet, a monumental effort. Her legs leaden, she went to the door, opening it to find Renzo and her mother's guard waiting with expectation so bright and dread so thick that she had to grip the door handle to keep from bowing beneath the onslaught.

"Take the queen to her chambers and call a healer for her. Send word round the city for anyone still able to attend that there will be an emergency meeting in the council chambers—"

"At least have it in the tower, so you'll reduce some of the input. And it's more defensible if the Destrye enter the city."

She nodded wearily, no longer spending the energy to protect the sensibilities of the guard. She wasn't thinking clearly. "All right, that makes sense. Emergency meeting in the third-level salon in my tower. I'm going there now. All of you—get as much information as you can about what's going on. Send messages as soon as you know anything. I believe the Destrye have plans and the means to open the gates and let their warriors into the city. There may be no one left to stop them."

They made sounds of protest, but subsided when she shook her head. "Find out if I'm wrong. Make sure someone stays with the queen, should worse come to worst."

"I'm staying with you, Princess," Renzo said, face grim.

"No, I—"

"Begging your pardon, Princess, but if what you say is true, it's possible you are the last surviving member of the royal family. Who is capable," he added, carefully not looking toward Queen Rhianna. Hating that truth, Oria cast one searching glance at her shattered mother and queen as one of her guards gently picked her up and carried her from the room.

"We must protect your life at all costs," Renzo urged quietly.

With no energy to argue and no thoughts to muster, Oria nodded. Then went to drag herself up the long climb to her tower, to find out whether any pieces remained to be put back together.

~ 7 ~

B Y THE TIME Oria reached the third-level salon, the sky beyond the open windows had brightened with dawn. She went to the window; the view wasn't quite as good as the one from her garden several floors above, but there was little to see of the conflict. Bára lay eerily quiet.

Most likely any citizens who hadn't been summoned to the battle were barricaded in their houses, and any who had answered the call to defend Bára would still be trapped outside the walls. The main gates weren't visible from her vantage point, which came as something of a relief, though that might be the wrong response to have. A good leader would want to see everything for herself. But it might be more than she could withstand, the sight of Bára's gates hanging open like a wound, Destrye barbarians streaming through it to spill more blood, to finish the job of crushing her people.

And her. So far she hadn't broken, had withstood more input than ever before in her life, but it felt as if one more blow would do her in, leaving her shattered beyond repair.

"You're doing very well. Besides, there is no 'beyond repair.' Where there is life, there is always the possibility of healing."

"But where there's death, there is no healing, only corruption of the flesh." She sounded bitter even to herself and Chuffta did not reply. The image of her mother as a corpse in her chair still filled her head. She couldn't quite grasp that her father might be dead. Perhaps her brothers, too. All that seemed far away, muffled behind a curtain she dared not draw back.

A scuffling sound at the door made Oria turn from her morbid thoughts, and High Priestess Febe entered, leaning heavily on her walking stick of carved bone, accompanied by her aged husband, Vico. Both wore their golden masks, both alive, if not necessarily well. Vico had earned his mask fairly, of course, but expressed the merest trickle of magical power. He served Priestess Febe well enough to siphon off her powerful energies when needed, but theirs was far from a perfect marriage and he couldn't muster any of the greater defensive or offensive magics. No one had worried about it, because the high priestess used most of her sgath to sustain Bára, with the help of the junior priestesses. Vico mainly functioned to keep her balanced.

"I've sent word to the head priestesses of the temples in the other cities, Princess," Priestess Febe said, sitting heavily. "I don't know if they'll be able to help—though they owe us—but they will at least know of Bára's peril."

"Thank you, High Priestess." Oria hadn't thought of that. So much she didn't know, such as why or what they owed Bára. Except she did know that Bára was the capital of them all for a reason. None of the others sat atop such a potent and constant source of magic.

A few other priests and priestesses arrived, a dozen or so, all similar in magical power and physical strength—which was why they had survived the night. All were too elderly or not useful enough to have been called to battle the Destrye. The only others would be those too new to their masks to have ascended the walls or taken to the field, or those of the noble families who'd not yet qualified to take their masks at all. Who knew how many among them would find *hwil* and become useful?

Folcwita Lapo arrived, breathless, for once not perfectly assembled and groomed. Pausing in the doorway, he surveyed the small gathering, then scrutinized Oria. They'd interacted very little. Mostly she'd seen him at court functions, but as someone unmagical and not at all trained in *hwil*, he'd kept his distance from the sensitive Oria. Even though it felt as if she could absorb no more, his prickly energy hit her from across the room, forcing her to breathe through it. Ambitious, ruthless, and determined, the folcwita had served her father well in managing all nonmagical aspects of running Bára, and by all accounts did it well. Oria should be grateful to have his assistance at this time.

If she could stand to be in the same room with him.

"Folcwita," she greeted him. "What news do you bring—are we invaded?"

"Obviously," he bit out.

"Not quite, Princess," Ercole, captain of the city guard, answered, pushing through the doorway. "The main gates remain closed, but only because a few of the faithful city guard hold them. There's intense fighting there, both inside and out. I have to say, without the battle mages, we're bound to lose. Our numbers are not great and their warriors exceed our skill."

"Then why are you here instead of there?" the folcwita demanded.

Ercole shook his head, his lined face gray with exhaustion and despair, his once splendid uniform soiled with blood and other matter Oria couldn't identify and didn't care to examine too closely. "One man will make little difference at this point, though I will go back as soon as I'm released. I'm here at your summons, Princess. To give you the information you request-ed. What do you need to know?"

Oria fought back a headache, an aura forming at the edges of her vision such as she hadn't experienced since early adolescence, when her hormones and burgeoning magic collided and conspired to send her to bed for days on end in a darkened, soundproofed chamber, with only Chuffta's quiet thoughts for company.

"I'm still here."

"What of—" not just her brothers "—the sorcerers and our forces still outside the walls?"

"We don't know for sure what their status is." Captain Ercole looked at his hands, scrubbing absently at the blood-stains. "It's certain that they cannot return with the gate closed, so they're likely in dire straits, pinned between the wall and the Destrye forces. With the priestesses dead, they're down to their own reserves of magic, if they have any left at all. The golems have all fallen, which surely means Priest Sisto is dead. They have no help there."

Priestess Febe, Priest Vico, and Folcwita Lapo all startled at that—not at the news of his death, but something else. Through the roar in her head, Oria tried to parse what upset them. Something they didn't want her to know.

"Priest Sisto's golems were outside the wall?" But Ben had said something, hadn't he? *"Harrying them with golems all the way."* She'd only partly listened at the time, concentrating on keeping her brothers' bristling grien out of her head.

Captain Ercole rubbed a hand over his face, chagrin oozing off of him. "They'd become the mainstay of our defense."

Oria hadn't known that, but why would she? Aside from the occasional family meal, she had rarely participated in discussions of the particulars of Bára's defenses. She'd only encountered Priest Sisto's golems a few times, the most salient during a demonstration at the temple, as part of her lessons, probably a good ten years before. With an otherwise minor magical ability to manipulate silicates, the priest had refined his art to ambulate creatures made of the stuff. Nasty things with no intelligence, the golems did not move quickly or with any agility. The lesson primarily demonstrated how even minor magics manipulated with inventiveness and ingenuity could produce large-scale results.

They'd become useful for menial work around Bára, she'd understood, particularly for unpleasant tasks that humans preferred to avoid, such as clearing sewage pipes of blockages. Her father and Nat had discussed it once.

"I know of the golems, but how are they useful for defense?" she asked.

The folcwita stepped in, preempting Captain Ercole. "Why use human men when the golems served the same purpose with no loss of life? The golems made far superior soldiers."

The captain glared at the floor, obviously disagreeing but not arguing.

"Priest Sisto gave them fangs, Princess," Priestess Febe explained into the gap. "And long, very sharp claws. They served as a solution to several problems."

"Most of which are not relevant at the moment," Folcwita Lapo inserted with a quelling glance at the priestess.

"I imagine I have no time to learn about them with the enemy literally at our gates." Oria's eyes throbbed, focus blurring in and out, and she pressed her fingertips to them. "But I will want to hear about them in detail later. Your advice, Captain?" she managed to say.

"Open the gates, Princess."

"What? Are you mad?" Folcwita Lapo roared, slamming

his hand on the table.

The literal and emotional impact drove through Oria's temples with knifelike intensity. Green fire rolled across the table, sending the folcwita reeling backwards, frantically batting at the silk sash of office that had caught flame. Everyone stared in astonishment at Oria. No—at Chuffta on her shoulder.

"I will protect you." His mind-voice came through with grim certainty.

"Watch your volume, Folcwita. The princess is fragile." Priestess Febe said, with sgath that nevertheless reverberated. It spread through the room like a cooling balm, easing Oria's pain considerably.

"That...that *creature*," the folcwita sputtered, his fear palpable.

Oria understood his reaction, though she judiciously hid that thought from Chuffta. The derkesthai Familiar had never shown aggression like that, typically saving his fire for roasting bits of meat and vegetables. But then, they'd both been pressed far that day.

"So far as we know, Princess Oria is the only functioning member of the royal family we have left," Priestess Febe continued. "Let's do our best not to sacrifice her this bloody day also. If her Familiar even allows it."

"Apologies, Princess," the folcwita gritted.

Oria nodded at him, saving her energy. "Explain your reasoning, Captain Ercole."

He spread his hands, palm up. "We've lost. The gate will be opened. If we fight, every man who does will die and the gate will still be opened. As long as the gate is closed, our people outside are trapped away from shelter and succor. They will be killed and the gate will still open. We might as well offer our surrender."

Folcwita Lapo choked out a sound, but subsided with a wary glance at Chuffta. "I disagree," he said softly enough, though his emotions raged. "King Tavlor would never surrender, Princess. Think of your father, out there battling for us. Bára cannot simply throw open her gates to the Destrye and offer her tender belly to the enemy for them to rend and tear. We must fight with all we have. What would he say upon entering Bára only to hear you already gave it away?"

"My father is dead." Oria hadn't meant to state it so baldly, but she lacked resources to cushion the words. As it was, they echoed with hollow finality in the salon, the morning sunlight pouring in with ironic cheer, a playful breeze fluttering the sheer curtains framing the windows, hung there to be drawn on hot afternoons.

"You can't mean it, Princess," whispered Priest Vico. "Queen Rhianna yet lives, I'm told, and she wouldn't if..."

"My mother felt him die and, yes, it nearly killed her, too. I don't know about my brothers and the other priests, but we must prepare for the worst news there also. Captain Ercole is correct. We've already lost. Now we must decide what to do about it. I say we offer surrender."

"There is another alternative," the folcwita said. "We can invite the Trom."

"That's hardly a viable option," Priest Vico retorted. "We might as well throw ourselves in the chasms."

"The Trom?" Oria groped for the information, her mind stupid with overload. Captain Ercole looked similarly baffled. She recalled the word vaguely from some long-ago tale. Some sort of mythical elder race?

"These teachings are sacred to the temple and those who've taken the mask," High Priestess Febe said, her featureless mask making the order resonate with hollow echoes. "I discussed this eventuality in a general sense with the folcwita of the council once news came of the devastating losses of our priestesses. The Trom are ancient guardians who can be summoned in times of extreme need. Many are the cautions against calling on them lightly, as the price they demand is high. That's all any of you need to know."

"What is the price?" If Oria hadn't squandered so much time not learning *hwil,* she wouldn't be scrambling to assimilate all of this new information. She'd be privy to the temple's sacred knowledge.

"I know some and will share that with you."

"The specifics may be shared only with those who have achieved *hwil.* The inherent power is far too dangerous otherwise." High Priestess Febe nodded, several of the priests and priestesses echoing the gesture knowingly. "Suffice to say that the price is different every time, chosen to suit the time and place. I urge we look at every option before we choose this, only at the hour of extreme need."

"Aren't we there already?" Folcwita Lapo demanded. "Look around you!"

"No," Captain Ercole said quietly. "Not if we surrender."

They all looked expectantly at Oria.

"Don't give them more opportunity to argue. You are queen for the moment."

"Princess Oria, you are inexperienced, fragile by your own admission, have no mask, and can't know what a grave step—"

Oria cut the folcwita off, happy to also shut down the frustrated rage he sent her way. "I am also the royal princess and, in the absence of anyone who outranks me, my word is law. Captain Ercole—how do we go about offering surrender?"

Folcwita threw up his hands. "Without my help, I can tell

you that. I'm not eager to die."

"We need an emissary," Priestess Febe said. "Someone brave enough to approach the enemy within the walls, to make the offer to discuss terms. The folcwita is correct—the risk of death is high. They may not wish to listen. The Destrye are a bloodthirsty and barbaric people, who live to destroy. It's entirely possible they won't withdraw until they've slaughtered every one of us."

Captain Ercole nodded. "I will do it."

"No." Oria smiled at him. If they survived, she'd remember his stalwart loyalty and courage. "We need you to continue to lead the guard. I will do it. They won't kill a woman under flag of surrender."

The group exchanged uncomfortable glances. Finally, Captain Ercole said, "Princess—we believe they won't hesitate. They murdered the priestesses on the walls in cold blood."

But not her. *She wears no mask. She isn't one of them.* "They will recognize me as no priestess. I have the the best chance of speaking to them of any of us."

"It's too great a risk, Oria," Priestess Febe said in a gentle, insistent tone. "You may be no sorceress and perhaps can never take the throne, but we cannot afford to squander your potential, just in case."

Oria shook her head, pressing her lips against the regret. "Such is the fate of a figurehead." One about to collapse at that. "You have Queen Rhianna. She is strong and will recover. Perhaps my brothers yet live. It's worth the risk to my small life to perhaps get them back and save what we can of Bára and her people. To protect the magic well beneath the city, as is our sacred legacy."

A short silence settled over the room, no one mustering an argument against her logic.

"Prepare a horse for me, dress it in white tack. White is for surrender, yes, Captain?"

He nodded unhappily, but with respect in his eyes. "I'll prepare a banner for you also. Would you like some help with the words to speak, Princess?"

"Yes. Thank you. I'll don white also and be down as soon as I am able." She hesitated. "I hate to ask, but with Alva gone, I'll need someone to help me dress."

"It would be my privilege to assist, Princess," Priestess Febe said with a grave nod.

It seemed they all would be taking on new roles that day.

"I'm going with you when you ride out, Princess," her guard Renzo said from behind her. "I won't let you be completely undefended."

"Thank you." She stroked Chuffta's long tail. "But I have my own defenses, too."

"Yes. We will do this together."

She smiled at the lizard's fierce thought. And maybe felt a little fierce, too.

~ 8 ~

I N A WAY, fighting human men came as a relief. Though the guard inside the walls put up a fierce fight, fueled by the desperation of men defending their homes and families, Lonen understood it better. And though exhaustion dragged at him, that bleak despair no longer clouded his mind. This kind of battle at least made sense.

These men would not give up easily, either. Though the sun had risen to midmorning, making him entirely too hot in his furs, with no opportunity to doff them beyond shoving his cloak behind his shoulders, the Báran guard showed no sign of flagging. Lonen and his men had formed a defensive wedge inside the gates, holding it in the narrow passage against the city guards who came at them, but they hadn't yet found a way to open the massive doors. Could be magic, knowing these sorcerers.

Destrye from outside arrived to supplement their forces, finding the ropes and scaling the wall, then dropping over. But more Bárans joined the guard attacking them—common folk by their dress, mingling with the brightly uniformed guard. The Destrye who added themselves to Lonen's defense were men separated from their units, still doggedly following the primary mission of getting up and over the wall, then throwing into Lonen's fight for lack of any other objective. None had news of the rest of the army, at least not that could be transmitted between pitched skirmishes.

Much depended on the Destrye forces outside the walls, because they had arrived at a stalemate within it. It sounded like utter chaos on the other side of the doors and, if Lonen's people weren't going to make it through soon, it could turn his occupation of the gate into a long-term proposition. Something they had meager supplies to outlast. At least the narrow alcove just inside the gates made it relatively simple for a small group to defend.

They might as well implement rotations and settle in.

Sending several of the recently arrived men to push the line of defense forward, to gain them a bit of breathing room, Lonen stepped back behind them. Then he shucked the damn cloak, grateful for the immediate cooling. Too bad he couldn't discard it altogether, but he'd need it if they found themselves still outside when the cold night settled in on them again.

"Alby!" he called, waiting for his man to disengage and similarly take refuge behind the wall of fighters. Alby also immediately doffed his furs.

"What kind of monstrous land has burning days and freezing nights?" Alby panted, leaning hands on knees to take full advantage of the breather.

"I begin to understand why they came to Dru for water, brutal as this place is," Lonen agreed. "We need to set up shifts. Only enough men to hold the gate, rotate out the ones who've been fighting longest, fresher ones to the fore."

Alby eyed him wearily. "There's not a man here who *hasn't* been fighting all night."

"Best judgement then. And find me whoever's come over the wall most recently. I need to know what's going on out there."

"Yes, my prince, but—" Alby's eyes widened just as a trumpet pealed. "Holy Arill incarnate!"

Lonen spun to follow the direction of Alby's gaze, tired muscles singing into life as he lifted his axe to meet the challenge, then lowered it again in slow bemusement. A white banner rippled over a blaze of copper hair. The woman from the window. Another dream made flesh in this nightmarish and impossible place.

The clank of weapons fell from cacophonic levels to bearable. Enough for the men to hear Lonen as he called the command to desist but remain alert. He pushed to the fore, ready for a trick. If she did wield magic she might be able to obliterate them all, and he'd be responsible because he could have killed her at her window.

All for youthful idealism and a soft heart he'd long since thought shredded by the golems' claws.

Quiet spread outward, reverse ripples that stilled the fighting, bringing a welcome respite as she approached. Men continued to face off, holding their poses, ready to reengage at the slightest hint of betrayal.

She rode a pale horse, decked out in exotically smooth fabrics that caught the sun and shone with reflected light like Grienon, all in shades of cream and crystal white. The gown she wore distorted the slight frame he recalled from her silhouette, an impressive display of wide shoulders and voluminous skirts. It put him in mind of a small cat arching its spine, every hair on end to appear bigger and more ferocious. She dripped with laces and shimmering pearls, jewels from the sea he'd only read about or seen in illustrations.

That bright rain of copper hair was the only color about her, a stubborn note of resistance against her vigorous demonstration of surrender. That and the armed guard who walked at her stirrup with a determined mien, and desperate emotion in his eyes. He loved his mistress, whoever she might be.

The white dragonlet on her forearm moved, spreading its wings and blinking at him with those green eyes so brilliant they vibrated against her vivid copper hair.

Lonen tore his gaze away from the mythical creature and forced himself to focus on the woman's face, to read her intent. Though if she opened the earth beneath them, there was precious little he'd be able to do. Rationally, he should not let her approach.

But he seemed to be far beyond rational thought.

Normally her skin would be golden-kissed by the sun, he guessed, but something had made her unnaturally pale. Lines of strain rode her forehead and bracketed her mouth. She looked to be in pain, possibly injured in the fighting? But she didn't look like a fighter, all soft limbs and graceful slenderness. Young, too. Younger than he'd first thought, when he'd glimpsed the curves of her woman's body in the candlelight.

Barely more than a girl, in truth, especially to be apparently negotiating a surrender.

But then he wasn't that far into his own majority. Only last season his father had scolded him about flirting with girls more than he practiced with his axe. How things changed in a short time. Look at him—war-weary and in the position to discuss terms for the Destrye armies. War had aged him far beyond the demands of daily life. What he wouldn't give for those irresponsible days.

The woman reined up before him, her eyes narrowed. Another sign of pain.

"I believe you can understand my words?" she asked in an accented but clear use of the trade tongue.

"I do. What is your intention?"

"I will speak with the leader of these men—is that you?"

"Yes. I am Prince Lonen, son of King Archimago of the Destrye. In his absence, I may speak for him." He hoped. His father was in no position to disagree and Lonen would pass off negotiations to him soon enough.

"I am…" The woman swayed a little in the saddle and her guard cast her a concerned glance. She recovered, however, straightening her spine. "I am Princess Oria, interim ruler of Bára. I wish to negotiate a surrender."

A susurrus of surprise ran through her people. Not what they'd expected, despite the banner she carried. Probably, in their arrogance, they'd never witnessed or even contemplated such extremity. Well, they would now.

"Total surrender," he stated, his voice harsh to his own ears. "You, your people, and your city agree to complete subjugation to King Archimago of the Destrye. In exchange for your lives, you will yield everything else."

Princess Oria looked to the lizard on her arm, her lips moving ever so slightly. Talking to the animal? Perhaps they'd dressed up a crazy girl to bargain, to distract them from a sneak attack. Backing up a step he summoned Alby. "Keep out a sharp eye, in case this is simply a ruse."

"Yes, my prince."

Oria fastened her gaze on him. The same color as her hair, her eyes gleamed brighter with shrewd intelligence. "You offer death, not life, Prince Lonen. Abject slavery is no way to live. The people of Bára might as well expend all our effort and the last of our lives taking as many of you barbarians with us as we can."

Her people cheered at that and Lonen kicked himself for the misstep. No cause inflamed people faster than that of the martyr. He should know. "Who do you call barbarians?" he challenged, his men shouting in accord. "You sit in your fine city draped in jewels and send your monsters to slaughter our children. Who is barbaric in their behavior?"

She flinched—though she covered it well—more color draining from her face. Her lizard mantled, hissing at him, eyes burning with green flame, as if he'd injured the princess in some way. She soothed the creature, stroking a hand along its scales, and Lonen suppressed a shudder of revulsion. Oria's eyes flicked up to his again and a small smile twisted her lips, as if she'd somehow read his discomfort and found it amusing.

"Look around you, Prince Lonen. It is you who attack us, our people who are dying. We can debate the specifics later. For the moment it seems to me that it gets us nowhere to hurl insults and accusations at each other. The fact that we are enemies has been well established." She waved a graceful hand at the scatter of bloodied bodies on the stones, and Lonen didn't miss that she averted her gaze. "The challenge is to find common ground for setting terms to end this conflict."

"I offered grounds for your surrender," he all but growled. It rankled that she remained so calm in the face of utter destruction.

"No, Prince Lonen." She emphasized his title with the same mild reproof his mother might have in correcting his manners. "You flung out the most extreme ultimatum, likely to challenge how easily I'd fold. I can tell you quite plainly that yes, you have cornered us to the point where we offer surrender, but we are not defeated. Given the choice between utter subjugation and death on our own terms, the people of Bára will choose death—and we have the means to take you with us." Her people broke into cheers again, raising their weapons.

She was bluffing. She had to be or her sorcerers would have hurled magical weapons at them already. Still, he had to give her credit. Young princess and interim ruler or no, she had a gift for rallying her people. Something about the way she held herself communicated her commitment to that path. She *would* rather die than give up entirely. The sudden image of her white gown bloodstained, her throat cut and those brilliant copper eyes going dim with death raked at him. He had no wish to see her dead.

He'd had plenty of death already. In fact, it suddenly felt as if he might agree to anything to be able to set down his axe, wash off the blood, and sleep for a few days. Could she be that sort of witch, to influence him that way?

"What terms do you propose then, *Princess?*" He made the question hard and sneering, so she wouldn't catch on to his weakness.

She steadied herself, raising her eyes as if reading from a mental list. Someone had prepped her. Not a fool then.

"We will agree to cease all fighting, both in and out of the city. You and your men will be granted safe passage. We will open the gates and you will inform your forces that a temporary truce is in effect. We will similarly inform our forces of such. At a date and time we agree upon, the highest ruler of each of our peoples who yet survives will meet to discuss further terms."

It sounded reasonable, though his tired brain could be missing a loophole. Or whatever she was doing to cloud his intentions and incline him towards sympathy. "The truce includes the use of magical weapons against us."

"Of course."

"Including any witchcraft you or your creature may be working on me at this moment."

She cocked her head, ever so slightly, but he noted it. He'd surprised her. "I'm working no magic on you at this moment," she said. "And Chuffta is magical by nature. He cannot cease being who he is. However, I offer my personal guarantee that so long as you do not violate the truce, magic will not be used to harm you or your people."

"And your personal guarantee is worth how much, exactly?"

A shadow flickered across her face, beyond whatever pained her, something hard behind that pretty oval face.

"I might ask the same of you, Prince Lonen, you who wears the fur of animals and is covered in the blood of my people. I am not the one with a battle-axe in my hand and hatred in my gaze."

No. If anything, grief and exhaustion clouded her eyes. She had no right to play the high moral card, however. She might be pristine in her garments, but her people's hands were bloodstained with the guilt of causing this war.

She must have read something of his anger in his face because she held up a hand, as if to ward him off, briefly closing her eyes. "I cannot offer more than my word. Either you and I trust each other enough to stop the fighting long enough to set terms or we might as well all go back to slaughtering one another."

Once again, she set him back, had him feeling chagrined. Fine then. Lonen lowered his axe, wiped it ostentatiously on the uniform of a fallen guard of her city, then sheathed it on his back and held out his bloodied hands. "You have your temporary truce, Princess. Open your gates. You, however, will go through them with me."

~ 9 ~

ORIA MANAGED TO keep her expression smooth, drawing on years of faking enough *hwil* to escape lessons. She couldn't let this Prince Lonen—if he was indeed a prince, as that seemed a lofty title for such a brutish man and people—perceive how much he frightened her. Up close the Destrye were every bit as vile, ferocious, and bloodthirsty as the worst of the illustrations she'd pored over with such sick fascination.

Even the wild dark hair that hung to his shoulders was matted with blood, indistinguishable from the black fur vest he wore, which left tanned arms as bare as his thighs. He bled from a half-dozen wounds and seemed not to notice. It must be abhorrence that transfixed her, that made it so difficult to look away from the play of corded muscle as he sheathed that enormous axe.

And now he expected her to go with him through gates she'd never passed through in her entire life.

"You likely cannot withstand it. You are already close to collapse."

"I've been 'close to collapse' for hours and hours," she muttered at Chuffta. "So far it hasn't happened."

"That doesn't mean it won't. You've been able to forestall it through strength of will, but even you will reach a breaking point—and it will be all that much worse for pushing yourself so far."

"This is not helpful advice."

She'd tried to keep her lip movements small, but Lonen frowned at her, black suspicion on his face and angry revulsion pouring off him like the stench of a decaying animal. It made her stomach lurch. Several of his men made hand signs at her, hate and fear oozing from them.

"Cease stalling," Lonen sneered at her. "Do we have a deal or not?"

"I cannot go through the gates with you. I can stay just inside the doors and—"

He cut off her words with a chopping hand and furious glare. "Then I can only conclude you are without honor and mean to betray your word. Do your men wait outside the gates to slaughter us the moment we step out? Perhaps the earth will open beneath our feet or a wall of fire will immolate us? No deal, *Princess*."

Oria sighed. "There is no such plan, but I understand your fear."

"Fear?" He visibly bristled. "I am not afraid. I am a warrior of the Destrye, a prince and my father's son. I am simply not a fool to be tricked so easily."

Instead of retorting that she could sense his fear as palpably as the sun on her skin—and that it made her want to empty her guts except she hadn't eaten in so long that nothing sat in her stomach—she nodded in resignation. "I shall go through the gate with you."

"Oria, don't do this."

She didn't reply to Chuffta, partly because there was nothing to say and partly to forestall more of that glowering hatred from the Destrye. Not that she cared what he thought of her, but the toxic energy dragged at her fragile control more than any other variety. In a better frame of mind, she might appreciate how much she'd learned about her own capacity to endure various energies in the past hours.

"Renzo, would you help me down?" She held out a gloved hand to him, not trusting her legs to hold, especially in the heavy court gown meant for sitting and looking impressive, not walking. With a mental grumble, Chuffta climbed to her shoulder, winding his long tail around her waist.

"Princess, I can't let you walk among armed enemy soldiers with no protection," Renzo whispered, harsh and adamant, as he handed her down.

She dipped her chin at him, doing her best to ignore the way the ground squished beneath her silk slippers, moisture soaking in along with the violently fractured energy shed by the dying. Perhaps she'd reached a similar saturation point, where she simply couldn't hold any more energy, so it ran off an overflowing roof cistern in a good monsoon year. That would be helpful. Chuffta snorted his opinion of that in the recesses of her mind.

"My man comes with me, to guard my back," she said, hoping she sounded firm.

Lonen acknowledged that with a grim twist of his lips. "Mine, too, then." Another man, equally shaggy and blood-soaked stepped to his side.

"They need to form an aisle," Renzo murmured to her, "and lay down their weapons."

Lonen overheard the quiet words. "Not happening."

"You can't ask Princess Oria to walk a gauntlet of the enemy," Renzo snarled at him.

"If they wanted to cut me down, they could have already," Oria said in a mild tone, letting Lonen overhear that, too. She held his gaze with her chin high. "My people are largely dead, our defenses falling around us. One more death would hardly matter." She'd surprised him with that, enough to abate his fury, the relief like a cool evening breeze after a sweltering afternoon. "I shall walk your gauntlet."

He eyed her, gaze slipping to Chuffta. "Leave the dragonlet behind."

A laugh escaped her, shocking and raw. Mostly at her Familiar's indignant and inarticulate reaction. She shook her head. "Not happening." It gave her some satisfaction, too, to throw his words back at him.

They locked eyes and wills. His, densely fringed with black lashes, were a dark gray, like the granite their sister-city to the north, Arvda, sent in trade. Surprisingly lovely, they would have made him look feminine but for the angry line of a recent scar that dragged from his forehead, skipped his eye, and continued down his cheek. Nearly missed losing that eye to whatever had sliced at him, something thin and sharp by the look of it.

"Every moment we waste allows more of both our people to die," she said softly. "Chuffta remains with me or I don't go. Give your men the order to let us through and I'll give the order to open the gates."

With a grim nod, he turned to face the gate, standing on the side of her away from her Familiar.

"Dragonlet," Chuffta fumed.

She ignored him, knowing perfectly well that he was attempting to distract her from the trial of stepping beyond the boundary walls of her world. She didn't understand how it worked—yet another temple secret that would be shared only if she fully realized *hwil*—but something about them buffered the wild energy of the larger world just as her tower did. No sensitive who hadn't taken the mask even came close to the gate, much less set foot outside.

All she had to do was get through the next minutes and remain conscious long enough to get the message through to stop the fighting and get word to her brothers. Hopefully at that point at least one of them lived and could take over.

"And plan your funeral," came Chuffta's sour thought. His worry came through clearly or she might have been annoyed.

"Don't put attention on a result you do not want," she told him. Then, before Lonen could say anything or make that sign against evil, she called out in a louder voice, "Open the gate!"

Lucky for them that Priest Vico had enough magical ability to do that much, with Priestess Febe feeding him from her still vast reserves. It seemed a grave miscalculation to Oria to have left the city without sufficient sorcerers to even open the gates again. Why had the king committed *all* of the most powerful to the battle? It didn't bear thinking of at the moment, but if she survived and didn't end up a Destrye prisoner, she resolved to learn more about strategy.

She'd wasted a lot of time pretending to meditate and chasing elusive *hwil* that she could have spent studying useful knowledge.

Magic streamed in a thin swirl past her, then burgeoned, touching the massive doors. Without a sound, they slowly opened, admitting the roar of battle that had been muffled before.

Frenetic, fragmented energy slammed into her like a physical assault.

Chuffta loomed large in her mind, soaking up what he could, but she swayed on her feet. A hand grasped her wrist, where the lace cuff bared her skin, burning with raw, undisciplined energy, scorching her unmercifully.

"Princess Oria?" Lonen peered at her, much too close.

"Don't touch me." The request came out ragged, nearly

begging him, and he snatched his hand away, eyes firing with renewed offense and fury. She turned away from it, feeling top-heavy and bottom-light, a festival cake piled too high. The doors opened enough to show a raft of Bára guard just outside. They turned, swords and spears ready.

"Stand down," Oria commanded, fastening her gaze on one she recognized. "Lieutenant. We have a temporary truce."

The men sagged, their exhaustion and despair swamping into a kind of dreadful relief that blackened the edges of her vision.

"Bring my brothers—or the highest in command who's still alive. I've offered surrender in exchange for cessation of hostilities." She got all of Captain Ercole's words out, though it seemed she heard them from a vast distance, down a long tunnel. "Someone needs to take over negotiations."

She pushed the final instruction through the onrushing black. Then succumbed as it crashed over her and washed her away, Chuffta's mind-voice a wail in the distance.

"Oria!"

LONEN CAUGHT ORIA as she fell, an instinctive grab he would have stifled if he'd had a beat more to recall her hissed directive not to sully her with his touch—and to consider her reptilian defender. As it was, she passed out so precipitously, as if that last word uttered took her final breath, that he nearly didn't catch her before she hit the paved road. The dragon creature took wing.

Bemused to find himself holding her as he would a Destrye

bride, but dressed in white, he kept one wary eye on the man Oria had called lieutenant and the other on the dragonlet circling his head. He'd throw the princess to the ground if either of them attacked. He owed her nothing, not even this courtesy. Except...

Except she'd said she couldn't exit the gate and he'd insisted on it. Perhaps it hadn't been a trick or missish timidity. What did he know of magic? He'd thought of her as a puffed-up, spitting cat before—holding her this way now, she seemed like one soaked that turned out to be skin and bones beneath a wealth of fur. She weighed practically nothing and most of that had to be the gown.

He nearly did drop her when talons sank into his shoulder. "Gah!"

Bright green dragon eyes stared fiercely into his. "I'm not hurting her, curse you, beast," he hissed. Amazingly the thing seemed to understand because the wicked points retracted some. Not entirely, but less painful. The thing's long tail curled up like a snake about to strike, then wrapped around the bare skin on Oria's forearm, a slight strip of creamy flesh, slightly darker than her glove and sleeve.

A moan sighed out of her, a faint hint of color returning to her death-pallid cheeks.

"Let me take her from you," her guard said. "She'll do better inside the gates."

Lonen hesitated. They could cut him down without her, but a Destrye didn't use a woman as a shield. No more than he already had, to his chagrin. Hopefully her faint didn't indicate she carried a disease.

He held her out and the dragonlet hopped from his shoulder onto Oria's chest, folding its legs and wings to curl up there, gaze intent on her face, evincing an unnatural intelligence and affection that made his skin crawl. As her man took the princess away, Lonen noted how her formerly pristine gown bore blood smudges in the shape of his arms and hands, the shadow of his grip like an injury. The crimson, both bright and drying, on her white dress looked like a bad omen.

But for her people or his, he didn't know.

Possibly both.

~ 10 ~

To Lonen's vast relief, his father and Ion soon arrived at the gates, the Báran guard parting for their passage with hard faces but lowered weapons. Much as Lonen wanted to embrace them and pound their backs in the great good consolation at seeing them still alive, he held himself back. And told himself Arnon must be out commanding the Destrye forces, in case of treachery, not fallen in battle.

Before they could converse, another two men arrived wearing the crimson robes and eyeless golden masks of Báran sorcerers.

They ranged into sides. King Archimago and Ion flanking Lonen, and the two sorcerers standing shoulder to shoulder across from them. How could they see to walk in those masks? A silence stretched between them, neither side willing to concede by speaking first.

"Where is the Princess Oria?" one of them finally demanded, the metal mask making his voice echo like the ghosts of campfire tales. "We were told she was here, outside the gates, but she clearly isn't. We won't fall for the tricks of barbarian scum."

Lonen clamped down on a childish quiver of fear. It was only a man wearing a golden mask, nothing supernatural. And one with his magic fled, bled out undefended during the night on the high walls above. Anger surged through Lonen that this man hid behind a mask, flinging insults when they'd been the ones who'd forced Lonen to commit the unthinkable, the murder of women.

King Archimago turned to him. "I understand a princess of this city gave formal surrender and we are to negotiate terms."

Lonen nodded. "Yes, my king. Princess Oria approached us and offered peace if we would allow her people outside the walls to return within, with no further fighting or fatalities."

"Oria?" The other, slighter masked man sounded incredulous and young enough that his voice cracked a little. "Our sister outside the gates, offering terms? I find this so unlikely as to be impossible."

Lonen bristled at the dismissal in the boy's tone. He hadn't much cared for the witch, but she'd met him with bare-faced bravery. "She recognized the gravity of your defeat and conducted herself with honor in an attempt to salvage what she could—including your cowardly lives. She accompanied me here, gave the order, and then was…overcome by some sort of fainting spell. Her man carried her back within. All here witnessed it. You can ask your own guard."

"It's true, Prince Nat," the lieutenant confirmed, addressing the older man. "The Princess Oria, in the flesh, rode to the gate under banner of surrender. She asked that you take over negotiations." The words he didn't speak, of what occurred after, rang with quiet significance.

The featureless mask seemed to glare, the man's bony shoulders stark lines beneath the draping robe. Not a lot of muscle there. Not a warrior then, not like the Destrye. No wonder they relied upon magic and the golems to fight their battles.

"We do not honor the promises of a girl made under duress," he said. "There shall be no surrender."

The younger sorcerer started, glancing at him.

King Archimago, surprising them all, laughed, the harsh, hoarse sound that rattled in his voice ever since Nolan was lost. "And I do not negotiate with a mere prince. Where is your king?"

They both lost their bluster at that, the formerly brash boy turning his masked face down in apparent grief, the one called Nat going slack before regaining himself. "I am the king now. As my father's heir, I step into his place."

A murmur ran through the people, a sound of further defeat, and—surprise? Another moment that should have been triumphant and fell far short of the mark.

"Very well," King Archimago said. "You have two choices, boy. You can honor the terms of the surrender offered by the Princess Oria or we can finish the job of killing you, your family, your leaders, and any of your people still wishing to fight, until we reach a true surrender. I have no wish to destroy your people, but I will if you force my hand."

"No wish to destroy!" the younger man burst out. "*You* attacked *us*—unprovoked!"

Oria had said much the same thing. A strange defense, this protestation of innocence. One that the heir did not echo, however.

"You think you can defeat us so easily," Prince Nat snarled.

"Look about you! We *have* defeated you," Lonen put in, surprising his father and Ion, judging by their sidelong glances. But he'd had enough of it all. Had since the dark hours of the harrowing night. "Your sister nearly killed herself to make this truce. I don't pretend to understand your ways, but she and I agreed to terms at some cost to her. Would you throw that away?"

"She had no right." By the sound, the young Prince Nat spoke through gritted teeth. "It's not my fault the idiot left her tower."

"Your family politics are nothing to us." King Archimago gave Lonen a quelling stare. "Choose, heir to nothing. You agree to Princess Oria's surrender of your city and we negotiate terms, or we recommence battle. Before you answer, you may have a moment to speak to your lieutenant. So your understanding may rule, rather than your pride."

Leaving the enemy prince no choice, King Archimago turned his back. A deliberate insult that the Destrye, at least, would understand. Their forces had—against all probability— seized victory over the dreaded golems and sorcerers, and they deserved to know it.

"Lonen." His father beckoned Ion and him closer, for a low-voiced conversation. "What is your relationship to this Oria?"

The question took him by surprise. "None at all. I met her not an hour ago when she rode up to offer surrender." He left out the previous sighting as not relevant.

Ion gave him a strange look. "Why are you defending this woman then?"

The king dipped his chin at Ion, confirming the question.

The sun beat way too hot on Lonen's scalp, the blood drying and drawing the skin tight, an irritating harmony behind the growing chorus of aches and pains from various wounds. "I found her bravery in the face of defeat admirable. And…there's been enough death this night and day. But for a vain princelet blinded by his pride, we could be done."

His father clapped his shoulder, squeezing. "You did well, my son, breaching the wall. I won't ask what you had to do, for I see the shadow of it in your eyes, but we know you won this battle for us. Much as I do not wish to censure you in this moment, I must caution you to harden your heart against this princess."

Lonen gaped at him, scrambling for a reply.

"It happens," his father said in a softer voice. "Some part of you thinks that by saving her you can expiate this guilt you carry for whatever dark deeds haunt you. But she is the enemy as much as any of them. When we are done here, you can make sacrifice to Arill. The goddess will lighten your heart."

"My king, I don't—"

Ion, who'd been leaning in, trying to overhear, broke in. "He means don't let a bit of foreign pussy make you think with the little head instead of the big one." Ion grinned at him. "There. That manned you up again."

"That is not what—"

"We have a decision," Prince Nat called out, sounding considerably less arrogant. "If you will, King Archimago."

They returned to face the two sorcerers. "We agree to the surrender," Prince Nat said, defeat and sullen anger manifest in his voice and shrouded form. "What now?"

"Now, I will send men to occupy the city," King Archimago said, "to ensure continuing peace. My son, Prince Ion, will accompany them and remain in charge of the Destrye forces within the walls. Your men may reenter the city and see to your dead and injured. We shall do the same, camped outside the walls. We shall agree to meet just after dawn tomorrow morning, to discuss terms going forward. The least hint of hostility toward my men will result in immediate cessation of the truce. We'll finish what we started and there will be no further pause for mercy. Tell me you understand."

They didn't like it, the desire to protest clear in the tense lines of the princes' shoulders. Lonen himself barely squashed the urge to speak against Ion's assignment to command the occupying warriors. After all, he'd been the one to establish diplomatic relations with…with Oria. *Don't let a bit of foreign pussy make you think with the little head instead of the big one.* Ion was wrong on that. Oria might be exotically fascinating, but the strange witch held no attraction for him. Not like his lovely Natly. He simply wished to—what? Be assured of the princess's well-being, perhaps.

As if by making certain that he hadn't harmed her irreparably, he could wash the blood of all the others from his hands.

His father, always wise, was right. He needed to purify himself and make sacrifice to the goddess to begin to shed this terrible guilt. The sooner away from this place the better. Somewhere out there, even at that moment, Natly and his real life, the normal peaceful one, moved step by step away from him.

Perhaps he could take solace in that aspect of victory. They'd nearly reached the end of their consuming quest to free the Destrye of the golem incursions. With this crushing defeat of the enemy, they could return to the fertile forests and meadows of home. The place he'd marched away from, certain he'd never see it again. Suddenly, it seemed he might.

The prospect gave him unexpected hope. Enough to banish the unfortunate Oria from his thoughts and firmly replace her visage with Natly's. As was good and right.

~ 11 ~

Though a bath wasn't in the stars for him in this sunbaked, goddess-forsaken land, Lonen scrubbed away the worst of the bloodstains with sand, while a medic cleansed his wounds with alcohol—a fiery purging he welcomed as the beginning of his penance. He bore more injuries than he'd thought, but far fewer than he deserved, having slaughtered so many.

The wide, wounded eyes of the first woman he'd murdered hovered in his mind, overlapping with that long-ago doe, then overwhelmed with Oria's grief-dark copper ones.

But he didn't speak of it. Not to Alby. Certainly not to his father. Nor to Arnon, who had indeed survived the gruesome battle. Odd that he didn't want to say anything to Arnon about meeting Oria, even when he shared a flask of hogshorn with his younger brother. Arnon had listened many times to Lonen's trials with the elusive Natly, always offering a patient ear and decent advice when asked. Though this…encounter—really only the one, because the semi-vision didn't count—had nothing to do with pining as he'd done for Natly.

No, it was as his father had said—a product of guilt and post-battle nightmares. It would remain between him and Arill, all part and parcel of the peculiar shameful guilt he carried, hopefully to be relieved in time. But even after he shoved food into his aching belly and toppled onto his sleeping furs, naked but for his many bandages, Oria's eyes haunted his dreams.

IN FRESH GARMENTS, his hair oiled and tied back, if not particularly clean, Lonen, with Arnon and their father, made the trek up the road to the city gates at dawn. Destrye guarded them now, saluting and then bowing—acknowledging their commander and king—following with broad, even jubilant, grins. Lonen wasn't the only one who hadn't expected this day to come.

Within the city walls, a far more morose atmosphere prevailed. Ion, who met them at the gates to escort them in, had of course stationed Destrye throughout Bára, which looked desolate otherwise. Most of the population must be keeping indoors. Unless more had perished than he'd thought.

Occasional denizens observed their passage, the lightly clad and slender people, mostly fair-haired, a clear contrast to the occupying Destrye. With the leisure and daylight to pay more attention to the city itself, Lonen found it surprisingly attractive for a place constructed of so much stone.

Like the high rocks behind, the towers of the city speared up in rounded shades of gold, rose, and gentle browns. As if the people had taken the harsh colors of the desert and blended them into something gentler, more forgiving. Window openings laced every building, often giving glimpses of blue sky beyond through yet more windows. White net fluttered in many of them—some drawn across completely, some were tied to the sides. Open-air balconies and terraces held all manner of plants and trees, with flowering vines draping over the edges. Between the towers, arched stone bridges traversed dizzying drops, both spectacular and fearsome. And yet other paths that bordered the canyons were studded with benches, presumably for people to sit and enjoy the view.

Combined, it all gave an impression of delicacy, verdancy, and peace at odds with the forbidding city walls, deep chasms, and dry salt plain that encircled it.

They'd mentioned a tower in reference to Oria, as if it were a specific and special one. Which seemed unlikely, given that the lion's share of buildings in Bára could be called towers. Could it be the tallest among them? It wasn't so easy to judge relative height from below—rather like trying to pick out the tallest tree from the forest floor—but one seemed to tower above the others, fat in circumference, with a profusion of balconies and what must be an extensive garden at the very top.

"Looking for someone?" Ion's tone was snide, his expression forbidding.

"Observing the city," Lonen replied, as if the question had been sincerely asked, not barbed with innuendo. "It's lovelier than I expected."

"For the home of rapacious monsters? I suppose it is."

"Is this the behavior of my heirs?" King Archimago asked in a mild tone. "Now that the enemy has fallen, must you fight amongst yourselves?"

"I don't even know what they're poking at each other about," Arnon protested.

Ion didn't comment, so neither did Lonen. Odd how, with the battle crisis over, they so quickly reverted to old roles and arguments. Except that Nolan should have been there to act as peacemaker, cracking jokes instead of lying broken at the bottom of one of those dramatic chasms. The thought brought grim reality crashing back. They might be walking through a city that could have been drawn from storybooks, but they traveled over the corpses of too many people.

As if they felt it, too, the other men fell silent until they crossed one more bridge over the deepest chasm of all and entered a complex of towers near the one Lonen had picked as the tallest. Tracing the line of the surrounding outer wall with his eye, he reconstructed the encounter from the fragmented images of that long night of assault, deciding that it could indeed be the spot where he'd stood and seen Oria in the window.

"Is this the palace then?" he asked Ion, figuring it for a reasonable question.

Ion nodded brusquely. "So far as we can discern. We haven't been sitting around chatting. But apparently this is where their council meets and makes decisions. Prince Nat sent me a message—a surprisingly deferential one—that this would be the logical site for negotiations, as they had the room for plenty at the table and for as many guards as each side felt comfortable bringing. He offered to accede to our wishes for an alternate meeting site, but as I had no better to offer..." He glanced at the king.

"We shall see when we arrive, but I imagine I would have chosen the same." King Archimago put a hand on Ion's shoulder, gripping it much as he had Lonen's the day before. "I'm proud of you for how you've handled this occupation. Of all three of you. And of—" He broke off, not naming his fourth, lost son.

The council chamber occupied a vast space indeed, with many windows, a cross-ventilating breeze blowing between them, fluttering the pale curtains made of sheer, shimmering cloth reminiscent of Oria's white gown. Destrye guard ringed one side, the Bára guard on the other.

The two priests, masked and in their crimson robes, sat at one end of a long table, a dozen other Bárans, mostly elderly, ranged along the sides near them. Though women made up part of Prince Nat's council, some of them in golden masks and others not, none had Oria's distinctive hair. King Archimago took the seat at the far end, Lonen and his brothers taking the chairs to the sides.

Just as well. It would be a long day, hammering out a lasting agreement. Not that Oria's presence would have distracted him, but the less trouble from that direction, the better.

She floated through a gray mist.

Amorphous, numbing, it calmed her for an endless time. She felt nothing, sensed nothing, was nothing.

Restful nothing.

But after a while, as she became aware of the passage of time, the nothing began to bother her. The dragging muck of sleep went from comforting to cloying to confining, keeping her wrapped tightly like the silkworms succumbing to their lovely cocoons. Only she would not emerge into a night-winged moth. She'd remain trapped in this place, blind, deaf, without touch or scent of anything. She struggled against it, wanting to scream and finding that, too, entirely missing.

Was this death? She was alone, bereft of the world.

"Oria. Oria, you're alive and I'm with you. I'll never leave you."

She didn't know who that was or who Oria was, but she clung to the calming voice, as if it were shelter in a sandstorm.

"Yes. I will shelter you. Rest. Heal."

No longer so afraid and alone, she allowed the sleep to rise up, grateful for the black to replace all that clinging gray.

"…WHAT TO EXPECT…"

"…never before…"

The disjointed phrases cottoned through her mind. At first the words held no more meaning than the soughing of an afternoon breeze just before sunset stilled it. After a while, they began to retain their shape, sticking longer, with edges that signified something. "…no more mind than an infant's…"

Hot rose light beat through her eyelids, burning away the last of the mist that had obliterated her senses, and she registered a breeze on her skin, the scent of day-blooming lilies.

"…prepare yourself for the worst."

"I've already lived through the worst," a voice she knew well cut through. She reached out for it, blindly seeking.

"Mama?" No sound came through her stiffened, dry lips, which cracked, bringing bright pain that she actually welcomed. She *was* alive. She fought to make that final escape. There were things living people did—opening their eyes, moving their limbs.

"She's here, Oria. We're both here. Try harder."

"Mama!" she called, some part of her remembering that time when she'd been unable to feed herself, calling for this woman who—oh yes. There. That cool hand on her forehead, then slipping behind her neck, dribbling cool, sweet water between her lips.

"I'm here, baby girl. Wake up now."

"It may not be wise to—"

"I'll care for my daughter. Leave us now."

The room went blessedly silent, of both sound and a certain anxiety that had strummed unpleasantly. A smoothly scaled tail wrapped around her wrist, caressing, affection flowing in as restorative as the water in her parched throat.

"Swallow the water, Oria."

"Can you open your eyes? Come on now. Wake up for me. Chuffta is here."

It took a monumental effort. One she had to carefully think through, finding the old nerve pathways, cranking at them like a servant girl working a well pulley. That helped, to imagine the stiff wheel turning, the rope pulling, tugging at her lashes painfully.

"Wait a moment, baby. Hold still." The hands went away and Oria whined an inarticulate protest. They came back, a cool cloth on her eyelids. So much better. "There. Try again."

They moved more easily this time. The light hurt, but she squinched against it, seeking her mother's face—unmasked and lined with worry. "Mama."

"Yes." The familiar brown eyes filled with tears and spilled over, running down her face, choking out her next words.

"Why are you crying? Don't cry." The words only came out partially, mostly in a voiceless whisper. She tried to raise a hand to wipe the tears away, but couldn't.

"She is happy, Oria. Grateful to have you back with us. As am I."

"What happened to me?" The words came better this time,

but with effort. She managed to move her eyes, though not her head, to spot Chuffta on her pillow, green gaze intent on her face.

"It may be best for the moment not to try to remember too much. Just know you've been ill and must recover. Slow and steady wins this race."

She didn't like it, the not knowing. But it also made her head hurt to think about it, a much less welcome pain.

"Swallow a little more water. You need to drink," her mother urged.

Oria obeyed because it was the easier choice, and because she suddenly discovered a raging thirst, as if her belly, too, had only just awakened.

"Not too much. Not at first." Her mother set the cup aside, then wiped her tears away. "Sleep if you can and I'll wake you in a bit for more."

Succumbing to the suggestion—or, more truly, giving up fighting the onrushing darkness, she did. "Love you," she muttered before she went under.

"We love you, too, Oria. We're with you."

She sank again, with her mother's hand stroking her forehead and Chuffta's firm presence in her mind, tail wrapped around her wrist.

And a puzzling fragmented memory of granite eyes searching hers, asking some question she couldn't answer, before strong arms swept her up, holding her close against his heart.

~ 12 ~

T HEY'D BEEN TOO many days at the negotiations. Stalled, in the most galling way.

The young king, hastily ratified by his people the evening of Bára's crushing defeat, so they'd been told, proved cagey and stubborn in his arguments. Far too much so for the ruler of a conquered people. To Lonen's ongoing puzzlement, his father seemed to be losing ground in this war of words. Certainly King Archimago had never had to debate in these subtly insidious ways before. Among the Destrye, his word was law—none argued with him, on the battlefield or off.

These sorcerers and priestesses, however, with their ex-pressionless masks and endless picking apart of details—they wielded arguments as the deftest warrior would a set of sharp blades.

And the Destrye king…well, he wasn't the man he'd been when they set out on this quest, much as Lonen hated to acknowledge that much, even in his darkest thoughts.

He'd learned a great deal in the past few days that would serve him well should he ever have to take the crown, an unlikely event with Ion heir before him. Still, he'd never expected Nolan to perish and leave him one step closer to the burden of rule, so he filed the lessons away as a precaution, trying not to fret over how his father seemed to fade with every passing hour under the desert heat. Beyond that, the disquiet of wondering what had happened to Oria nibbled at his peace of mind like the biting insects that came in the open windows in late afternoon, until someone thought to summon servants to draw the sheer curtains. He needed to step away from it all, clear away the nattering worries. So when they broke for a midday meal, Lonen went walking instead.

He followed the path along the gorge that separated the palace complex from the other parts of the city. Clearly some long-ago ancestor had set it up so the bridges could be quickly destroyed in case an enemy breached the walls. If the people supporting Oria the day Bára fell had been smart, they would have advised her to do just that, and to remain in her tower. Maybe they had and she'd ignored the advice—she seemed stubborn enough for it, even on brief acquaintance.

It's not my fault the idiot left her tower.

Indulging himself, he squinted up at the structure, reason-ably certain she must be up there somewhere. He hadn't seen her at all since the surrender—and her subsequent collapse—and he couldn't exactly ask after her health. Giving it up, he resumed his walk, nodding at the Destrye guards stationed here and there.

The Bárans had begun to emerge more with every passing day, slowly taking up the business of daily life again. Another strangeness, seeing the Destrye warriors and their enemy interact over such things as putting the city back to order, or even bartering for pretty objects to take home to their women. Lonen should think about getting something for Natly. Maybe some of that fine fabric that gleamed with its own light, for a gown or scarf.

Hopefully they'd hear from the Destrye women soon. Fast-riding messengers had gone out but had yet to return with word.

A few young Báran women passed him, bare faces tanned and hair streaked with sun, though none with Oria's distinctive copper. Nor did anyone he'd seen have a pet dragonlet like hers. They nodded to him cautiously, one eyeing him with more boldness, then fell to whispering among themselves after he'd passed. King Archimago and Ion both had been firm in orders that the women of Bára were not to be touched. They'd leave no Destrye blood behind to be fouled with their witchcraft and magic.

To his surprise, he encountered Ion approaching on the path from the other direction. His brother lifted a hand in greeting, as if they hadn't parted less than an hour before. "I see we have the same idea."

Lonen nodded ruefully at an elderly priestess he knew from their meetings by her tower of platinum braids, and who sat on a nearby bench, unmoving, nearly a statue in her stillness, only the midday breeze stirring her crimson garments, sun reflecting painfully off the golden mask. "I can't bear to sit any longer. How do they stand it? I feel as if I've been moldering in my grave."

Ion cocked his head in the other direction, indicating they should move away. After they made it a short distance down the walk, he said, "I'm concerned about how long this is taking."

Lonen blew out a short breath—both relieved that he wasn't the only one to be disturbed and bothered that Ion felt the same. "Do you think they could be deliberately stalling, that they've somehow called for aid that could be on the way?"

"It's what I would do." Ion had his hands clasped behind his back, brow furrowed. "We know next to nothing about these people. The Destrye have—or had—allies. Why wouldn't the Bárans?"

"That's my take, too." Lonen hesitated before broaching the difficult question. "Then why is Father allowing them to drag their feet?"

Ion flashed him a dark scowl and Lonen braced himself for his older brother's withering scorn. He should have known better than to question the king aloud. But Ion's forbidding expression crumpled and he rubbed his brow with a sigh. "I don't know," he finally admitted. "The same is bothering me. Arnon has noted it, too, and pulled me aside last night with the same concerns."

At least they all three agreed. "Do you think," Lonen ventured, tentative in this new territory of being aligned against their father, "that they could be working some form of mind magic against him? Something subtler than fireballs, thunder, and earthquakes, but just as powerful?" If they could do such things, it might explain the way thoughts of Oria clung to him.

Ion's dark brows rose as he considered that. "It hadn't occurred to me. Arnon and I thought to blame it on Nolan's death. That grief is still fresh."

"It is for all of us," Lonen pointed out, taking a moment to choke back the black emotion that wanted to rise at the very mention of his brother's demise.

"Harder, though, for a parent to lose a child, a king to lose an heir, than for us to lose a brother."

Was it? Ion had sons out there with his wife on the Trail of New Hope, so perhaps he understood something Lonen did not. In many ways, he had a hard time coming to grips with Nolan being truly gone. For long spaces, he could forget about it. Until moments like this one.

"Perhaps so." He hesitated, then voiced one of the ideas he'd been mulling. "We've had no opportunity to say the prayers to Arill to guide Nolan's feet to the Hall of Warriors. With his body lost in battle, it could be that his shade wanders until we do. It's a plaguing thought."

"Do you—" Ion cleared his throat, gazing into the chasm. "Has it occurred to you that he might not be dead? He could be down in something like that, hoping we'll come find him. He could be hurt and…"

Lonen put a hand on his brother's shoulder when Ion's voice choked off, his own throat going tighter. "Yes," he said. "In dreams, I see him, falling, lying there broken, calling to me." A pall settled over them. Lonen had thought he'd be the only one to be plagued with such morose phantasms. Ironic that he and Ion should bond over this, of all things.

"Remember when he was seven?"

"And fell in the river? Yes." Lonen shook his head, a smile alleviating the strangling grief. "And you jumped in after him, fully dressed, sword in hand."

Ion laughed, which was better. "Father nearly skinned me alive for that one—for ruining good boots, nearly dropping my sword, and because I was supposed to be watching all of you, not flirting with that girl. I can't even remember her name." He'd gone back to sounding bleak.

"Nolan wasn't a little kid, Ion. He was a grown man in charge of a battalion of Destrye who fought bravely to save our people—including you and me and that girl whose name you can't remember. It's not your job to watch us anymore." A strange place to be, offering such comfort to his eldest brother.

From Ion's sidelong glance, he thought so, too. "That's not how it feels. But enough of this. Tell me why you think they're working some form of mind magic on the king."

He absolutely would not mention Oria. "I don't have any good reason. More…a feeling?" Lonen waited for his brother's disdain, but Ion said nothing, only listened. "I've told you how it was, killing the priestesses who stood on the walls that night."

"Yes." Ion's voice and face were grave. None of them liked that they'd won the battle on the broken bodies of women.

"It seemed—this will sound strange."

"Can any of this be stranger than it already is? We've already witnessed the unthinkable. Stop dithering and tell me straight."

Lonen had to smile. Ion, back to being himself with his didactic ways, but also a changed man, wanting to hear the strange thoughts of his fanciful younger brother. Once Ion would have rubbed his face in the dirt for saying such foolish things. In a sudden glimpse, Lonen could see his brother as king after their father's death. Something that had once been unthinkable. Now it seemed not only possible, but that Ion might make a good king.

"When I killed the first one, not knowing she was a woman, I did so because she faced out toward the battle. At least, I told myself it was only that. But—thinking back to that night, I must have felt something else at work. Something about those masks and… Have you noticed the way they seem to glow sometimes?"

"A reflection of the light," Ion offered, but not dismissively, simply as an alternate argument.

"I thought that, too. Metal reflects and the gold is bright, highly polished." Oria hadn't worn a mask. So far every man and woman of higher rank who'd spoken in the negotiations did, while the bare-faced denizens of the city all seemed to be of lower status. But everyone who spoke of her freely acknowledged her as a princess. As if of their own will and not his, his eyes strayed to her high tower. He wrenched them away before Ion noticed. "It makes me wonder is all. Why do they wear them? It seems they shouldn't be able to see, but they behave as if they can."

"It's cursed unsettling, I can tell you that." Ion pursed his lips behind his thick beard. "He hasn't said, but it could be that Father meant to leave them some measure of dignity by allowing them to retain the masks."

"Or because none of us really wants to see what lies behind them," Lonen said, before he rethought the jest.

Ion nodded to that, however. "That could be part of their trickery. Like the Xyrts who paint their faces blue to frighten their enemies."

"It makes it more difficult," Lonen said slowly, thinking it through, "to guess at their intentions when we can't see their faces. I'm not adept at negotiations, but that bothers me."

"None of us are skilled in this arena, which is why we shouldn't have accepted their surrender and simply continued the battle until they could no longer fight."

Lonen bristled at the implicity accusation. "I know you think you wouldn't have done the same in my shoes, but—"

"But nothing," Ion cut in, more the brother Lonen knew well. "You were swayed by a pretty face and a sorrowful smile."

"What makes you think Princess Oria is pretty? You've never laid eyes on her and I certainly never said so."

"You didn't have to. It was writ all over your face when you defended her actions—to her own people, I might add. Besides, plenty of Destrye witnessed your conversation with her and described how you saved her from falling, all noble and full of concern. You have a soft spot for females and always have. Didn't you consider how it might look, that you showed such care for one of the enemy?"

Lonen clenched his teeth, keeping his response measured. "No, I didn't think at all. She fainted and I caught her. Any man would have done the same."

"Not any man. I wouldn't have. But that's always been your problem, Lonen. You follow your heart, not your head."

"The big one or the little one?" Lonen snapped back, tired of this old argument.

Ion clapped a hand over the back of Lonen's skull, hard enough to make his ears ring. "The one is empty and the other attached to your heart. See if you can figure it out. Still," he said, while Lonen fumed, "your points are well taken and I will bring them to Father's attention. We should demand they remove the masks or we will rejoin the fight and see who wins."

"And if they don't agree?"

"They will, because even their proud and stubborn boy king will see that they cannot prevail against us."

"Unless they have aid coming," Lonen replied, full of the foreboding that had plagued him these past days. Ion called King Nat a boy, but he was their age. He might seem younger and softer, not being a warrior, but that did not make him foolish or without weapons of his own.

"All the more reason to insist on this measure immediately."

~ **13** ~

O RIA LIVED IN a world of alternations. Asleep. Awake. Dark. Light. Drink. Sleep. Eat. Drink.

Sleep.

Sleep.

Sleep.

Every time she awoke, her mother and Chuffta were there, ready to offer her a glass of cooled water and affectionate reassurances. A bouquet of lilies sat in a vase on the table beside the bed, wafting a sweet, thick fragrance. She'd gaze at their vivid colors, feeling as if she'd forgotten something, but she always fell asleep again before she could determine what it was.

Eventually she stayed awake long enough to string several thoughts together. Her mother attended her constantly. No one else did. Where was Alva?

"Don't worry over these things. You have one concern—to rest and heal."

"I've been doing that."

"You've been doing what, baby?" her mother murmured. "Have some broth."

"I don't want broth. I want to know what happened. Am I sick?"

"Yes." Her mother looked away as she said it. "You've

been very ill and you must take care not to relapse. You must rest and heal."

"That's what I just told Chuffta—I've been doing that."

"He's wise and you should follow his advice. That's why you have him. This is not something to be quickly overcome. Recovery follows its own calendar."

Oria struggled to sit up, to look around, not sure who or what she sought or why her body responded so sluggishly. Then realized her mother was holding her down by the shoulders, the slight pressure more than Oria could muster the strength to resist.

"Why am I so weak?"

"Because you've been ill," her mother replied with strained patience. "It's not good for you to become agitated. Sleep. Rest. Heal."

The familiar calm of her mother's soothing energy spun through her. Reminding her of something. Her mother, face creased with devastation, unresponsive. In a chair, overlooking the wall, where a Destrye warrior covered in blood, carrying an axe, paused in a pool of light, just as in those lurid paintings that had aroused the fascination of adolescent self. So vividly real and—

With a choked gasp, her eyes flew open. "The Destrye!"

Her mother winced in regret. "Don't think about it. It's done. You must—"

Harsh reality cut through. "Father is dead. What of Ben, Nat, and Yar?"

The queen passed a shaking hand over her face. "Nat and Yar are fine."

Oh no, not Ben. Not her gentle brother, who'd never once teased about her lack of *hwil*. Who'd taken his mask after his little brother and never showed bitterness or any kind of grudge. She'd secretly hoped Ben would even things out by finding his ideal wife first. Now he never would. She lay back, letting the deep and formless grief move through her. Something else. "And the Destrye?"

"Try not to—"

This time Oria managed to struggle up to a sitting position, mostly because her mother seemed unable to resist further. Oria's body protested, stiff as a corpse and weak as a newborn's. What in Sgatha had happened to her?

"I have to know." The memories came back, jagged, sharp-edged scenes, and her head began to throb. Descending from her tower. Her mother unconscious. Enemy within the walls. Her brothers without. Meeting with what remained of the council.

The granite-eyed Destrye prince. Something in her shied away from thinking past him.

"You were overcome," she said, touching her mother's arm. "Are you all right?"

"I will live. Thanks to you." Something in her tone made it sound more like an accusation, but only sorrow showed in her mother's face. "Though I shall always regret that I failed you in your hour of need."

"Failed me?"

"I'm so, so sorry, my baby girl." With a broken sound, she stood. "I need a moment."

Oria watched her mother, the unflappably *hwil*, ever cool and composed queen and priestess, as she hastened out to the terrace, a hand over her mouth to muffle the sobs that nevertheless blew back in on the breeze. Chuffta remained on the light blanket beside her, the tip of his tail lightly clasping her wrist. Steadying her. As he always did.

"She believes you would not have fallen ill had she remained

cognizant," he explained with great gentleness.

"What does my being sick have to do with…" But the rest came back, reverberating through her skull. The excruciating agony of stepping through the gates, the cascade of energy and emotion, along with vibrations she'd never before encountered, one upon the next, until—

"*Stop it.*" Chuffta's sharp thought cut through the rest. "*That's in the past. You survived it. But thinking of it can recall the damage. Exercise some self-discipline and cut it off.*"

Gaping at the lizard, whose green eyes sparked with unprecedented ferocity, she wrenched her thoughts from that moment. The pounding in her head receded, a welcome reward. "Tell me what happened after." She put a finger to her temple to stop the distracting pulse beat. "Are they—gone?"

A pair of stone-gray eyes in a scarred, blood-spattered face.

"*Will you promise to remain calm? Let me walk you through a meditation first.*"

"I don't want to meditate." Her voice came out too sharply impatient, a bit of wobble beneath. She let out a long breath. "I'll be calm, just tell me."

Chuffta appeared satisfied and folded back his wings. "*The Destrye accepted your offer of surrender. They occupy the city, negotiating with your brother, who is now king.*"

Nat was king? Why wasn't her mother ruling in the waked of their father's passing? Nat had no wife yet, not even an imperfect one to feed him energy. He couldn't be king.

"*The Destrye king does not know your laws. Nat and the council stall for time.*"

"Time? What good will more time do?"

Chuffta's hesitation was palpable. "*They have invited the Trom to Bára.*"

That memory came back with force. Folcwita Lapo arguing that they should send for help from the Trom. The fear and heightened excitement some of the others felt at the suggestion. "But we decided not to send for them."

"It appears your decision was overruled." Queen Rhianna, composed again, stood in the doorway, framed by brilliant sunshine. "Something else I blame myself for."

"Why?" Oria frowned, more for the fact that she'd suddenly realized she'd never before seen her mother so often without her mask of rank. "You didn't call them, did you?"

"No. High Priestess Febe did."

"With…Priest Vico sending the call? I didn't think he was powerful enough."

"He's not. I think—" She sighed heavily, sagging against the doorframe. "I think Nat must have done it. Had I been cognizant, I would never have allowed such a drastic, foolish move." Moving like a woman twice her years, she came to sit beside Oria on the bed, gripping her forearms over the long sleeves of her sleeping gown, preempting further questions. "Let me resume my apology. I regret, so very much, that I failed you. I lost *hwil*—an unforgivable breach. I apologize with all my heart and will spend what is left of my life trying to make it up to you."

The bed seemed to sway under Oria, the sense of dislocation, of the bottom falling out of her world so profound. "You can't lose *hwil* once you find it."

Her mother wouldn't meet her eye, squeezing her hands too tight. "I did. It's…it's thought that when your father…" She choked on the words.

A chill of horror-filled grief dragged over Oria, followed by beads of cold sweat down her spine.

"*Steady,*" Chuffta murmured.

"That I broke," her mother managed to get out. "Thus I no

longer deserve the mask of a priestess."

"They took your mask away?"

Her mother nodded, weeping again. No composure at all. "When Tav fell, I—" She couldn't continue, her wild grief, despair, and a black rage beneath it all pouring into Oria. Gasping, she reeled under it, aware on one level of Chuffta's tail winding between their hands, breaking her mother's grip— too much, even through the silk. As soon as the contact broke, Oria could orient again, begin to separate her mother's grief and anger from her own—though they had so much interface, like mirrors of each other, that she couldn't disentangle all of it.

"Rhianna." Juli, a junior priestess, new to her mask, was suddenly there. "Come away. This isn't good for Oria."

"I let him die," Rhianna sobbed. "I wasn't enough. The union cracked and…" Her words devolved into a garble as Juli led her away.

Stunned, Oria lay back, trying to process it all. Letting the emotional energy drain away. "Why does she say she let him die?"

"Because her failure resulted in his death." High Priestess Febe entered the room, golden mask implacable, hands tucked into the billowing sleeves of her crimson robe. "A priestess's responsibility, even more so a wife's sacred obligation— particularly in a temple-blessed marriage of perfectly matched partners—is to keep her sorcerer husband fed with sgath. Queen Rhianna failed in this, no matter the reason, and her husband died. How are you feeling, Princess?"

Chuffta bellied onto Oria's chest, folding his wings so he rested his pointed chin on his thumb claws, eyes green and shining as the leaves of the fruit trees in her garden.

"Listen," he soothed, no doubt sensing Oria's ire. *"Perhaps*

we shall learn something."

"Better, but I don't understand, High Priestess."

"Of course you don't. Had you achieved *hwil* and taken the mask before all this happened, you would be better prepared." The high priestess sounded weary, on top of the eternal stain of disappointment. "Knowing what we know now about Queen Rhianna, perhaps we erred in letting her have such a strong influence over you."

Though Oria, of course, could not see Febe's eyes, she nevertheless felt certain they rested on Chuffta. Much as Oria wanted to bristle, it seemed that the High Priestess emanated something through her careful *hwil*. Uncertainty?

"Anything you can tell me that the temple will allow would be helpful, High Priestess Febe." Oria pulled off the humble tone reasonably well. Chuffta agreed with a mental snort of amusement.

Febe paced over to a window. "Some of it, naturally, is a question of whether your mind and spirit have the maturity to understand. However, the situation is grave enough that I believe I should endeavor to teach you, though it may be pouring water into a bucket with no bottom."

Fortunately, the promise of information had Oria restraining a smart remark in response to the not-so-subtle insult.

"Despite all that has been studied on the flow of sgath to grien, there is a great deal we do not consciously understand, that lies in the realm of *hwil*. Testing showed your mother and father to be a perfect match. There were no indications otherwise, else the temple would not have blessed their marriage. To all appearances, she'd always provided him an unending source of sgath, which made him a powerful sorcerer and king."

"I know all this," she muttered softly enough that the high

priestess could not hear. Chuffta, however, heard clearly.

"No, you know what you've always believed. What your parents believed and taught you in turn. Listen to a new truth."

She didn't want to. Stubbornly, she stared at her ceiling, the mosaic of clouds and sky not as restful as usual.

"Or, if you are not ready to hear, if you need to rest, we need not do this now. Tell her to keep her secrets for later."

Chuffta's mind-voice, while solicitous, held enough reproof that she unbent. At the gate, facing down that bloodied warrior prince, she'd resolved to improve her knowledge. That included the painful things.

"Particularly the painful things, some would argue."

"We've since learned that perhaps some individuals are able to falsify the appearance of *hwil*, of compatibility with a mate." Febe's voice held suspicion, stopping short of accusing Oria of faking *hwil*. Though Oria had never claimed to have reached that miraculous state. Had others done so? Simply said so without really doing it? Had her own mother? It had never occurred to her to pretend, and yet…what a simple answer that would be, to gain access to the temple knowledge, to buy time to cultivate control of sgath in secret.

"King Tavlor relied on that bond heavily," Febe was saying, "believing it to be unshakeable, that with his temple-blessed marriage and the combined pool of power from all the priestesses, the sorcerers could not fail. Then the Destrye began killing the priestesses, an unprecedented event, at least in recent memory."

That was why he'd committed nearly everyone to the battle. Her father had believed they couldn't fail. Had he realized the truth before he died? She hoped not. What a horrible thing to realize, then to die without being able to rectify such a terrible mistake.

"We knew killing a priestess would obviously sever the bond between her and the sorcerers. We did not predict what might result if a number of priestesses died in rapid succession because it never occurred to anyone that it could happen. The walls of Bára have never been breached in such a violent and sudden way. Now that you know it could and did, knowing what you know of sgath magic, what do you predict? Think it through."

Oria quelled her stubborn impulse to disobey the high priestess's pedantic instructions. Her obstinacy had held her back in the past and she needed to learn to do better. She tried to calm her emotions. One of the clouds in her ceiling mosaic had always looked like a winged horse to her, ever since she was little. She found it and traced its lines with her eyes while she thought about it. "Priestesses absorb energy from all living things, particularly the focused and purified magical sources, as below Bára, and transform it into sgath."

"And some nonliving things. Perhaps an exacting point, but an important one for this puzzle," Febe said. "What are some examples?"

"Magical energy also comes from the sun, from Sgatha and Grienon, and from certain kinds of rock and heated gases in the earth below Bára. Depending on her nature, a woman might absorb one kind of energy more than another." Oria had no idea what her nature tended toward, which had always been part of the problem. Without *hwil*, the energies just piled up into in a meaningless jumble. "A priestess releases sgath ideally to a priest who's her perfect mirror. Through their bond, he converts that into grien, supplementing his own and repurposing it into whatever element his nature dictates."

"And for those without marriages, let alone without temple-blessed ones?"

"Those priestesses direct their sgath into a kind of pool that all sorcerers can dip into." The logic began to take shape. She wrenched her gaze from the winged horse in the mosaic sky to Chuffta's discerning, somber gaze. "When they died, if they were effectively bonded to the pool of magic, then all their energy poured into it, one after another."

"Yes. One life, even with the violence of murder, would not have made a difference. That energy would have been diluted into the rest. But, with so many powerful priestesses dropping their entire life energy into the Báran pool, within minutes of each other…" Febe sighed, her sorrow palpable.

"The priests overloaded. I can see how that would happen, though I don't think they could."

"No one imagined that scenario. But then, never before have so many priestesses been so actively contributing to a common pool, nor so many sorcerers drawing from it so heavily. The battle magics consumed so much that the priestesses offered more and more to sustain it."

"So what happened?" Oria asked, mouth dry with dread.

"It's difficult to explain to one without *hwil*, and the framework of teachings to support your understanding. But what you need to know is that King Tavlor overspent himself and died, which left Queen Rhianna unmoored. She should not have survived." There was a question there, an expectation, and Febe's mask faced Oria, scrutinizing her with uncomfortable intensity. "How is it that she did?"

"I—I don't know." She hadn't expected to feel accused of something, especially not knowing what she'd done, right or wrong.

"You were alone with her. Think back. What exactly did you do?"

"Nothing." Oria tried to think, so much of that a blur.

Aware also that maybe telling the exact truth would not be the smartest step. "I chafed her wrists, called her name, and she woke up."

"That can't be all." Though Febe remained serene, an impatience crawled through the room. "Tell me, moment by moment, how you—" Her chin snapped up, head swiveled to the window. "I must go. Don't leave the tower, Princess."

She swept out so abruptly that Oria frowned after her. "When she says 'overspent,' does she mean they broke?"

"Sounds that way to me."

"I didn't think men could break, because they can always release the grien."

"Now we know they can. Like you, they lost consciousness from the overload. Many of them died immediately."

"Did I... For a while I thought I was dead."

"We feared as much." His mind-voice became a gentle stroke. *"I couldn't sense you at all. I suspect that... Well, it's not relevant."*

"It is to me. What do you think?" She studied the jade-deep eyes, full of some uncharacteristic emotion.

"That perhaps you did die, that your essence departed your body, but then returned. Much as your mother's did."

"Why did I come back?"

To her surprise, he sounded vaguely amused when he replied. *"I don't know—why did you?"*

It took her aback, to contemplate that she'd somehow made this choice and caused it to happen. She'd think about that later.

Shouts reverberated outside. A new energy sliced through Oria's mind, unlike anything else she'd ever sensed. "What is that?" But she knew. That was why the high priestess had rushed out so precipitously.

"Unless I am mistaken, that is the arrival of the Trom."

~ 14 ~

T HE DESTRYE DEMAND that masks be removed had not gone over well. King Archimago had agreed with the wisdom of the strategic move—though Ion couched the proposal in terms of transparency of expression—with no mention of magical influence. Their father balked at discussions of magic.

All of them did, really, despite all they'd seen.

A rapidly heating argument seemed to be headed directly toward renewed combat, a prospect Lonen actually welcomed as it would be far better than this endless debate—killing a few of them would go a long way to releasing the building tension—when Ion's first captain ran into the room. He whispered urgently to Ion as Lonen's stomach dropped. And as shouts rose outside.

He didn't miss the way the young king, his adviser, Folcwita Lapo, and Prince Yar all exchanged glances that radiated smug satisfaction, even through the blandness of their masks. Most of the Bárans, however, looked confused and uneasy. As did many of city guard, who drew their weapons.

Shouts turned to screams.

Ion surged to his feet, his chair falling from the force of it, King Archimago a beat behind him. "You betray our truce!" Ion roared.

King Nat stood also, facing them down the long table. "You attacked our city. Are we not meant to defend ourselves?"

"You are a people without honor," King Archimago gritted out. "We should never have accepted your surrender."

"A surrender offered under duress," Nat snapped back, "by an untried girl with no mask and no authority to commit Bára to any treaty."

"She is a princess," Lonen said, before he thought better. He would never live down that decision. "Your sister."

"You know nothing of us, barbarian." Nat's sneer oozed from behind the mask. "And you never will because you'll all die under Trom fire."

"We waste time here." Ion signaled his man, sending quick orders. "Seal them in. No Báran leaves. King Archimago, we must move you to safe quarters. Lonen, Arnon—with me."

They jogged behind him, leaving a small crew of men to guard the city elders. At least they'd gathered conveniently in one room. The Destrye could ensure they'd remain there. All but the high priestess of their temple. He'd last seen her sitting on that bench by the great chasm, apparently meditating. Where had she gone?

"I'll stay with you," King Archimago said, drawing his great sword. "I won't cower behind my sons."

None of them argued. The king's word was law and they could not defy it at that moment any more than they ever could.

"What's the situation?" Lonen asked.

"Monsters," Ion replied, terse words shot through puffs of breath. "Attacking from the sky."

Indeed they were.

At the gut-watering sight, only hard years of training made

Lonen continue his headlong rush to battle the impossible. He recognized the creatures, however—giant versions of the dragonlet he'd spied with Oria. He still hadn't mentioned it to his father and brothers, though their men had seen it also and could corroborate his story. On top of everything, it had seemed…too much.

And not relevant until that moment.

Batwinged and bellowing fire, the dragons roared through the sky, barreling between towers and roasting Destrye and Bárans alike.

"Why would they call upon a savior that kills their own people?" Arnon cried out the question as they skidded to a stop at the edge of the chasm surrounding the palace. The confection of a bridge that Lonen had walked over less than an hour before had disappeared, cutting off the palace from the rest of the city. At whose behest?

"We cornered them," King Archimago said with weary resignation. "They saw no other way out. Desperate men take desperate measures."

"We could have come to an agreement," Arnon protested. "We only wanted to be sure they wouldn't come after us again."

"He's too young to be king." Their father shook his head. "I should have seen it before this. He'll sacrifice his people to retain his pride, to keep his grip on a throne he never earned. His people have become my responsibility now—unless we all perish together."

Helpless to do anything—not that any of the Destrye within the walls could do much to battle the giant monsters—the four of them watched from the brink of the chasm as people ran, some to the safety of the stone buildings, some in flames to collapse in heaps, burning into ash. Much as he wanted to look up to Oria's tower, Lonen forced himself not to, to bear grim witness to the destruction and terror before him. After a while it became clear that the beasts never crossed the chasm that surrounded the palace, though they could easily have flown over. Nor did they cross outside the walls, save for one section, toward the high mountains, where more streamed in.

If she was in her tower, Oria would be more or less safe. Along with her brothers and the others who'd so thoughtlessly sacrificed their people to destroy their enemy.

Within a short time, nobody remained outside shelter, the city as deserted as that first morning Ion and his men had walked them through. Less so, because no Destrye warriors could be seen. Not alive, at any rate.

A winged beast flew up, hovered, then landed on the far rim of the chasm. It looked like a snake with its unwinking black eyes, but with hind feet and leathery bat wings affixed. Talons the height of a man dug into the edge of the precipice, rocks falling way as they crumbled beneath its grip. Perched on its neck where it narrowed above the wing joints sat a creature that, while human in shape, bore no resemblance to any man or woman Lonen had ever seen.

The dragon creature snaked out its long neck, pointed chin coming at them like a spear. The four of them scrambled back, weapons drawn. Foolishness, in truth, as the dragon could have roasted them where they stood. Instead it laid its triangular snout on the ground, opaque eyes fixed on them. The man-thing on its back stood and walked with preternatu-ral grace along the sinuous neck. As it grew closer, more detail resolved. And yet Lonen still struggled to make sense of what he saw, even as the hair rose on the back of his neck.

It looked like a corpse that had been dried in the sun, skin shrunken over bones. Moving with a strangely articulated movement, almost insectile, it possessed no room in its angular body for the organs of a normal man. Black lidless eyes gazed unseeing out of the sockets of an overlarge, mouthless skull. Lonen had thought nothing could be more of an abomination than the golems. Another lesson learned.

"Arill save us," Arnon breathed, horror in his tone. "What is that thing?"

"If it lives," Ion grated out, "it can die, like any living thing."

It walked precisely, the way the forest cats do, one foot aligned exactly in front of the other, following a straight line between the giant lizard's eyes and down its snout, onto the rock of the palace promontory. Ion could very well be wrong, as the thing didn't seem to be living, beyond the fact that it apparently moved on its own initiative. A puppet on strings did the same. No expression showed on its smooth face, unnervingly like the masks the sorcerers and priestesses wore. A deliberate imitation of these monsters? If so, the Bárans were even sicker, more twisted than Lonen had believed.

King Archimago stepped forward, crowned by a wreath of bronzed oak leaves glittering in the sun, sword high, the polished steel bright. An impressive sight, though Lonen preferred the solid wooden haft of his iron-bladed axe. This creature could well be magically animated, like the golems, which meant the coarse iron would do far more than the king's sword.

"Halt!" King Archimago commanded, in the steel tones that had left more than one hardened warrior leaking into his boots. "This land belongs to the people of Destrye. You trespass uninvited. State your purpose here."

That was the king and father Lonen had always known—brave, commanding, the sun of his universe. With righteous wrath fueling him, King Archimago no longer looked old or worn. He blazed with glorious purpose. Protecting even the Bárans he found himself reluctantly responsible for. Lonen's heart swelled with pride. Despite all the terror and despair, the world also held honorable men who stood up for the good and the right.

The desiccated thing continued forward, expressionless and undeterred, easily a head taller than any of them. Nothing more than skin stretched over bone, it walked smoothly up to King Archimago.

Onto the point of his sword.

And kept going.

Somewhere Ion shouted a warning. Lonen sent slow messages to his muscles to raise the axe.

All moved as in a dream. The man-thing continued forward as if the sword didn't exist, the metal slipping through him like a hot knife through grease, the point emerging out its back. The moment spun out forever, a long, sticky summer's afternoon. And yet Lonen couldn't lift his axe in time to stop it.

Like a mother lifting her hand to test the temperature of her child's brow, like a lover caressing his beloved's cheek, the thing stroked spidery fingers over King Archimago's face.

And watched him fall.

King Archimago crumpled into a boneless pile of empty flesh, the sword and oak leaf wreath clanging down with him. Lonen's axe arced through the air, but Ion had been moving first.

Always first to defend, to protect, Ion swung his iron broadsword, releasing the battle cry of the Destrye warriors.

It went through the thing as if it didn't exist. A brush of light fingers and Ion, too, collapsed.

Somehow a sense of self-preservation kicked through

Lonen's wild horror and he checked his swing.

"No!" he shouted, his voice taking up Ion's still-echoing warrior cry as Arnon lunged past him.

~ **15** ~

ORIA FLUNG HERSELF through the doors to the garden terrace and pelted for the balustrade, gripping the stone with shaking fingers as her mind caught up with the sight that greeted her.

Derkesthai filled the skies—only they were hundreds of times Chuffta's size, and darkly shaded instead of white. When they weren't silhouetted against the sun, their deep metallic colors gleamed bronze, copper and gold. Their fire, though, blazed the same green as Chuffta's, and even more lethally, incinerating on a proportionally grander scale.

One swooped below her tower, broad-winged and chasing a squad of city guard who ran for the bridge to the palace. The men nearly made it across before the bellowing fire that chased them—so beautiful, like leaves fluttering in a cooling breeze— immolated them and the bridge, too. They plummeted into Ing's chasm, becoming floating ash as they fell, their death wails rising up to Oria.

It took her to her knees, the bruising pain of hitting the stones barely registering above the agony of so many lives pouring through her, with all their desires, sorrows and unspent wishes.

Chuffta landed on her shoulder, tail winding over her sleeve to wrap around the bare skin at her wrist, the pain receding. Not gone, but less intense, like the sun's heat fading behind a rare haze of clouds.

"You can't save them—at least spare yourself the burden of suffering along with them."

"Why?" The question sobbed out of her. She laid her palms flat against the softly gritty carved balustrade, peering through the openings, aghast at the scene playing out below, Bárans and Destrye alike running before their attackers, then vanishing into clouds of ash. "If Nat called to them for help, why are they attacking *us*, too?"

"That's why calling upon the Trom is a dangerous proposition, why the temple warns against it. They follow their own code. Once invited, they are as a beast released from confinement—killing indiscriminately."

"So they'll destroy us all. After everything we've suffered to try to make a peace, we'll simply all die at the hands of your brethren."

"Only distant brethren and those you see serve the Trom. We are similar, yes, as you are to the Destrye, but even more unlike. There are tales from long ago of a Báran mating and producing children with a Destrye. A derkesthai could no more mate with the Trom steeds than a Báran cat could with its larger, wilder cousins."

Obscurely that comforted her, that her wise and gentle Familiar wouldn't someday grow into the monsters that terrorized a city full of defenseless people. Angry as she was at the Destrye for bringing this blight upon Bára, she couldn't revel in their agonizing deaths. When Lonen dashed out from the palace entrance, recognizable even from her great height by the massive double-headed axe he carried, she cried out an involuntary warning.

A useless one, as he couldn't possibly hear her. Three other men accompanied him, one wearing some sort of golden crown and carrying a bright silver sword. Like the other Destrye, they'd abandoned their heavy cloaks, likely as a concession to the Báran heat, but still wore their furred vests and leather-strapped boots. They seemed as stunned as she, watching both peoples die in great numbers. Though she looked for them to appear, her brothers did not emerge, nor did any of the rest of the council.

She prayed that they remained under shelter.

The immense derkesthai never crossed Ing's Chasm that isolated the palace and temple, however, as if an invisible wall prevented them.

"It could be the temple's magic acts as a barrier, though I'm not sure."

How could Chuffta remain so calmly speculative?

"I don't even understand how that would work," she muttered, mostly to herself, stewing with frustration.

"Probably one of the many secrets they intended to teach you."

"Information that could be critical to know if we're not going to be incinerated. But no." She was as far from attaining *hwil* as she'd ever been in her life—and never likely to reach it under these conditions. The trials of the past week dragged her emotionally to the opposite pole of where her mind and spirit were meant to be for *hwil*. Instead of calm detachment, she jangled with death energy and despair. She became aware that her Familiar hadn't replied and turned her head to look at him. Chuffta also gazed at his giant cousins, soaring through the sky, a pensive look in the quiet green of his eyes. "Chuffta?"

He replied without looking at her. *"Maybe it's a time for rules to be broken. Perhaps also…"*

"What? Perhaps also what?"

"I hesitate to say too much, but they might have been wrong about you." Chuffta's mind-voice held regret and Oria tried not

to let it dig at her. She'd long suspected the same, of course, that she would never don her mother's mask, take her place among the least of the temple's priestesses, much less as a power of her own. Small and unimportant problems to have, in the face of such great ones.

With no one left in sight to char, many of the great lizards peeled off to make lazy circles in the sky. One, however, landed at the edge of the chasm, snaking its sinuous neck just as Chuffta would, creating a living bridge across. Something stirred at the wing joints that had blended in before that. A person?

"That is a Trom," Chuffta said with quiet emphasis.

"How do you know—have you seen one before?"

His trepidation leaked through the long pause. *"In dreams,"* he finally replied. *"Though I didn't know what it was when I dreamed it."*

Oria suppressed a shudder as the Trom stood, then walked along its steed's neck bridging the chasm to the palace side. "Why can they cross now?"

"The invitation might have been worded as such, to allow that individual Trom entrance, if no one else."

"And what will they—" She broke off with a strangled croak as the Destrye king first confronted the Trom, then fell to its touch. Then another man. Lonen aborted an attack he'd launched, dragging the third man to the side. Faint shouts rose up from them, audible in the silence of the empty city.

The Trom seemed to ignore them, walking on and disappearing into the palace.

"We have to go warn my mother, my brothers." Oria dragged herself to her feet and made for the inside, Chuffta spreading his wings for balance at her abrupt movements.

"How can they not know? Everyone in the city knows what you

know."

"Then I can't simply stay up here while they all die." She pushed through the outer doors, rapidly descending through the long spirals.

"What will it profit for you to die with them? Remember what happened last time. And you were at peak strength then. The last collapse weakened you severely."

"I don't care. I'm sick to death of being weak. If I die with them, at least I won't have to suffer the pain of outliving them all."

Chuffta said nothing more, though his disapproval—and fear for her—wafted through her mind. Or perhaps that was the smoke from the burning bodies carried by the afternoon breeze through the tower windows.

It seemed easier to lift the bar at her tower door this time, though she should have had more trouble, being weak from her days as an invalid. Perhaps having done it once before helped. This time no guards at all remained outside, not even Renzo. Shouts echoed down the hall, from the direction of the council chambers, and she ran towards them.

Then skidded to a stop.

Renzo lay in a heap, sword drawn, handsome face crumpled like an overripe fruit. She crouched, reaching out a tentative hand. Not to test for life, as he couldn't possibly be alive. Even with her inexperience, the lack of any animating force in the abandoned flesh before her was obvious. Rather, she struggled to understand what had happened to him. No evident wound and yet...

"I've heard it said that the Trom can dissolve that which makes bone strong."

"They chew the bones of their enemies," she whispered, remembering how the Destrye king seemed to simply collapse at the Trom's touch.

"Apparently more than a metaphor."

Needing to reassure them both, for Chuffta sounded unsettled, too, she reached up and stroked the silken scales of his breast, where the powerful wing muscles flexed. The shouts from the council chambers had faded, though voices harsh with anger occasionally echoed through, too vague for her to make out words. No clash of weapons.

Feeling her defenselessness, she took up Renzo's sword, easing it from his pulped fingers with the burn of nausea in her throat. It was heavier than it looked, dragging at her shoulder and elbow.

"It's not too late to go back. You walk into great danger."

"I wouldn't be able to lift the bar into place again. We'd be trapped up there while the great danger came after us." And she wasn't sure if she could climb all those stairs. Her body still didn't feel right, the enervation of her collapse exacerbating the poor condition brought on by her soft existence. Another fruit of Bára to be bruised and discarded. Too sweet and overripe.

Determined to be more than that, she headed to the council chambers, skirting the crumpled bodies—both Destrye and Báran—strewn about like the discarded skin and gristle from one of Chuffta's carnivorous meals. Nobody guarded the council doors, not even the ceremonial guard who'd remained there day and night all her life. The sucking sensation of crashing loss pulled at her, leaving her as boneless as all those dead.

Time enough to grieve later, if she survived.

She straightened her spine, imagining it lined with steel the Trom could not dissolve, and edged into the room.

And got her first close look at the Trom.

Not benevolent in appearance by any stretch, the Trom

looked like the reverse of the kills it left in its wake, as if it took their bones to make its own, then coated them with a layer of finely scaled skin.

It stood before Nat, who wore his mask and robes—and their father's crown. The sight shouldn't have made her angry, but it did. War must change all the rules, for none of the Báran or temple laws provided for Nat to be crowned king. Yar stood at his right shoulder. Both of them simmered with grien, drawing from the pool that must have been slowly rebuilding as High Priestess Febe put the junior priestesses to work. Nat seemed to be speaking to the Trom in low tones, gesturing to the group of Destrye.

She picked out Lonen easily—not for his double-headed axe this time, for he was barehanded—but because he was staring at her with a hard, even mean, expression. Perhaps the face of a man who had just watched his father and brother fall boneless to the ground in less than a heartbeat. He stood at the forefront of his men, not bloodied as he'd been the day of surrender, but no less intimidating for that. He pointed at her—no, at the sword she carried—then at the floor.

Feeling stupid as well as weak, she gripped the sword tighter, as if he could take it away from her from across the room. Even though her arm muscles already wept with fatigue so much that she'd love nothing better than to cast it away.

Nat's raised voice carried across the room. "I command you! Kill them all, now."

The Trom's reply slithered across the polished stones, like dry husks rubbed together, reverberating on a mental and emotional level that sawed across her raw sensibilities. "The Trom do not answer to you."

"I am King of Bára and I summoned you for this purpose," Nat proclaimed in ringing tones that nevertheless evoked his teenage arguments with their father. He'd never done well being thwarted, had always been too prideful and easily frustrated.

"You are not the Summoner," the Trom replied, without heat or interest.

"Princess Oria." The hissed whisper dragged her attention away. Lonen and his men had edged closer. She turned, struggling to point the heavy sword at him. He shook his head at her. "Drop the sword. It won't hurt you if you're not a threat."

Uncertain, she surveyed him. "Do you think it's a trick?" she asked Chuffta.

"It could be. But none of the Destrye hold weapons, so they must believe it to be true."

"Do as I command as King of Bára or face the consequences!" Nat's voice grew louder, along with the palpably building tension of contained magic and incipient violence, buffeting Oria like the hot desert winds that brought late summer sandstorms.

"Oria! What in Grienon are you doing out of your tower?" Yar had spotted her and sounded overexcited, his voice cracking with it. "Get over here now."

"Be careful," Lonen said, no longer bothering to whisper, holding her gaze, his own urgent. "If you offer threat of any kind or point a weapon at that thing, it kills with a touch. Blades pass right through it—even wielded by someone who knows how to hold one correctly."

"Oria! Attend me," Nat thundered.

Something changed in the tenor of magic in the room. The Trom looked at her now, matte-black eyes boring into her from even that distance. "Oria," it said. "Princess Ponen."

Her own roiling energy, still boiling over with all those

death agonies, surged within her at the Trom's words. Swelling up the way grien was said to, an irresistible force that yearned for release. If only she knew how. The Trom stepped away from Nat and Yar, turning in her direction. It lifted a hand that seemed to have no palm, only long, articulated fingers, like the desert spiders with bodies so small they seemed to be all leg. A kind of greeting? No more emotion showed in its still face than in the golden masks of the temple. With a start of near revulsion, Oria realized those masks must be modeled on Trom faces.

"Put down the sword, Oria." Lonen sounded less commanding than imploring. He might be her enemy, but she didn't think he wished for her death. A great deal of emotion surged through the room, liberally mixing with the barely leashed magical energy, but his stood out from the rest, something leafy, cool, and ancient to it. Not violence and anger—not toward her, anyway—but grief and keen-edged fear.

Following intuition and because her arm muscles begged for it, she bent her knees and laid the heavy sword on the floor. Lonen had seen through her on that—she wouldn't be able to swing it anyway. Straightening, she faced the Trom, refusing to be cowed by its remote, alien visage. "Greetings, Trom. Why do you slaughter the very people who asked for your aid?"

"Oria!" Nat surged forward, halting abruptly when the Trom pivoted its head to gaze at him. Though her brother wore the mask, nerves showed in the lines of his body. Behind him, Yar clutched white-knuckled hands together. The flavors of their barely restrained grien coiled and lashed. They planned to unleash something huge. "Don't presume to question our distinguished guest. Go back to your tower. I command you, as your king."

She nearly spat at that, mouth full of bitter grief that Nat would presume to command her, only days after their father's death, knowing as they both did that he could not have been truly crowned. All of it a ruse. He meant for her to move away from the Destrye, who faced certain death as soon as she did. A demise they richly deserved, so she should not interfere. She couldn't stop herself from glancing back at Lonen, though, not sure what she expected, but still feeling somehow as if she were abandoning him. If nothing else, she'd be breaking her word. He was still staring at her with a kind of ferocity unique to the Destrye, his eyes gritty and bleak as unpolished granite.

"I think it wise to move out of the line of fire." Chuffta sounded unusually subdued.

She made herself look away but did not leave the room. Instead she joined the group of masked junior priestesses, a brace of city guards protecting them. At least they'd learned that lesson. The Destrye warriors might have sheathed their weapons, but they looked as if they could kill with their hairy, brutish hands.

"Kill the Destrye, Trom," Nat said clearly. "It's why you were summoned."

The Trom had been watching Oria all this time, with skin-crawling focus. But at Nat's command, it swiveled its attention, not to the Destrye, but to Nat. "That may be why the Summoner called us, but it's not why we are here," it said, voice scratching over Oria's consciousness like a dull knife.

"Then we shall compel you." Nat raised his hands, magic pouring from the priestesses to him and Yar, who echoed their brother's movement. "In the name of Grienon, I command you to—"

As he spoke, as the magic sprang from his hands, the Trom

lifted a languid hand on an impossibly long arm and caressed her brother's cheek.

He sagged, crumpled, and fell in a heap.

~ **16** ~

IF LONEN EXPECTED Oria to scream—or perhaps faint again—at the sight of her brother's abrupt demise, she surprised him. She seemed vastly changed from the girl he'd glimpsed, candlelit in the window, or the young woman who'd ridden bravely to offer her city's surrender.

The last days had honed her. She'd lost weight, though she could hardly afford to lose any, her cheekbones and jaw line stark under her pale skin, copper eyes overbright in violet-shadowed sockets, her formerly shining hair braided back and dark with oils. As if she hadn't washed it in some time. As if she'd been abed all this time.

He should keep his attention on that foul creature the Bárans had so foolishly summoned, but his gaze kept going back to Oria, the white lizardling fierce on her shoulder, tail wrapped down the arm of her gray gown like a shimmering series of bracelets.

She didn't scream or faint. Instead she impossibly—showing incredible foolishness, not bravery—thrust herself in front of her remaining brother, taking his hands by the wrists, forcing them down. And turning her back on the monster.

He hadn't realized he'd stepped forward, fists clenched, until he became aware of Arnon's strong forearm around his throat. "My turn to save you," his brother hissed in his ear.

"Don't be an idiot. She makes her own grave."

The last years of Lonen's life had become a study in helplessness. His inability to stop the increasing golem rampages. The final, agonizing decision to send the women and children away, to abandon their home to the enemy's raids. That goodbye to Natly, certain he'd never see her again. The devastating losses of their forces. Nolan gone. His father dead. Ion, too.

Each death had carved another chunk out of him, as if every one of them took a piece of Lonen away to the Hall of Warriors. It seemed a man couldn't survive being gutted so many times, which explained why he felt so empty, so beyond the ability to feel anything.

And yet the sight of that slender, exhausted girl putting herself between her brother and a monster who killed with a caress filled him with a desperation that demanded action.

Oria stared up into her brother's gold mask, saying something low and urgent. Lonen's heart thudded in his empty chest as the monster raised its hand.

Closed the distance easily.

Drifted to touch her bright hair.

"No!" he shouted, the cry choked off by his brother's stranglehold.

Oria turned, still holding her brother's wrists, and flinched back at the spidery fingers hovering so near her cheek. Her cur of a brother wrenched free, backing up several hasty steps, and Lonen's heart shredded into panic as the thing made contact. Traced her high cheekbone, followed the line of her jaw. Brushed one deadly finger over her full lower lip.

And she remained standing.

The thing spoke to her in some incomprehensible language. It had a voice like an old warrior Lonen had known as a boy, a man who'd taken a sword wound to the throat. He'd lived, but spoke in a rasp, a cawing whisper.

"Nothing else." Her clear voice rang through the room without wavering. "Except to go, all of you. And do not return."

The thing caressed her cheek again, and she surely restrained a shudder, her slim frame tight as a drawn bow string, as it spoke to her again, at some length.

With that languid, unhurried, and jointless movement, the thing turned and strode away, out of the chamber. All in the room watched it go, silent, frozen in place, as if afraid even a loud breath might attract it back again.

Then erupted in chaos.

Prince Yar shouted something incoherent at Oria, then dove on the late king's pulped body. The princess reeled a bit, but caught herself, bolstered by the masked priestess with corkscrew red curls, who carefully supported Oria by the shoulders, saying something in her ear that made Oria nod sorrowfully as she gazed at her brother. The city guard advanced on Lonen and his pitifully small force of Destrye, who quickly scrambled for their discarded weapons. They were few in number—only the handful of warriors who'd been occupying the palace itself and guarding King Archimago, and who'd managed to evade the monster's touch. An amazingly simple strategy, to lower weapons and not attack the thing. It seemed to ignore everyone otherwise.

Except for Oria. Who alone had survived the thing's touch. Two exceptions at once.

"We have to recover Father and Ion," Arnon was saying in his ear. At least he'd released his throttling hold. Lonen supposed he should be grateful for it, but he burned with resentment—and an odd sense of betrayal. So many dead to that thing's foul touch, and nearly Oria, too. Not that he cared for her fate exactly, but it grated that she'd protected her brother instead of the other way around. Even now her brother paid more attention to a dead man than his living sister.

Or, rather, to the crown.

"Lonen!" Arnon urged.

"Their bodies are going nowhere," Lonen replied, his voice surprisingly even, given all that churned inside him. "Let's turn our attention on those still living—with the goal of keeping them that way."

Prince Yar stood, the heavy jeweled crown of Bára in his hands. "I am king now," he proclaimed.

"You are not." Oria overrode his words before he finished, making the boy turn to her in shock. If Lonen could have seen his face, the young prince would be gaping slack-jawed, an image that amused him greatly.

"Then who is in charge, Princess Oria?" Folcwita Lapo demanded.

"There are laws—both secular and prescribed by the temple—that decide such things, Folcwita. You know this as well as I."

"We are at war." Lapo thrust an angry hand at the Destrye. "We are invaded, occupied!"

Oria's chin held a stubborn tilt. "And yet we are not animals. We choose a ruler by writ of law."

"Surely, you don't think to claim the crown." Yar was still holding it, his voice full of anger. "You have no mask and are too frail to be—"

"Not me," she cut him off. "Our mother, Queen Rhianna holds the right to rule. At least in the interim, until protocols are followed."

"Oria, she…" The priestess who'd supported Oria trailed off, with a cagey glance at Lonen and his men. Following her gaze, Oria pressed two fingers to her temple, looking pained.

"Why are you holding blades at each other? Haven't you all had enough of death today?" Her voice wavered. "We need to get people out there to restore order to the city. Some of the burned may yet be helped. Others in hiding should be told it's safe to emerge. Why is no one thinking of these things?"

"We need to use this opportunity to evict the Destrye from Bára once and for all," Prince Yar said to her back, his snarl unfortunately a bit too much of a whine.

"We promised a truce and broke it," Oria said to Yar, but she looked at Lonen. "Will the Destrye accept a renewed truce, at least for the next few hours, so we may all tend our dead and wounded? I realize you have no reason to trust my word a second time, but it's all I have to offer. I shall remain here to see that it's kept." She threw a significant glare at the folcwita.

Yar and Arnon both burst into protest—a strange pair of bedfellows there—but Oria held Lonen's gaze. She kept her spine straight and chin high, both proud and humble at once. Her eyes held a special plea, as if she somehow asked this of him personally. He who'd risked himself to implore her to drop that ridiculously large sword she so obviously had no skill or strength to wield. Despite the hollowness of grief, the image of her straining to carry, much less lift the thing and point it, nearly had him smiling.

Even so, she seemed to be one of the only sane one of her entire tribe. Which was saying something, given she went everywhere with that white dragonlet that she seemed to believe understood her when she spoke.

He found himself inclining his head, a slow nod of acceptance that had his brother rounding on him. Tempting to knock Arnon upside the head with the haft of his axe, to silence him. But they needed every able-bodied man the Destrye could muster. Until they assessed the casualties, it could be that the balance had changed enough for the Bárans overpower the Destrye forces inside the walls. A daunting thought, even though the Bárans weren't warriors.

"Princess Oria, you have no authority to—" Folcwita Lapo started.

"In my mother's absence, I do. And I'm older than you, Yar."

"You wear no mask, Oria," the prince grated.

"And you have no wife," she retorted, then turned back to Lonen. "I'm asking for a few hours."

"You have them," he found himself saying.

"Lonen, you—"

"I'm older than you, Arnon." Lonen nearly smiled to be echoing Oria. It hit him like a physical blow that, with Ion and Nolan dead, along with King Archimago, that he—the dream-filled third son—would have to assume the Destrye crown. If they ever got out of this cursed walled city. "Let us tend to our people, Princess Oria. A truce until we can convene here again at sundown? I promise that any Destrye who lifts a weapon in violence to one of your people will die by my own hand."

"I promise the same, that any Báran who attacks a Destrye will be tossed into Ing's Chasm. Blades down, gentlemen, please." Oria seemed to sway a little on her feet, recovered herself. "Let the Destrye go about their business and us to ours."

Her guard bowed to her, sheathing their weapons. With another nod to his unlikely savior, Lonen returned his axe to its place on his back, mustered his men, and went to see about dealing with yet more dead.

~ 17 ~

ORIA WAITED FOR Lonen and his warriors to clear the room, then succumbed to Chuffta's chiding—and the sapping weakness in her limbs—and sank into a chair at the council table, cradling her throbbing head in her hands.

Nat dead, too. Only her mother and Yar left of their family. Her mother acting crazy, bereft of her mask and *hwil*, and Yar… What was this infection of power madness that had overtaken them? Her father had raised her brothers to be ambitious, true, and prepared them to rule. And Yar had been ever the most impetuous of them all, but everyone had laughed at that, saying he'd grow out of it. She'd never imagined her brothers would be so quick to claim the crown, especially with them so untried. Of course, never in her worst imaginings had she imagined such a vacuum on the throne of Bára.

Even so, everyone knew no one not stabilized by a marriage bond could rule Bára, or any of her sister cities.

"Perhaps that is the problem," Chuffta pointed out.

"Good point," she murmured to her Familiar, watching Yar and Folcwita Lapo argue, Nat's crumpled corpse at their feet. Somewhere in the mad jumble of emotions sandblasting her there had to be grief for her brother's death, but for the moment she couldn't find it. She'd passed into some state of callousness where she felt everything and nothing at once. High Priestess Febe entered the room, pausing to take in the scene. Her mask, naturally, gave nothing away, but she seemed unsurprised. Aha, it turned out anger still ran strongly in her heart. Oria called Febe over.

"Yes, Princess?" The high priestess emanated calm, her hwil unshakeable, which only fueled Oria's ire with the woman.

"We need Queen Rhianna here."

"Is that wise, Princess?" The high priestess's mask turned towards the fallen prince. "Can she withstand another death, the loss of her son? You saw how fragile she—"

Sick to death of talk of fragility, Oria fixed Febe with an imperious glare. "It's happened, whether she can withstand it or not. She is the queen and we need her. Please bring her here."

"But Princess…" Priestess Febe hesitated, her voice going kind in that tone Oria knew all too well. "You may not be in the best frame of mind to be making decisions since your unfortunate incident."

Just charming how the priestess said that, as if it were a tale written in illuminated letters and taught to children: *Princess Oria and Her Unfortunate Incident.*

Chuffta snickered in her mind. That at least remained the same.

The priestess noted something of her poor attitude, because she drew herself up, a thread of…something leaking through her cultivated calm. "There are things you should be aware of, Princess. Without *hwil,* however—"

"I'm aware of a great deal," Oria interrupted her, beyond done. "Mostly I'm *aware* that many people have lost sons and daughters today, while still mourning the thousands lost only days ago. I'm *aware* that my mother is also the queen of Bára and not even the temple has the power to strip her of her responsibilities, even if she did lose her mask. If there's precedent to remove a widowed ruler from the throne, that should be put before the Council of Law and judged according-ly. Until that eventuality, she is needed and she will step up to serve Bára as she's always done." Oria discovered she'd risen to her feet and that High Priestess Febe had taken a hesitant step back. "I may not be a priestess, but I am a princess who might be Queen of Bára myself someday—perhaps sooner than you think—and you *will* do as I command."

"Yes, Princess Oria." The priestess's voice sounded odd, but she hastened away with enough speed to set her crimson robes swirling.

"Well done, Oria."

She sat again, pressing her face into her hands, muttering into them. "Do you think so? My temper got away from me."

"Anger will fuel you in a way that despair will not. Use it."

"So much for seeking the calmness of perfect *hwil.*"

"It occurs to me that one can only beat one's head against a wall for so long before determining that the wall is harder than one's head."

"Is that supposed to be a profound teaching? Because I have no idea what you just said."

"Oria!" Yar shook her shoulder.

She lifted her face to narrow her eyes at him. This shouting of her name was getting old. A minor irritation in the face of all that had occurred, and yet...

"Stop nattering at your derkesthai and face reality. Either look about you or go back to your tower."

"I'm looking," she replied as evenly as she could. "I'm taking a moment to meditate while we await the arrival of

Queen Rhianna."

"Our brother is dead!" Yar shouted the words at her, as if she somehow didn't understand.

Oria took a breath and counted, trying to exercise patience and compassion for her obnoxious little brother, as her parents had always counseled, and her gaze strayed to Nat's jellied corpse. Her gorge rose along with grief that he'd never juggle fireballs for her again. Funny, the inane things that you remembered about a person. She should be mourning the loss of Bára's best heir to the throne. Not his cocky grin. Had his teeth dissolved, too?

"It's not him. Only a shell he left behind. He does not suffer."

"A lot of people are dead," she told Yar, swallowing back the sorrow. "Have you looked outside?"

"What are you saying?" Yar sounded young and uncertain. More the Yar she preferred, the adolescent boy overwhelmed by his formidably precocious powers rather than insufferably arrogant about them.

"The Trom arrived on giant derkesthai."

"As dumb as they are large."

"But not intelligent, like Chuffta," she added, to please her Familiar. "They burned everyone in sight, Destrye and Bárans alike. I saw it from the tower. And the halls are strewn with corpses like…like Nat's." Her throat grabbed on his name. "That Trom who walked in here dropped anyone who attacked him."

Yar sat heavily. "I didn't know. The Destrye kept us trapped in the council chambers, under guard."

"Well, now you do know. The bridge over Ing's Chasm was burned to nothing. I imagine the Destrye are working on something to allow us to cross into the city, to help all our people. But magic might come in useful, if you have some to spare." She allowed a little doubt to leak into her voice, to prick his pride.

Yar spread his hands, palms up, as if he knew she could see the grien in them. Perhaps everyone could do that. One of the temple's many secrets—but the temple did publicly teach that sensitives perceived magic differently, depending on their natural affinity. "We were building it up," Yar said faintly. "Priestess Febe and the junior priestesses had been feeding us sgath for days while we stalled negotiations. Nat said… He and Folcwita Lapo said the Trom would kill the occupying Destrye in the city and we'd take out the ones in here with one focused blast." His mask raised to face her, forlorn in its featurelessness. "It was a good plan."

Oria put a hand on his forearm over his robe. It was not the time to point out the utter foolishness of a plan that opened Bára to the Trom—not the least because Nat's poor judgment got himself killed. "We can only do our best, going forward. One step at a time. Go find Prince Lonen and help them bridge Ing's Chasm."

"You want me to work with the enemy?" Yar jerked his arm away, the moment of uncertainty gone, replaced by the brash pride of the arrogant young man who'd declared himself king over his brother's corpse. "I won't do it, Oria."

"We have no choice," she explained with more patience than she'd thought she possessed. "We have a truce until sundown and not enough people left to waste in fighting each other. Go help build the bridge, Yar. Use that grien you built up to help Bára. To help us, not the enemy."

"Okay." He nodded. Then stood. "Okay," he said again. Straightened his shoulders and left the room.

Folcwita Lapo glared at her from a cluster of council members near the windows, but none of them approached her. Which was fine with Oria. Nat's menservants arrived with a litter and managed to move him onto it, by dint of lifting his robes, then covered him with a pall. She didn't envy them that job. Or all the servants of the palace doing likewise with the casualties of the Trom's lethal caress. A further punishment for the survivors, having to cope with this horror.

She shuddered, for that and at the memory of that thing's touch, how it penetrated to her bones, touching intimate places that should belong only to her. The peculiar sensation of being...tasted. In all her life, only her mother and father had touched her skin-to-skin, besides accidental encounters. And Prince Lonen. The contact with him, however, while searing and possibly contributing to her collapse, hadn't unsettled her the way the Trom's did. But it hadn't hurt her, either.

And those things the Trom had said to her. *Princess Ponen. We have satisfied the call of the Summoner. You do not yet command our obedience. Perhaps you never will. I look forward to our next meeting. Thank you for the invitation.*

She hadn't liked it a bit.

"*I did not like it either, even filtered through you.*"

"Why didn't I die?" She asked the question with hesitation, certain she wouldn't like that answer either.

"*I don't know.*" Chuffta sounded apologetic. "*Logically, however, there are two explanations. Either the Trom can control the result of its touch, deciding whether to kill or not with it. Or you are in some way immune.*"

"Both of which would be followed up with the bigger question of why."

"*Agreed. But...*"

"But what? Be straight with me, Chuffta." She'd spoken a bit too loudly, one of Nat's servants starting towards her, then backing away when she waved him off.

Chuffta hopped off her shoulder and onto the table, keeping his tail in a loose bracelet around her wrist, gripping the wooden edge with his talons and straightening with mantled wings, so they looked eye to eye. *"Oria—I don't know everything either. Your mother visited my flight when you were a little girl and asked for one of us to be your Familiar. I agreed because I was young enough to bond with you and my family said such service to your line could be a great honor, if you turned out as your mother hoped."*

"What does that mean?" Oria's throat had gone dry.

"It means you're special. Your mother knew it. My family knew it. Maybe it's related to this."

"Well, if we're waiting for me to find *hwil* to get answers, we might be dead before that happens. It would be very helpful if someone would share a secret or two before it comes to that."

"Perhaps it is time to ask your mother."

"Perhaps so. But—you left others that you loved to be with me?" The question had never occurred to her. Chuffta had always been there, from her earliest memories. She'd never considered that he'd had a life outside of being her Familiar.

An odd conversation to be having at that moment, but she'd make no further decisions without the queen's approval, and at least this helped calm her.

"Family, friends, sure. But my flight is still there. We are a long-lived people and I will see them when I return. I thought it would be interesting to wander in the world of humans for a while."

"The way things are going, that might be sooner rather than later," she told him seriously, then stroked the curve of his neck. "But I'm grateful for you, now more than ever."

"I'm glad to be here, now more than ever. And I fervently hope I won't have cause to return home for a long, long time."

~ 18 ~

To Lonen's surprise, Prince Yar appeared to help bridge the chasm. At first the Báran prince stood to the side, managing to be both arrogant and diffident, watching them build an anchoring assembly in tandem with the Destrye team on the other side. Wary of the prince's intentions, Lonen detailed Alby to surreptitiously observe him.

But when the opposite team brought out arrows to carry ropes across, Yar stepped up. "Ah…Prince Lonen?"

"Yeah?" First time the kid had used his title. Interesting. Too bad it was now out of date.

"I can make the bridge—with stone."

Arnon bristled. "We don't want any part of your foul magic, you—"

Lonen held up a hand, swallowing his own knee-jerk revulsion. "Yes, we do. If we can spend effort elsewhere, I'm all for it. There's plenty to do." On the other side of the chasm, groups of Destrye and Bárans edged around each other as far as the eye could see. Observing the truce but not embracing it. He wanted to get over there as soon as possible, to start everyone coordinating for the few hours they could. He didn't care who built the bridge. "We'd appreciate it, Prince Yar."

The unsettling mask turned to him for a moment, and he thought the boy might ask a question, but he didn't. Just squared his shoulders and faced the chasm, raising his hands as they'd seen the sorcerers do in battle, the sight giving Lonen a habitual rush of terror before he reminded himself that it wouldn't be directed at his men this time.

"Clear your men away," Yar commanded. "So there are no accidents." The addition came in a less certain tone, revealing a young man's anxiety. Much like a young warrior still learning to trust his skills.

Lonen passed the word, using hand signals to the men across the chasm. Bemused, they obeyed, standing back to watch the sorcerer work, for the first time able to observe without the duress of battle. It seemed that nothing happened immediately and Arnon shifted restively, then stilled as he saw the same thing Lonen did.

The edges of the chasm seemed to blur. Lonen narrowed his eyes, searching for the illusion. Then the stone actually moved. Like the soft clay worked by Destrye potters, the rocks transformed as if under a giant hand. Extruding from each side, thickening as more stone flowed to join in, then extending again, the two fingers of stone met in the middle, blending seamlessly together into a low arch very similar to the bridge that had been burned away, though devoid of ornamentation.

It took only minutes, but Yar lowered his hands with a long breath, sweat streaming down the sides of his face at the mask's edge as if he'd exerted for hours. Then he faced Lonen. "It's solid. They can cross. It takes more, to build a thing, so I kept it simple." He sounded apologetic, but also hopeful, a puppy hoping to be petted.

Lonen gestured to his men that it was safe, grimly amused to see Destrye on both sides pause to knock fists against the stone and slide their feet to test the surface. Caution paid off, to be sure, but their doubt stemmed more from distaste for the magic of the Bárans than from concern that the structure would fail. The stone bridge looked as solid as the sharp rock edge of the chasm, all of one piece. It might, in fact, be difficult to take down again without the help of a sorcerer. But that would not be Lonen's problem.

"An impressive feat, Prince Yar." He nodded his respect, willing to throw the boy a bone.

The boy actually shrugged. He might be younger even than Oria. In fact she'd said as much, hadn't she? When she set him back on his heels. An intriguing glimpse of fiery spirit in an otherwise gentle-seeming personality. "Earth is my affinity and I'm unusually strong," Yar was saying. "But breaking it open is much easier than molding it."

A rock of angry grief plummeted through Lonen. Those cracks in the earth, like the one that took Nolan. Still, it might not have been this boy. "Is it...usual," he asked, trying to sound neutral, "to have that 'affinity'?"

"Oh no." The prince shook his head, sounding proud. "It's a rare gift. I'm a prodigy, in fact."

Full of himself and oblivious to the impact of his words on Lonen, who curled his fingers into fists to stop himself from wrapping them around the sorcerer's throat to throttle the life from Nolan's killer. *Haven't you all had enough of death today?* Oria's weary voice echoed in his head and he loosened his fists. Yes. Yes, he had.

"Perhaps you'd best go help your sister," he suggested, turning away.

"She doesn't want me." The prince sounded far too petulant. "She sent me out here to help you."

Ah, that explained a great deal, and he couldn't really blame her. "Then let's go see to our people."

CLEARING AWAY THE dead took less time than tending to the many injured. That is, once both peoples resigned themselves to collecting a small portion of the ashes that were all that remained of their friends and loved ones, identifying them by jewelry or metal weapons, which was all that didn't burn. The remaining ashes they swept onto wagons and dumped into the seemingly bottomless chasms.

Expedient, if nothing else.

And filthy work, too, both physically and spiritually. Lonen's soul would be begrimed beyond purification by the time they made it back to Dru. His body certainly was. They experienced a bad moment when the Bárans brought out golems to assist. His men cut three to quivering, gelatinous bits before the protesting Bárans explained these would help with the uglier tasks. Only then did they note that these had no fangs or claws as the ones outside the walls had.

The Báran healers also surprised them by offering to tend to the Destrye injured as well, citing the truce and that Lonen's warriors had helped so many survive to reach the hall where the healers worked. Still, Lonen assigned to them only the Destrye who seemed unlikely to survive the short journey out the gates to their own healers with the encamped army outside the walls.

In a stroke of good fortune, the Bárans' dragons had only attacked inside the walls, so the already much-reduced Destrye army outside had escaped further losses. Especially welcome as most of those men weren't stationed inside Bára because they'd already been too severely wounded. While speaking to the Destrye captains, Lonen relayed the news of King Archimago's and Prince Ion's deaths, along with the remains of their bodies, such as they were.

A curse of this benighted land, that death took his family without leaving bodies to properly anoint, to guide their steps to the Hall of Warriors. He could only pray they'd find their way regardless. Surely Arill would not be so cruel as to turn her back for a technicality of ritual.

They would burn the Destrye dead that they could, and decamp the next day in stages, dividing the army into groups by travel speed. There would be no more delays in negotiation. Lonen intended to put as much distance between the Destrye and Bára as possible. They'd be done with this place if he had to browbeat Oria and Yar into staying up all night. And this Queen Rhianna, if she showed herself. She had not thus far.

The sun was declining to the flat horizon by the time Lonen walked over Yar's stone bridge to the palace, weary in mind and body, and filthier than he'd been in his life. His skin itched to be rid of the ashes of the dead, but he'd made an agreement. The Destrye kept their word.

To his surprise, Oria met him just inside the doors. She'd changed from the gray dress she'd worn earlier, and had washed her hair. No longer braided, it floated around her like a cloak of copper, contrasting with the slim outline of the deep green gown she'd donned. The white dragonlet sat on her shoulder, iridescent scales catching the firelight from the sconces in the dimming hall, reflecting back Oria's colors.

He scrubbed a hand over his eyes and looked again. "Princess Oria," he acknowledged. "It seems the sun is setting."

"As it does every day," she replied, in the manner of someone returning a ritual greeting. Then shook her head slightly and gave him a rueful twist of her lips. "I think I don't want to know what grime coats you. I've arranged for you all to have access to the palace baths. Several of your captains, your lieutenant and your brother are already there." She gestured at a young serving boy. "Bero will show you the way."

"Thank you." It took a moment for his numb brain to process. "The truce—"

"Can we agree to extend it until you are not soiled with the remains of all our dead?"

"Yes." As much as he longed to be clean, he lingered a moment more. "I appreciate your thoughtfulness."

"In turn, I appreciate your long afternoon's toil on behalf of my people," she returned gravely. "I've heard many reports of your efforts and a proper bath seems a small favor in return. Go bathe. There are clothes for you to wear while yours are cleaned. I'm having food and drink brought to the council chambers. Everyone can eat freely."

"So we can stay there as long as necessary to come to an agreement."

He must have sounded harsher than he meant to because she flinched. The dragonlet's long white tail snaked around her wrist, coiling and uncoiling.

"I think it's best," she said, in a reasonably smooth tone. "Then we can all be done with each other."

As if it were so easy. "That will depend on you, Princess. We'll go when I'm satisfied with the terms."

"You and I made one agreement before. I feel confident we can come to another."

"Perhaps so." Uncertain what moved him to do it, he bowed—a slight incline—but a concession Ion would have smacked the back of his head for. Ion, however, now walked with the dead and Lonen lived. "I shall return shortly and we will find out."

<h1 style="text-align:center">~ 19 ~</h1>

ORIA LINGERED IN the entry hall until she felt certain all the Destrye who were going to had returned to the palace and found the baths. Thankfully all of them had been appreciative of the consideration and none had argued. She'd been uncertain how they'd receive the courtesy, as they were hardly well groomed at the best of times. Apparently being covered in the ashes of human bodies crossed the line, even for them. Or they were too exhausted. The cleanup efforts had been grim, all the men emanating dark thoughts. Some angry, some in despair.

Lonen, in particular, was a tumult of rage and guilt, all underlain with a grief that matched her own—energy he projected as forcefully as he swung that axe.

"He will not go easy on you," Chuffta observed.

"I don't need easy. I need them to go. We'll agree to their terms, watch them leave us be, and then set about rebuilding." She didn't want to think about the Trom's promise to return.

"You don't know what terms he'll ask for."

"Does it matter?" She sounded bleak, even to herself. "We are a decimated people. Prince Lonen already understands that we wouldn't agree to total subjugation. Anything else we can live with."

"Perhaps he'll ask for that again."

"If so, we'll ask Yar to build that bridge when we come to it." She smiled a little at her own joke, making her way down the hall to the council chambers. In truth she was proud of her little brother. She'd expected him to pitch in with heavy lifting, at best, and stay out of her aura at least—not create an entire bridge. And then he hadn't returned immediately, instead staying out and assisting with the cleanup. Something he wouldn't have stooped to before now. But then, before now she wouldn't have possessed the audacity to send him off on a task, either.

The temple taught that the crucible of crisis built character. *True growth is uncomfortable, even painful.* Of course, the priestesses meant by testing the strength of *hwil* under intense pressure, but perhaps the horrors of this week would mature both her and Yar. A small benefit for all they'd suffer—and would still face in the days to come.

Yar had dragged himself back to the palace before Lonen did, but not by much, exhausted and utterly defeated. Witnessing what horrors he and Nat had wrought affected him enough to agree to let Oria handle the negotiations, saying he no longer trusted himself. Then he shuffled off, uncharacteristically despondent, to bathe and eat in his own rooms, then to sleep.

More than a little weary herself, Oria envied him the respite. She wanted nothing more at that moment than the remote isolation of her tower. But she'd slept for the past several days—she could make it a few hours more.

"You were unconscious for days because your body shut down to keep your spirit attached. It's not exactly the same thing."

"I feel all right. Nothing like I did before I collapsed. I'll ask for a recess if I feel it coming on."

"Did you feel it coming on before?"

She didn't bother to answer as they both knew she hadn't. Yes, the pressure and input had been building to unbearable levels—and blew up exponentially once she stepped outside the city gates—but she'd expected to feel the onset of actual collapse. Instead she'd simply blanked. Gone from agonizing consciousness to clawing her way out of that gray fog, days later. Not something to dwell on.

A number of people waited in the council chambers and she hesitated outside the doors, not ready to go in. Lapo, along with several other folcwitas, had Priest Vico in one corner, arguing in low voices. Priestess Febe sat nearby, apparently meditating. Freshly washed Destrye warriors prowled the laden food table. Even in the pale silk trousers and loose shirts of Báran men they stood out with their dark skin and wild hair. No sign of Queen Rhianna. She'd said she wouldn't come, though she'd received the news of Nat's death with her former outward calm.

She and Oria had spent an hour together while the queen's handmaidens washed Oria's hair and fetched her a clean gown from the tower, so Oria wouldn't have to make the climb. The queen had put her off when she asked why the Trom called her *Ponen*, though Oria thought it wasn't that she didn't know, but rather she couldn't bring herself to care enough to muster an answer. Her mother also listlessly refused to advise Oria, telling her that whatever terms she set with the Destrye didn't matter to her.

With Oria on her feet again, her mother seemed to have again lost the brief spark of her old self.

"She may yet recover," Chuffta comforted her.

Oria fervently hoped so.

Folcwita Lapo spotted Oria and waved her over. "Does he think I'm a servant girl to be summoned?" she muttered, irritation crawling up her spine.

"Don't go then."

"I'm not going to." Instead she waved him off in the same preemptory fashion and ambled to the buffet table, picking up a plate and filling it slowly, deliberately dawdling. The Destrye gave way, nodding with more courtesy than she would have credited such rough men with. Ironic that she'd rather be in their company than the folcwitas'.

"Princess." Lonen greeted her with a nod, taking up a plate of his own and scowling at the table. He'd tied his still-wet hair back with a piece of leather and trimmed his beard to a neat scruff. Between the two, the hard line of his jaw stood out more, along with the scar that dragged down his cheek. He shouldn't look so appealing, nor should she be battling an unsettling urge to run her hand over his beard, to discover if it felt soft or scratchy. She never wanted to touch people, as it only led to disaster.

Lonen noticed her intent stare and raised dark brows. "Problem?"

"I didn't expect you so quickly, Prince Lonen."

He tilted a wry glance at her, a glint of something in his slate-gray eyes. "Your baths were such a treat I thought it best not to linger, lest I get too comfortable and fall asleep. A strategy of yours, perhaps, to incapacitate me before the negotiations."

"I'm sure you must be exhausted." She clutched her plate, glad of something to do with her hands, and focused on not stepping back, though the Destrye stood much too close for her to screen out his emotions. A great deal going on under that remote expression, but...a flicker of humor there, like a blue flame licking up from banked coals of darker feelings.

"As you must be also," he returned. "We have not had the

opportunity to speak since you fainted in my arms, but I believe you've been unwell since."

"I did not faint, certainly not in your arms." She used the excuse of making room at the table for new arrivals to put a bit of distance between them. That was better.

"Actually, the Destrye did catch you when you collapsed."

"Not helpful," she muttered through clenched teeth.

Lonen stepped back also, the scar on his cheek pulling with displeasure. "Is there no meat?"

"Meat? Animal flesh?"

A ghost of a smile twisted the man's lips, the frown smoothing. "Generally, yes—meat is animal flesh. The Destrye are rarely cannibals."

"No," she replied a bit tartly, feeling the sting of embarrassment that she'd implied as much. Surely they weren't really and he was teasing her. "Bárans eat only fruits, vegetables, grains. There's some cheese you could try."

"No wonder they're all so weak," one of the nearby warriors said to another, to a crack of laughter.

"Don't try it—that stuff is rancid."

"Stand down," Lonen snapped. "Get your food and go. If I want to hear from you, I'll say so."

They bowed and hastened away with admirable discipline while Lonen peered doubtfully at the round of cheese. He took a bite, then spit it out with a grimace of distaste. "It *is* rancid. Do you mean to be rid of us with food poisoning?"

Oria risked drawing near again, reaching a hand around him to snag a piece of the cheese, biting into it and chewing. "No. We don't think of it as rancid. It's more…cured over time."

He frowned at her in such consternation that she nearly laughed, an odd bubble rising through all the dark despair.

"Did my brothers bring in meat for you before this? I didn't think to ask the kitchens for it. We don't have much, but…"

Lonen was slowly shaking his head, expression opaque, but a tendril of curiosity winding through his bleak emotions. "You are the first of your family to offer us food."

Oh. Maybe she'd erred in doing so. Probably a conquered people didn't play host to their overlords. She made a terrible diplomat. Another course of study to add to the list, should their lives ever return to normal.

"You're doing fine. I'll tell you if you make a real misstep."

Holding her gaze, Lonen bit into the cheese again, a smaller bite this time, chewing it thoughtfully. He swallowed, the ridge in his throat moving with it. Her fingertips tingled to touch him there, too. "An acquired taste, perhaps," he said and she had to drag her thoughts back to the subject at hand.

"Try this," she said, not certain why she felt hot. Though the curtains lay slack along the windows, no breezes to catch. Reaching for the crock, she dabbed some honey on his hunk of cheese, smiling as he bit in, his brows raising in pleasure.

"It's sweet. We have something like this made from the sap of trees in winter."

"Ours comes from insects. They make it to feed their young."

He made such a grimace at that, setting the cheese down and pushing it aside, that she realized she shouldn't have told him. It did sound odd, put that way. "I can ask for—"

"It was thoughtfully done—" Lonen said at the same time, a faint smile for their mutual gaffe. Surely he wouldn't be as nervous as she? "Thank you," he continued, "but we have meat at the encampment, if the men wish to find some."

"Oh." She had no idea what armies ate. "Where did you get it?"

Two lines made brackets between his thick brows, a definite sense of puzzlement coming from him. "We brought some with us, dried, and we've been sending parties back across the bay to hunt for more."

"Oh," she said again, feeling like an idiot. Hunting. Of course. She had no idea what animals lived across the bay, but would not ask and further reveal her ignorance. Averting her gaze, she noticed Folcwita Lapo prowling the other side of the room, throwing her black looks. The force of his displeasure crawled over her sensitive nerves even from that distance, a headache pounding into her temple.

"Careful, Oria."

She was sick to death of being careful, of being so cursed weak. But she really did not look forward to sitting at that table and having everyone's anger shout at her for hours. How could she make good decisions under those conditions? Especially when only she and the Destrye prince need agree to the terms, as they both spoke for their people at the moment. The rest was courtesy and she had used up her quotient of that commodity.

"An excellent idea."

"Right." So great was her relief at the suggestion that she forgot herself and spoke out load, reaching up to scratch Chuffta's chest.

Lonen gave her a startled glance, then scrutinized her Familiar, distaste wafting off of him. That time she didn't care. She took a physical step back, bringing his stormy gaze to hers again. "I have a suggestion, Prince Lonen. Is there any reason you and I can't sit down alone and discuss terms one on one—do we need all these people?"

She'd surprised him, which at least backed off the worst of the disgust. "My brother will be annoyed," Lonen said slowly, thinking it through, "but I outrank him. What of your advisers, your council?"

"They will also be annoyed, but I outrank them." She nearly smiled at the flicker of amusement that lit the stormy gray of his eyes. "Arguably they have had their opportunity for days now to make their opinions known."

"Believe me, Princess, they have. Repeatedly."

She didn't ask why the Destrye had tolerated the obstructionism. From the resolute set of Lonen's jaw and the determined anger rising out of him, he, at least, was done with it.

"Then I see no reason you and I shouldn't sit down privately to discuss. Come. I know a place." She set her plate down, not hungry in the first place, and beckoned to Juli. She liked the junior priestess, who possessed both a solicitous nature and discretion, and asked Juli to relay that Oria had withdrawn to her tower and should not be disturbed—after a suitable delay. They'd see how long that lasted before Folcwita Lapo and the others realized she'd circumvented them. She started to go. When Lonen didn't accompany her, she turned back. "Problem?"

"Shouldn't we include a guard of some sort?"

"Why—are you afraid of me?" She regretted asking it, because his reaction stabbed at her, that severe distaste, shaded with suspicion and distrust. His eyes flicked to Chuffta and away.

"I don't know." He paused for a long moment. Then his mood shifted and he smiled in truth, a bright emotion echoing it, a flash of who he might be when not at war. "It depends on if you have that sword on you. My life could be in danger."

"A risk you'll have to take, Prince Lonen." She made herself stay somber. And did not further draw attention to Chuffta by mentioning his ability to guard her well-being.

~ 20 ~

"I T'S KING LONEN, by the way," he told Oria as he followed her out the doors. The dragonlet had swiveled its head backwards on its neck, keeping those bright green eyes fixed on him, unblinking, reminding him uncomfortably of its enormous lethal cousins. He wouldn't let it unsettle him. Or her, with her uncanny gaze that seemed to see more in him than he liked.

Could she read his thoughts? It would be interesting to test it. Something to discomfit her from that unshakable poise. Like working up a vivid image of tossing up her skirts and ravishing her until she screamed his name and—

"When did that happen?"

He nearly asked what before he caught himself. She cast him a questioning glance, which at least seemed to prove she hadn't eavesdropped on those prurient thoughts. Something that felt like a reprieve, after the fact. Still—what witchy powers did she possess? He wanted to pose the question, but it seemed…intimate. Not appropriate for the conversation they needed to have. About politics. So the Destrye could finally leave this cursed place and go home, find their own women again.

What Oria—or any of the vile Bárans—could or could not do should no longer be his problem. A fine goal for the negotiation.

Oria frowned slightly, and the dragonlet leaned into her, tail coiling so much like a snake that he fought the impulse to throw it to the ground and stomp on it. "*King* Lonen?" she prompted, emphasizing the title.

"As soon as my brother the heir died," he said shortly. "There's no need for discussion, ceremony, or…law committees, among us, as it seems you Bárans have."

She nodded, looking thoughtful, neither confirming nor denying. They arrived at a set of closed doors, two of the city guard outside it.

"Admit no one but Queen Rhianna," she told them, and they bowed, opening the doors for her. She began to ascend a winding set of stairs, but Lonen paused, taking a moment to observe the weight of a large metal-clad bar settling into place behind them, as if by magic.

"Operated by a secret external mechanism," came her explanation, and he turned to find her copper gaze on him, again discerning far too much. "But it can be lifted from the inside with a bit of effort. I managed it, so I'm sure you could."

"Ah." He restrained a comment that her slim arms looked barely able to lift the weight of the dragonlet, much less that bar.

"I hope you don't mind climbing," she said as he joined her on the step. "It's a bit of one."

"Not a problem." He took in the spiraling stairs, made of stone and clinging to the curved outer wall of the tower, circling an echoing space from the ground floor to the dizzying heights above. Flaming sconces studded the walls at intervals, but failed to illuminate the ceiling that must be there, somewhere, high above. Open windows looked out on the city, though the night seemed too still for breezes. "Do you intend to be queen?" he asked, earning a startled glance.

"Is that one of your terms?"

"No." He didn't know why he'd blurted out that question. "I don't care about your government, as long as you keep it far away from the Destrye."

"Then why do you ask?"

He gestured at the endless rise of stairs. "Making conversation. It looks like a long walk."

"I apologize for that. But it's the best place for me to be for a number of reasons."

"Why's that?"

"No one will be able to interrupt or interfere with our conversation. I want a solution, not more arguing and delay."

"I meant, why won't they be able to interrupt?"

"It's my tower." She shrugged. "No one may enter without my permission, by sacred law."

"Interesting. To protect your virtue?" If so, he shouldn't be alone with her. Certainly the thought shouldn't give such a punch to his gut.

He surprised a breathy laugh out of her. "It's more complicated than that."

"Try me."

She threw him a repressive glance, all humor sapped from her expression. "None of it is relevant to our negotiations. To answer an easier question—no, I have no desire to be queen and there are...reasons I should not take that role. Suffice to say, we have a queen. My mother is alive and well. There will be decisions to make depending upon what you and I agree the Destrye role in our government will be."

He mulled over her words—both spoken and what she cagily withheld. When she'd first offered surrender, he'd proposed total subjugation because he'd been thinking in battle terms. Fighting made things simple. You won or you lost. Usually if you lost, you died. Or wished you had. But this would not be so straightforward. He had no desire to rule Bára from afar. During that interminable wrangling, his father had never gotten to the point of giving his vision for the future of the two peoples—one of many things Lonen would give a great deal to know that his father would never be able to relate.

None of them had discussed what would happen if they managed to stop the golem incursions, other than a vague idea of going back to a way of life already thoroughly destroyed. But King Archimago had died in part because he'd taken responsibility for the innocent portion of the population of Bára. Rage at the injustice of it all boiled through Lonen. Against all odds, they'd triumphed...and yet, what had they won?

Oria paused, putting a slim hand against the stone wall. She'd paled, her breathing labored.

"Are you well?" he asked, though clearly she wasn't. The dragonlet peered around her hair at him, the stare oddly accusing.

She raised her eyes ruefully at the remaining stairs. "I am not in condition for extensive exercise, to my great chagrin. Also, as you observed, I've been unwell these past days."

Something told him that wasn't the entire truth, but before he could question her further, she pushed away from the wall with a grim set to her jaw, gathering up her long skirts, and set to climbing again.

"Why pick a place so far then, that takes so much effort?"

"I'll need to get up there eventually tonight, it might as well be now. And...I'll be able to think better." She hadn't been looking at him, but did then with a slight grimace. "I should probably not admit such things to my enemy."

She was likely right, but for a few moments—to his own chagrin—he'd forgotten that about them. Also he wasn't entirely sure what she'd admitted. "I could carry you," he found himself offering, then regretted it instantly.

Already shaking her head, she brushed him off. "Really it's better if you don't touch me."

Don't touch me. Her desperate command of before still rankled. "I'd hardly rape you," he replied, stiffly furious. "None of your Bárans have been bothered that way."

"I did not know that," she said quietly, perhaps because she lacked the breath for more. "But that's not what I meant. I intended no offense, King Lonen."

Feeling like he should apologize but unwilling to, he remained silent for the rest of the ascent. Better for her not to waste breath talking anyway. Finally, they reached the very top and she led him through a series of rooms to an open-air terrace full of flowering trees, blossoms luminous in the night, and the rustle of trailing vines. Oria lifted her face to the sky, Sgatha high and rose-colored, sighing in what could only be relief. No sign of Grienon, so he must be in his dark phase.

Lonen wandered to the balustrade, struck by the view of Bára below, all falling away beneath her eyrie. Beyond the high city walls the Destrye camp blazed with campfires, the long dry plateau moonlit around them. Oria's tower. It tugged some emotion from him, a strange tenderness that felt misplaced amid all the rage and grief.

"You live up here, all the time, alone?"

She joined him at the edge of the balcony, though still a good distance away, well out of touching range. As if he'd try after she'd sounded so horrified by the possibility. "I go down sometimes. And I'm not alone. I have—had—attendants, teachers. My mother, too, spends time with me here. A few others. Also, there's always…"

When she didn't finish the thought, he turned his back on the staggering—and stomach-dropping—view. The torchlight made her hair even more coppery, if possible, and the moon gave a pinkish cast to her fair skin and the winged lizard's white hide, both more otherworldly than ever. How she could both fascinate and repel him, he didn't know. Unless she practiced sorcery on him as he suspected her brothers had been doing to his father. What he needed was to get away from her unnatural influence and this place of monsters and death.

Superstitiously, he moved away from that dizzying drop. She might look fragile and become sickly climbing stairs, but he knew firsthand how powerful the Báran magic could be. He did not care to sample what a long fall that would be.

"There's always what? That lizardling you cart about everywhere?"

"His name is Chuffta." She sounded stiff. He'd annoyed her, insulting her pet. Good. Better than feeling that strange tenderness.

"You don't really believe you can talk to that thing, do you?"

She gave him a long look, then went to a set of low chairs around a table with a freakish violet fire burning in the center of it. Pouring from a pitcher into two transparent goblets, she nudged one in his direction, then sat back, cupping the other and drinking deeply. She heaved such a sigh of relief that he couldn't restrain his curiosity and went over to pick up his. The goblet was made of something very thin that felt as if it might shatter in his grip. He sniffed at the contents. Fruity and sweet. He tasted it. Juice, not wine. Figured.

"Shall we get to the subject at hand?" she suggested in an

even tone.

"You didn't answer my question."

"Because the answer doesn't matter. What I do or do not believe has no bearing on our negotiations. We could argue all night about our differences and it seems both our peoples have wasted enough time doing that already. What terms do you propose?"

"You don't have an offer?"

She actually made snorting noise, at odds with her regal poise. "No wonder you all spent so many days discussing. If I'm not mistaken, you're in the position of power. It seems to me that this conversation should consist of you, the conqueror, giving terms to me, the conquered—at which point I attempt to weasel out whatever concessions I can."

Abruptly tired, he sat across from her, dangling the goblet between his knees, reminding himself to handle it gently. He felt strangely naked wearing the soft garb of the Báran men, the loose material of the shirt and trousers so thin he barely felt it on his skin, but also grateful for it in the overly warm night. Something about sitting there with her, with the softly burning fire—pretty, even in its strangeness—and the moonlight turning the night-blooming garden into an oasis in her stone city surrounded by an unforgiving desert, made all the war and politics feel far away. For a wild moment, he entertained what it might be like to be there under other circumstances, to be courting her as he would Natly, seeing if he could make her laugh and—

He shook off the romantic notion. That was exhaustion getting to him, and being so long away from feminine company. Natly was waiting for him to return, a normal, beautiful and spirited woman of his own people. One with a strong, lush figure and vitality to run and ride with the best of the Destrye. And he'd be returning as king, which should be enough to finally persuade her to marry him.

"Mostly I just want this done." His turn to be admitting to the enemy what he shouldn't.

"Why don't we start with what you came here for—were you after the source of Báran magic?"

"Arill, no!" The shock of her suggestion had him rejecting that foul notion too brusquely, because she physically flinched, making him feel absurdly guilty, as if he'd punched her. "No, we want nothing more than to keep clear of your magic," he said more smoothly, rolling the fragile goblet between his palms. It reminded him of Oria, in a way—both easily crushed but also exotically lovely, unlike anything he'd seen or touched before. Not trusting himself not to shatter it carelessly, he set it aside.

"Why did you attack us then?"

Glancing up sharply, he opened his mouth to retort, but her expression, wide, wondering, and without guile made him pause. An act perhaps, but... "You attacked us first, Princess."

She shook back her hair, frowning. "How can that be true? Our peoples have battled in the past, I know, but the peace has lasted for centuries now. The Destrye live far from here. *You* came to Bára. We only defended ourselves."

It could be that she truly didn't know, isolated in her manmade fancy of a garden. He gestured to the trees, the lavish vines with their hand-sized pearlescent blossoms, faces turned towards Sgatha and visited by pale-winged moths that hovered over them as they drank. "Where does the water come from for all of this?"

Her frown deepened and she looked around, as if seeing it all for the first time. "Well, servants haul it up, but I gather that's not the answer you mean. They bring it from stores, cisterns below the palace. All the city buildings have them, as reserves for dry weather."

He gazed out at the sere, moonlit plain. "Is it ever not dry weather?"

"We have a monsoon season, though it's been very light the last few years. When it does rain, we have roof cisterns to gather it. A good monsoon season gives us water to last until the next."

"And if it's a bad monsoon season, very light, as in the last few years?"

She shrugged. "Well, obviously we've had enough stores to be getting by. My trees aren't dying so we haven't run out."

"*Or...*" He held her gaze. "You've been sending those unnaturally puppeted golems of yours—only equipped with fangs and claws—to steal our water and kill any living creature that stands in their way. Mothers, children, livestock." A bleakness washed over him at the memories.

To his surprise, Oria's expression echoed that.

She looked horrified, even. "You mean, similar to the ones we used to defend the city when you attacked?"

He barked out a laugh and swallowed some of the juice to salve his dry throat. Too sweet, but the flavor was growing on him. "They didn't just look like them, Oria. They were the same. They've been attacking us for years, decimating our people and driving us out of our homeland. We tracked them back here to make it stop. We had no choice."

That last came out too forcefully, too defensive. She needed to know the truth, though. He ran his hands through his hair, remembering belatedly that he'd tied it back in an attempt to look more appropriate for a meeting with her in her lavish gown. Impatient with it, he tugged off the leather tie and tossed it on the table. She might find him brutish and unkempt, but what did he care?

"Everyone has choices," she said, as quiet as he'd been loud.

"You have to understand, Princess of Bára. You—or maybe not *you*, I don't know, but your people—you drove us to this. Yes, we had choices. We either had to stop you, die trying, or die by the claw of your golems."

"I see. A moment, please." She rose, seeming restless, moving back to the balustrade and gazing out. The quiet murmur of her voice drifted on the night air like the heavy scent of the moon blossoms.

She must be talking to that dragonlet. The absurdity annoyed him, but weariness softened the edges of the irritation. Oria was right that they'd argued enough to last years. Along the rim of the fire table, a series of animal figurines paraded, made of the same delicately transparent material as the goblets, catching and reflecting the violet firelight. He picked up one that reminded him of one of the forest cats of Dru. Amazingly lifelike, the cat seemed to be stalking something.

The white lizard hopped off Oria's shoulder, wings unfurling for balance and catching Lonen's eye, then took a perch on the balustrade, green eyes glowing. Oria ran an affectionate caress down the thing's neck with long, slender fingers that stirred Lonen in deep places that felt long forgotten. She turned her back to the drop, facing him with hands folded over her belly, chin high and steady. "So, if this is the case—and I know nothing of it, but have no reason to disbelieve you— then you've succeeded."

It took him a moment to drag his thoughts back and she tilted her head, with a wry smile. "Your men killed the sorcerer who created the vicious golems," she explained. "That was a singular gift."

Anger burned through his stupidly besotted brain. Perhaps Ion had been right about his lack of judgement—and now Lonen could never tell him so. "A singular *gift*?" he snarled.

She held up a hand, both fending him off—though he hadn't moved toward her—and acknowledging his protest. "A poor choice of words, I apologize. That's simply how we refer to the magic. *Affinity* might be a better word. At any rate, no more of those golems will be sent against you because the man who piloted them is gone."

"We've seen others of those golems around the city."

"Piloted by others with far less ability, as manual labor only, and…it's something I cannot explain, but if they go too far, they lose their animation and collapse. I don't know exactly how the late Priest Sisto was able to send the water-seeking golems all the way to Dru, but I do know—from conversations among us—that we have no one else in Bára who could. I can also assure you that we won't launch attacks against you of any other kind, if you agree in turn to leave us alone."

He wanted nothing more. "How can you guarantee that?"

"What else can I offer?" She held up her palms, copper eyebrows forking as she thought. "I'll add a personal promise. If you are attacked by anyone or anything of Bára, I vow to do whatever it takes to protect the Destrye."

"A sweeping promise."

She smiled, ever so slightly. "Easy enough to make, as I can be sure Bára won't attack you again. We have other problems than warring with the Destrye."

"And you…have the ability to protect the Destrye?" Seeing her in that violet and rosy light, he believed that perhaps she did.

The brief moment of amusement fled. "I hope so, because

Bára will need that, too. I can only promise that I'll do my utmost for the Destrye, as I would for Bára."

"I'll have to settle for that, then."

She nodded, crisply. "So that's agreed. You say you have no inclination to govern us. What else do you want?"

Nothing, he realized. His father, Ion, even Nolan might have sought to take more, but he himself would be hard pressed to simply put things back together again. Still… "You must agree to keep those other things away from us, too. The dragons and the monsters that rode them."

She folded her hands again, expression shadowed. "I have no control over the Trom, but I believe them to be our problem. They came at our call and have a long history with our people. I don't think they have reason to pursue the Destrye in any way."

He nodded, wishing that made him feel better. The way that thing had caressed her cheek… "What did it say to you—and why didn't its touch kill you?" he asked, unsure if he wanted to know for her sake or his.

"I don't know. It's something I shall have to discover more about in the days to come." With her body silhouetted against the moon, the violet fire not quite enough to reveal her expression, he couldn't read her reaction to his ill-advised question. Some tremor in her voice, though, made him think she was afraid.

"You don't know what it said, or why it didn't kill you?"

"Why it didn't kill me. The words were…an old dialect, and were not important."

She was lying about that, which shouldn't annoy him as much as it did. "Are you in danger from it?"

She cocked her head slightly. "If so," she said in a measured tone that revealed he'd pricked her pride, "that also would be my problem, not yours, King Lonen. Do you require anything else?"

He searched for the words to express it. He wanted his youthful idealism back, to know that magic could be wonderful, the way he'd imagined it as a boy, the way it seemed possible in her enchanted garden. Not watered with the blood of countless Destrye dead. He wanted to be rid of the crushing grief, to rewind time so none of this had happened. Except that he would never have met Oria. Which didn't matter anyway as this meeting sealed their goodbye. He'd return to Dru elevated in station but impoverished in heart and spirit.

Nothing Oria could give him would change that.

"No," was all he said.

"All right." She scrubbed her hands briskly, as if shaking off dust. "Let's write it down and end this terrible day."

He agreed. Though once again, the final victory felt lacking.

~ 21 ~

ORIA STOOD AT the balustrade, the rising sun scalding her eyes as she watched the Destrye army decamp. Chuffta perched on her shoulder, similarly fascinated by the spectacle. She should be feeling a sense of triumph. She'd achieved what she'd wanted all those days ago, standing in that same spot, straining for any sign of the battle.

Don't put attention on a result you do not want.

For the first time, the import of that lesson came clear. She'd wanted quite desperately to know more about the battle, to see and hear and experience it up close. She'd gotten exactly what she'd wanted, hadn't she? And it had left her an empty shell, able only to feel grief and regret.

"A fine sight this is." High Priestess Febe said, stepping up beside her. "Who would have believed even a day ago that they'd leave so easily?"

"It was hardly easy," Oria replied, toying with the strip of leather Lonen had used to tie his hair. He'd left it on her fire table and she'd picked it up, first out of curiosity, not sure what it was, this foreign object in her otherwise unchanging world. Then she'd held onto it for no reason other than it gave her something to do with her hands. "It only took the near total destruction of our people." A destruction brought upon them twice over by her own family, something she still didn't know how to reconcile. A destruction that still loomed in their future, if what Lonen had said was true. If Bára had gone to such lengths to steal so much water for so long, did they have any reserves at all? The cloudless sky and heating plain mercilessly glared in confirmation of her worst fears.

"The arrival of the Trom frightened them." The priestess's mask inclined as she nodded at her own insight, oblivious to Oria's point—and probably Bára's dire circumstances. "Else they would not have agreed to terms so speedily afterwards. However you managed that, particularly without the advice of the council, at least they are gone."

Oria bit her tongue, keeping her opinion on that to herself. There would be time enough to sort out all of that, once the Destrye left. Already Bára felt different with none of them in it. In exchange for her promise that they would not be attacked or pursued, Lonen had withdrawn every last warrior the night before. Perhaps the vacancy in the usually humming energy of the city could be attributed to the loss of so many lives.

Or perhaps to the long shadow cast by the advent of the Trom. The people of Bára looked to face a rapid extermination by fire and bone-crunching, or an extended demise by starvation and drought. Removing the threat posed by the Destrye had only changed the cause and the timeframe—Bára still stood to fall as surely as she'd predicted the week before.

But if Oria had learned nothing else, she understood now that fretting changed nothing. Her mother would be proud. If she could see past her mourning.

Resolutely, she put her mind on next steps. "What can we expect of the Trom now, High Priestess?"

"That's not something for you to worry about, Princess Oria. This is a matter for the temple."

Chuffta made a snorting sound in her mind, one she'd love

to make aloud. She wouldn't, however. Though she'd lost much of her respect for the temple in the past days, she would not demonstrate it overtly.

"I disagree. The Trom indicated that it would be back to visit me, personally."

"Surely the Trom meant the temple, where the priestesses are trained to interact with them. Without having received your mask, without *hwil* and the teachings that follow, you are ill-equipped to deal with such an important entity."

Oria turned with angry incredulity on the woman. "The important entity that dropped my brother with one touch, that killed him and countless others for no reason at all?"

The priestess's mask gazed back at her with equanimity. "I understand that such emotional outbursts are difficult for you to control, as you have no *hwil*, but do try to restrain yourself from wild accusations, Princess. Clearly Prince Nat, while seemingly worthy of his mask, was in truth lacking."

Back to "prince" for Nat, demoted again, if he'd ever been truly elevated to king. "By that logic, I was not found lacking because the Trom's touch didn't kill me," Oria snapped back.

The priestess didn't reply, turning her face back to the Destrye army. Aha.

"Indeed," Chuffta echoed the thought. *"Something there."*

"It called me Princess Ponen," she said, noting how the other women tensed, ever so slightly. Not enough to break *hwil*, but a lick of bright emotion leaking through.

"I don't know that word," Febe said, voice blander than the gray fog that had cocooned Oria. A lie. Oria felt it in her bones.

"I need training," she told the priestess. "If I'm ill-equipped to deal with the Trom, then it's the temple's responsibility to teach me what I need to know."

"You know the rules, Princess. Only those with *hwil* can be taught. The knowledge is too powerful to be entrusted to the unstable." Priestess Febe attempted to sound regretful, but the untruth radiated off of her. Did she not know how easily Oria could sense that?

"Perhaps not." Chuffta sounded thoughtful. *"I don't have access to anyone else's experience, so I don't know how they perceive magic. We know yours is unique, with your unusual sensitivity. We've learned much about your magic in the last days."*

She really wanted to be able to discuss this with Chuffta, a surge of excitement lifting her spirits from the morose depths. It seemed wrong to feel hopeful when they faced so much mourning and such severe trials ahead. And yet the prospect that there might be an alternative solution to her problem, some other way to access her sgath—maybe without all that endless and futile meditating!—to end this crippling sensitivity and maybe have a weapon to fight that loathsome Trom, to find other sources of water for Bára…

The possibility gave her reasons to keep going. She sorely needed those.

Once Lonen had said goodnight and goodbye, she'd expected the relief of aloneness. Having his jangling, angry, and grieving presence gone should have given her a whole other level of palliation. Like stepping into the rooftop garden after all the chaos.

And his departure *had* given her some of that respite. But it left her with an odd feeling that had taken her time to identify. She'd even let Chuffta guide her into meditation so she could sort it out before she tried to sleep. Finally, she'd identified the emotion.

Loss.

For the first time in her life, she experienced real loneliness. *You live up here, all the time, alone?* His incredulous question kept rattling back through her brain. That and the feelings he'd emanated, sensual and rich, that heated her inside as if the sun's midday rays penetrated her. Waking feelings she hadn't tasted outside of those illicit illustrations of the Destrye that had so fascinated her.

They'd lingered long after his departure, touching her even in her sleep. She'd wakened from an intense dream of impossible sensations—of his hair in her hands, his mouth on her body, and their skin slicked together. Things she was unlikely to feel other than in dreams, as she'd never be able to bear such contact with anyone other than an ideal husband, which the temple wouldn't grant her even the opportunity to test for until she earned a mask.

Certainly she would never be able to touch Lonen so intimately, even if he wasn't gone from Bára forever.

She wrapped the leather band around a forefinger. Perhaps she kidded herself that she only held it to give vent to her restless fretting. The scent of the leather, maybe something of the man's energy, lingered in the tie. The Destrye king was such a creature of the larger world, with his exuberant masculinity. She'd watched him from her tower, greeting his men, slapping backs, and shouting happily about going home. The words had echoed clearly even to her heights.

Unable to sleep after those restless, unsettling dreams, and telling herself she was only performing her duty to the Bárans, she'd kept vigil all night, watching them pack up and go, just as she bore witness as they streamed away into the rising sun.

It had all left her strangely bereft, which seemed impossible on top of all her other sorrows. So this renewed purpose would put her back on track to do what she needed to serve Bára and her people, however she could. No more wallowing in grief over the past or of what would never be. The next step would be to get real answers.

"That would be helpful, indeed," Chuffta agreed wryly.

She scratched his chest in silent solidarity and gratitude that he didn't comment on or judge her preoccupation with King Lonen.

Not without some petty pleasure, she broke the cloud of smug satisfaction surrounding the high priestess. "Tell Queen Rhianna and Prince Yar I'd like them to meet me for breakfast in the salon, as soon as they can manage it."

Febe stiffened. "Am I your handmaiden, Princess?"

"The temple has not yet seen fit to supply me with a replacement for Alva, and *you* seem to be available." She let the pause hang, tasting the woman's rancor, learning what she could from it. If they wouldn't teach her, she'd discover her own truths. How had the first sorceress learned, after all?

"An oversight, Princess," Febe replied. "With all the tumult and you being an invalid all those days. We believed you near death, not in need of tending from one of our few remaining priestesses. A pity that your fragile psyche cannot withstand the company of someone less trained. They are a precious resource, not to be squandered on frivolous whims."

Oria ignored the escalating barbs, easier to do with the promise that she might not be so fragile forever. "An excellent point," she said in her mildest tone. "Fortunately, I don't require a great deal of tending, especially as I will be out and about in the palace and the city."

"Is that wise, Princess? Your fragile condition—"

"Grows no less fragile for this sequestration. I faced the worst and survived."

"We don't know that for sure."

"You can't be sure of that, Princess. Perhaps your condition is more akin to those sensitive to the sting of the honey-makers—the first reaction is merely a shadow of successive ones."

Oria flashed Chuffta a glance for sounding so much like the priestess. He resettled his wings, a gesture remarkably like an irritated shrug.

"If that's the case," she told Febe, "then I shall find out. In the meanwhile, a junior priestess to come by from time to time will suffice. While I'm away from my rooms, regular servants can assist with upkeep."

"I could carry messages for you," Chuffta offered, *"if you would like to see how you fare without me for short times. That might be a good test of your endurance."*

Gratitude for her Familiar's understanding welled up. That felt good, too. Enough to disperse the feedback from the high priestess, who seethed with that buried something. Nevertheless, Febe inclined her head. "I shall see if any junior priestesses will volunteer to be assigned to you."

"Thank you. On your way to take care of that, you can pass along the message to my mother and brother."

Without another word, the high priestess glided out, her fulminating resentment swirling in her wake.

"Well, that made her a bit angry," Oria commented.

"You sensed something else, too, beneath the resentment and irritation."

Had she? She sorted through it, as she had the night before, peeling away the layers. "Fear?"

"Yes, a kind of alarm. And maybe… jealousy. You unsettled her. I wonder why?"

"We'll see if my mother has answers."

~ 22 ~

THE QUEEN AND Prince Yar arrived together, she leaning heavily on her son's arm. When she saw Oria already waiting, Queen Rhianna opened her arms, a sad smile breaking over her face. "Oh, Oria."

Oria slid into her mother's welcome embrace. Even filled with the ragged shadows of grief and failure, the cool serenity of the woman felt like a balm on sunburn. "Mother," Oria whispered.

Yar waited stiffly, his mask of course impassive, control in place. She sensed nothing of his state beyond a faint burn of…more resentment and fear? After he'd been so much better the night before. And she'd had such high hopes that he had matured. Something had happened, she sensed it in the rapid shift of his emotions.

"Let's sit and eat," Oria said, gesturing to the table. The sight of the greens and fruits gave her pause. How much longer would they be able to grow food?

"I already ate in my rooms, where I'd intended to stay and rest, but I was *summoned*." Yar stalked broodily over to the window. "And we shouldn't be breakfasting while the Destrye army might yet turn around and attack us."

She didn't point out that resting in their rooms would be no better in that case. "Should they do so, our watching them will change nothing. We've reached treaty agreeable to both sides. Let it go."

"I'm only relieved to have them gone," Queen Rhianna said, sitting and nodding to her servant to fill her plate.

"Yes, and for so little on our part." Yar paced the room restlessly. "It makes me wonder what my lovely sister promised—or gave to—Prince Lonen in exchange."

"Oh, of course." Oria stabbed a berry, wishing it could be her brother. Never mind that her illicit dreams and their lingering effects made Yar's sally rather closer to the mark than it should have been. She felt sure he'd eaten, or lied about having eaten, because he didn't want to remove his mask. He was definitely hiding something. "I can barely stand the most casual touch from a carefully shielded and trained masked priest or priestess, but you believe I bedded the enemy so he'd take his army away? I suppose I should be flattered that you think my charms sufficient to accomplish such a great task."

"Then why were you closeted with Prince Lonen?" Yar retorted. "Folcwita Lapo is furious. I wouldn't have gone to bed and left things to you if I'd imagined you'd exclude the council! I thought you'd be smart and let them handle things. You were supposed to be only a figurehead."

She bit back her frustrated response to that. "What do I care if the folcwita is angry? I accomplished what he could not—what you and the council didn't, I might point out. Besides, I invited our mother. She did not attend."

"I couldn't have offered anything. Without my mask, without Tav, I am nothing." Queen Rhianna focused on her plate, eating methodically but without relish.

"Exactly." Yar paced over. "Which is why Oria, who also has no mask, should have left the decision-making to the council."

"Yar..." Their mother sounded infinitely weary and wounded. "We're still family. Sit with us and eat."

"Is that a command from my queen—or should I say, former queen?" he snarled.

Their mother's face crumpled, and she stared at her meal, a tear rolling down her cheek. Oria leveled an accusing glance at him, which must have worked, because he finally sat, if sullenly, but still did not remove his mask.

Probably better to direct the conversation away from the erratic bore tides of personal issues and onto the problems Bára faced. "So, did both of you know that Bára had been sending golems to raid Dru for water?"

The queen set down her fork, pressing her fingertips to her eyelids. "I warned Tav that would come to no good."

"What water?" Yar shifted in his chair, restless and unhappy. He'd never been much for politics, even at his best. "Why are we talking about this now?"

"Bára's water, all of it," Oria explained patiently. "Priest Sisto sent the fighting golems to Dru to bring back wagonloads of water, because we'd run out. That's why the Destrye attacked."

"The Destrye attacked because it's in their nature. They're barbarians." Yar got up to stare out the window again.

"We were desperate, Oria," her mother said, at least sounding bolder, more alive. "So were our sister cities. The drought has gone on for too many years. Dru was the only place close enough with plenty of fresh water still."

"So we slaughtered the Destrye for it—even their children?" Oria couldn't keep the incredulity out of her voice. Her mother opened her mouth but swallowed the reproof Oria expected.

"The Destrye weren't supposed to die," she said instead.

"We never intended that. Sisto claimed he'd found a way to create the golems with a kind of ongoing spell. It acted like a packet of sgath. He embedded them with both the command to carry out the task—to fill the barrels with water and bring them back—and also provided them with the magic to keep them animated. No one realized that would result in them going through anything—or anyone—who stood in the way."

"But you knew," Oria whispered. "You and Father, Vico and Febe—you knew afterwards."

"Not at first. Not until the Destrye began to fight back. They discovered that iron would kill Vico's golems by neutralizing the packet of sgath. He felt them die."

"So you—" no, Oria shared the responsibility as a member of the ruling family of Bára "—*we* sent more."

"Yes." Queen Rhianna looked sick with it. "We chose our children over theirs. It was supposed to be only for a short time. Until the monsoons returned. But they never did and then, before we knew it, the Destrye had traced the golems back to Bára."

"Oh, Mother."

"Do you hear yourself?" Yar sounded incredulous. "Were you even listening? It was us or them. They made the same choice—only we won in the end."

"That's highly debatable," Oria said without looking at him. The question applied even more to him. "Though the Destrye let us off lightly, Bára still faces utter destruction. Do we have any reserves of water left?"

"Enough to last a few months," the queen replied, poking at her salad. "Longer if we stop trading it to our sister cities, but that will create backlash from them."

Oria rubbed her temple. "Because of the goods they trade in return?"

"Food we don't grow here, yes, but also because they will see us as weak with no one on the throne, with our temple so depleted. Why not simply come and take the rest of our water? They need it as badly as—probably even worse than—we do."

Fragments of family dinner conversations turned around and fit together to make a new pattern. Her father and Nat boasting of Bára's power, how the other cities sent wealth in tribute, that King Tavlor ruled them all, with Nat gleefully planning to follow in his footsteps.

"It wasn't just about keeping our people alive, was it?" Oria laid her hand over her mother's. "Maybe at first it was, but then it became about the wealth and power."

Her mother turned her hand to grip Oria's. "Your father was a good man. He only wanted the best for us and for Bára. We cannot leave our cities, not now, after so many generations living above the source of magic. If we go outside our walls for very long, we'll die. Some of us waste away, effectively starving. Others, like you..."

Blasted apart by it. Her mother didn't have to say it. Yar sat still, finally, absorbing the conversation.

"Then the answer is a strong front," he said. "We have water reserves. We have the Trom, which means we have more power than ever before. We can get more water and force our sister cities to continue to pay tribute to us."

"We can't do that—"

"There is no *we*," Yar cut Oria off, popping to his feet. "I will do it because I will be king. Our mother cannot be queen, not without a mask."

"The law doesn't say that."

"He's right, Oria." Her mother withdrew her hand, patted Oria's once, then settled it in her lap. "The law may be silent on the issue, but only because no king or queen has survived the death of their temple-blessed spouse. I've spoken with High Priestess Febe. She, the temple, Folcwita Lapo, and the rest of the council no longer consider me to be the queen. The throne of Bára belongs to a matched, masked husband and wife. As we sit, there is only one candidate."

Yar held out his hands, as if expecting congratulation.

"But Yar cannot be king—he has no wife."

"I'm one step closer than you are, sister dear. At least I have a mask. If I cannot find a match here—though I'm testing a few of the junior priestesses—I'll command our sister cities to send theirs for testing. There's a perfect wife for me out there somewhere. In the meantime, I'll act as king."

"Our sister cities know perfectly well that you won't qualify. One of their matched couples will come here and claim the throne."

"Not with me as their sole source of water—thank you for that solution."

"We have only a few months left!"

He shrugged. "We'll get more from Dru. I'll command the Trom to do it."

"The treaty prevents us from attacking them again, Yar. You can't do that."

"Oh yes I can." Yar prowled over to her. "And it's all your fault. Your treaty means nothing because *you* had no power to sign."

Oria glared up at him. He'd always been precocious, and the baby of the family, so spoiled for both reasons. But she'd never imagined he'd be so foolish. "You saw the Trom. What they did to Nat, to so many. They do not serve us."

"Correction. They do not serve you, but they do serve me. *I* summoned the Trom, not Nat. That's why they didn't listen to his commands. I realized the answer when I awoke this morning."

"Why—what happened?" Oria rose to her feet. Grien, bright, nearly uncontrolled, rolled off Yar, along with a kind of triumph twisted together with sheer terror. This was what had changed from the night before. "Is that why you won't remove your mask?"

"Why are you obsessed with me removing my mask?" Yar snarled, clenching his fists, impotent rage and fear billowing through his *hwil*. Oria nearly flinched, anticipating the blow to follow.

"He'd better not." Chuffta's fierce thought bolstered her courage.

"What are you hiding behind it, little brother?" Oria replied, all reasonableness to his tumult.

"If you must know." Without waiting for a servant, Yar wrenched the mask from his head, the ribbons leaving wild tufts of hair in their wake. Oria and her mother both gasped, Rhianna putting an involuntary hand to her throat, as if choking back further words.

Yar's eyes had gone entirely black, like the Trom's, matte and without pupils. Horrified, Oria extended a trembling hand to her brother, not sure how to help but moved to try. He yanked out of her reach.

"Can you see?" she asked, for want of other pertinent questions.

"Only with grien, just as I always do with the mask on. It's no loss. Especially compared to what I've gained. You! Come tie this on me again." The servant scuttled over, taking the mask with shaking fingers.

"When did this happen?" Oria asked.

"I noticed when I awoke this morning, when I washed, before I donned my mask."

"Did the Trom do it, touch you in some way?"

"You know they didn't. The Trom touched *you* and you're fine." Yar oozed bitterness. "I'm the one who performed the summoning ritual. It should have been me the sacred one paid attention to. Not my magicless, maskless sister."

Oh, Yar. "What was involved in the summoning ritual?" And why had Nat put their brother up to it? But she kept it to the one question. Not that it did any good, as Yar exploded out of his seat.

"You look to steal my secrets, my power—but I won't let you!" Yar's unmasked fury poured out and Oria staggered back from it. Chuffta spread his white wings, wrapping them around her in a shield as Yar's grien followed his shout. Green fire shot out, incinerating the blast.

Yar's turn now to fall back with a thin scream as his robes caught fire. His valet rushed forward to put out the flames, but he pushed the man away with an incoherent roar, patting them out himself, featureless face fixed on Oria. "How can you do that?" he whispered, hoarse. Frightened. "You shouldn't be able to do that." Then he ran from the room, the valet in his wake.

Oria met her mother's stunned gaze. The queen had both hands around her throat, horror in her brown eyes.

"What did I do?" Oria asked her mother, though the queen didn't answer. "It was Chuffta who breathed flame."

"But you dissipated Yar's grien. You neutralized it."

She sank into the chair, pressing fingertips to her temples. Out of habit, though, because her head didn't hurt for once. It should. That amount of fury should have sent her screaming to the shadows.

"This is what I mean—you stopped it."

"How?"

"I don't know. But it would be most useful to find out."

"As much as I knew this might be," her mother said slowly, the quiet words slipping past her hands, "I never truly believed. And here we are."

"That what might be?" Frustration roiled up. "Ponen?"

Her mother closed her eyes, nodded ever so slightly.

"Explain this to me, Mother. I need to know."

Queen Rhianna nodded again with more conviction, finally dropping her hands. For the first time since her husband died, something of her powerful sgath welled up. "Yes. I have things to show you. Perhaps there is yet another way out of this mud trap."

Oria could only hope. Though through no fault of her own, she had still broken her oath—and she would do everything in her power never to be forsworn again.

~ 23 ~

WITH RELIEF, LONEN left the Báran desert behind him. It had taken days of slow travel to reach the dry scrublands, which then gave way to the cactus- and evergreen-studded border country, populated by neither Destrye nor Bárans. Much as he wanted to ride ahead with the faster scouts, he sent Arnon instead and kept himself to the back of their decamping army, moving with the slowest of the injured.

Ion might have made a different choice, but their father wouldn't have abandoned their many injured and Lonen hoped to be something of the king Archimago had been. If nothing else, he owed his father that, and the Destrye his father and brothers had died to save. They'd be remembered with honor, certainly. Already the musicians and poets among the warriors called him the Savior of the Battle of Bára. Several tales of the various battles with the Bárans—including increasingly more lurid descriptions of the golems, dragons, and Trom—were passing up and down the caravan of men and wagons and circling the campfires at night.

None of them mentioned Oria or her dragonlet, which suited Lonen just fine. The strange princess continued to plague his thoughts in worrisome ways, sometimes walking through his dreams, her hair copper fire, gaze full of some question. Sometimes her eyes were the bright green of the lizard's, her teeth the same sharp fangs as she hissed. Once she flew at him, white leathery wings capturing him and holding him still while she feasted on his liver, murmuring love words all the while, her avid mouth then fastening on his cock, milking him until he ruptured.

He woke from that nightmare in a cold sweat, his seed ignominiously filling the furs as it hadn't done since he'd been a randy adolescent. Too long away from women, from his lovely Natly. It seemed a king shouldn't be subject to such human frailty. He'd never expected to wear the Destrye crown, so he hadn't imagined exactly what it would be. Shinier and more noble, somehow. Without the disturbingly sexual dreams of a foreign sorceress or the persistent runs of the campaign trail.

Or the endless consultations on every matter, great or small.

The slow pace gave him time, at least, to learn the tasks of being a king, which seemed to be mainly making one decision after another, few of them compelling—a mountain of gravel, like the sands of Oria's desert, relentlessly piling into dunes. He longed to switch places with Arnon, to be riding fast and furiously to reunite with the rest of their people. The greatest irony of becoming king was learning that he'd lost a freedom he'd never fully appreciated—and would never have again.

BY THE TIME Lonen and the tail end of the returning warriors and litters of the injured sighted the forests of Dru that filled the deep and wide valley between the Snowy Peaks, they'd received word of those who'd been on the Trail of New Hope. The good news was that the refugees had turned around and traveled back to their homeland also, in another long caravan, spearheaded by the strong, followed by a long, straggling tail of the weak and wounded.

The bad news was that the women, children, and elderly had run afoul of more golems, suffering additional losses. Indeed, said the scouts who reported to him in the squalor of his inherited tent, much worse for wear from the long campaign, had the golems not inexplicably fallen dead one night, the refugees would have been decimated.

As it was, less than half those who'd set out returned to their emptied city. They turned out to welcome the final dregs of the Destrye army. They lined the road and drawbridges over the moats surrounding Dru, cheering with the forced enthusiasm of traumatized survivors, pitiful in their reduced numbers.

Once the Destrye had lived in cabins scattered throughout the lush deciduous forest of trees that towered as high as Bára's many towers. Some Destrye preferred to live alone, others in small family groups occupying one cabin, still others in extended families and communities in compounds of connected buildings. None had walls like Bára. Networks of roads had connected them, allowing for travel and commerce—all feeding into the broad, main road that led to Arill's temple.

Some holdouts lived in those outlying cabins and communities still, but the bulk of Destrye had fled their homes following the golem incursions, building new homes to cluster under Arill's sheltering wings. King Archimago had devoted considerable resources to digging wide, deep moats around the burgeoning city, filling them first with sharpened wood spikes, then iron ones to foil the golems. Those moats looked like a child's ditch compared to the chasms of Bára.

Never once had it occurred to them to build walls.

Lonen brought up the rear, riding over the last drawbridge through the gates of the city at the end of the column. Odd to see wooden buildings and leafy trees instead of stone balconies and towers, people with dark hair instead of light. The slapdash, panicked construction around Arill's temple had only deteriorated during the period of abandonment, but it had been ramshackle to begin with. One hastily assembled dwelling piled on top of another, the city was a hodgepodge of materials and design—except for Arill's centuries-old temple and the adjacent palace of governance—and nothing like Bára with her meticulously arranged and airy towers.

Still, the similarities shone through. The defeated Bárans had also been determined to cheer the smallest victory. The two peoples had chewed on each other's livers, it seemed, both cities crippled husks of what they'd once been, simply in different aspects.

Who had won what?

A woman broke from the throng, running up to him, long dark hair streaming like the tears running down her lovely face. Natly.

Though he was filthy, soiled in body and soul, Lonen dismounted, making his startled horse sidestep, and caught Natly up in his arms. She was both sobbing and laughing, her words incoherent. He held her close, inhaling the scent of qinn spices, the warmth of home. This. This was what he'd fought for, what so many died to protect. What his father and brothers had given their lives to rebuild. Through the exhaustion, a thin ray of hope wormed its way through. He'd made it home. Alive and mostly well.

Natly framed his face with her long fingers, her once elegantly jeweled nails short and broken. "You're king now," she managed to say, her gray eyes full of tears. "And returning victorious. I'm so proud of you. I love you so much, Lonen."

He kissed her, mostly to stop himself from saying this was no victory. All that time he'd waited for her to say those words, to be proud to be his woman—and now she said it because he'd simply managed to survive where others had not. And by committing unspeakable acts. "It still feels like dream. A long and terrible one."

"For me, too," she said, kissing him again and again. "But it's over now."

"Yes." Her mouth strange against his after so long apart. He threaded his chapped and dirty fingers through her black curling hair, grounding himself in Natly. His lover with dark eyes, not copper, who smelled of qinn and possessed no uncanny magics. She would make a good queen for the Destrye. "It's over now," he echoed her, wishing he felt that in his heart. Over her shoulder, a movement caught his eye.

Arnon stepped forward with Salaya, her hair shorn short in grief, holding the hands of her young sons, who'd never see their father Ion again. Natly made a sound of protest, clinging to him tightly when he tried to disentangle himself. "I have to talk to Salaya," he told her, and Natly also looked over her shoulder, thrusting her lip out in a bit of a pout that he'd always found so sexy.

"Do you have to? Talk to her later. Come with me and I'll bathe you." Natly scratched the back of his neck with her nails, a trick that had always made him crazy for her. But the devastation in Salaya's face, the haunted look in her eyes that reminded him strangely of Oria, cooled any desire he might have felt.

Gently, he unwound Natly's hands from his neck and

kissed her nose. "Go prepare the bath. And food if you can find any—I'm starving. I'll talk to Salaya and meet you shortly."

"You'll have to make it quick, Brother," Arnon said, gaze dipping over Natly and away. "I have a list as long as my arm of things for you to deal with as soon as possible."

"He's only just arrived home." Natly put her fists on her voluptuous hips. "Surely a conquering war hero—our new king!—deserves a bit of rest and celebrating."

Arnon shook his head wearily, squinting at the sky. "He'll be king of nothing if we don't figure out how to feed everyone. The first frost is only weeks away and it seems wolves scattered the herds we left behind. Not to mention we drained our water supplies when we left and the nearest source is at least a day's journey. We've brought some in, but it's slow going and not enough to keep up with everyone returning. Plus there's squabbles over housing and accusations of theft that have already caused several fights resulting in injuries."

"You're full of good news, aren't you?" Lonen scrubbed hands through his hair, slick with oil and dirt. He'd last bathed in Bára and it didn't seem as if he'd have another one any time soon. It would be unconscionable with their supplies so low.

"A fine welcome home for the King of the Destrye," Natly hissed.

Arnon only shrugged with a wry smile. "The good news is that we're alive to come home. The rest of it is pretty bad. We've got a lot of work to make it livable again."

Looking at his city made of wood, however ugly, Lonen let the weight of responsibility settle on him, heavy as Salaya's imploring gaze. He owed so much to his father's legacy, to Ion's forsaken family, and to Nolan's unrealized dreams, along with all the lives cut short, Destrye and Báran. He'd find a way to rebuild. His people needed him.

They needed a good king and he'd be that. Or die trying.

~ 24 ~

WRAPPED IN A cloak of night, Oria followed her mother to a place she'd never known existed, much less been to. Still within the city and somewhere beneath both the palace and the temple, they descended a set of stairs that seemed to be the mirror of the ones to her tower, spiraling around a dark pit that echoed with odd whispers, winding into the earth, possibly as deep as the chasms that cracked through Bára. Climbing these again, plus those to the height of her tower, might very well kill her.

Something to worry about later.

For the time being, feeling crushed beneath the earth occupied most of her attention.

"It's no different than being in a cave." Chuffta chirped the observation far too happily. *"I used to live in a cave. Cool in the hot weather, cozy when the chill winds blow. You'd like it."*

"So far I am *not* liking it," she muttered at her Familiar.

Her mother glanced over with a wry smile. "I found Chuffta in a cave. Is he telling you that?"

Surprised that her mother mentioned it, Oria latched onto the question. "Yes. Will you tell me about that? How did you find him and why? How did you convince him to come with you if you can't hear him now?"

"He can hear me, though, can't he?"

"Of course. I'm not stupid."

"I will tell you," Rhianna continued, "as we still have farther to go, no one to overhear, and all of this is a piece of what I wish to show you. Perhaps I should have told you more to begin with, but that's sand long since blown away."

Though she privately agreed, Oria kept silent, lest she stem this flow of long-awaited answers.

"Nat and Ben were but young boys when you were conceived. I knew right away that you would be a girl, the daughter I longed for, and more—I sensed that you might perhaps inherit the secret legacy of our family."

"The secret legacy?" she echoed.

"What my great-grandmother possessed, called *ponen*."

"That's the word the Trom used with me—I asked you about it."

"I remember. I wasn't ready then to explain it to you."

"Why now?"

"Circumstances have forced my hand. Yar is not ready to be king. He is far too proud and impetuous. The city guard agrees. They fear we'll be conquered by one or more of our sister cities if Yar takes the throne of Bára."

"Then you'll fight him for it—remain queen."

"Not me." Her mother flashed her a wry smile. "You."

Oria nearly stopped in her tracks, then had to hasten to catch up. "Are you saying you can help me find *hwil*?"

"Not exactly," she temporized, "but I can help you get your mask, which at least puts you and Yar on even footing."

"But…how?"

"*Ponen*," her mother said, as if it answered Oria's question, "is an ancient word, known primarily to the priestesses of our family, and recorded in only a few place. From the tales passed down, it's no easy burden to bear—as you've experienced in your life thus far. All of the women with ponen, however, had derkesthai to help them withstand the power of their affinities."

"What are my affinities?" Her question echoed with hollow immediacy, signaling the end of their journey. Indeed, the amorphous shadows of the center well showed blacker. They'd hit bottom.

"That is still your journey to discover."

Wonderful. It had been too much to hope that she might finally know that much. At least her mother hadn't advised her to meditate on it.

"Meditation is a useful exercise. You gain benefit from it when you exercise the self-discipline to truly quiet your mind."

"Yes, well, I gain benefit climbing up and down all these stairs, but that doesn't mean I enjoy it."

"What is Chuffta advising you?"

"To meditate, as always."

"No, I'm merely pointing out its benefits."

Her mother paused before an ironbound door set into a stone arch. The cool, sweet, and intense magic so characteristic to Rhianna swelled, swirled, and the door swung outward. Oria raised her brows at the nontraditional use of sgath. "Would High Priestess Febe approve?"

"The temple may govern most modern-day magical law," her mother replied crisply, striding through the doorway and into a dark hall, "but magic itself predates the temple. So does our family."

"And yet you allowed them to strip you of your mask."

Her mother faltered and Oria regretted the words. "I'm sorry, I—"

"No. You're right. I let them take my mask because according to temple law I no longer deserve it. However there are other, higher laws. The sorceresses of our line have had good reason to subject ourselves to the discipline the temple teaches. That is something for you to remember always. This knowledge is powerful—and can go badly if entrusted to the unstable."

The door behind them swung closed, plunging them into utter darkness. A breath of air against her face told Oria the other door had opened. That was why Oria shivered, not at the echo of Febe's words.

"Coming? If you're afraid, say so now, because it will only worsen." Her mother's voice held a hint of impatience.

"I can't see." Oria bit back the bitter words that begged to follow. No *hwil*, no ability to control her magic, no seeing in the dark. Or from behind a mask.

"I apologize." Her mother sounded chagrined, her hand touching Oria's sleeve, then guiding her to wrap her fingers around her mother's elbow. "Take my arm."

"I can't see either." The irritation in Chuffta's mind-voice perversely cheered her.

It bolstered her on the strange journey through pitch darkness, trusting to her mother's guidance. She kept wanting to put a hand out before her, to stop anything from smashing into her face, but it felt like that would be cowardly.

"There are no lamps or sconces in this section or I'd light them. I'd never before considered this a barrier to one who cannot see without eyes," her mother continued, apologetic, yet also thoughtful. "There are various guards set to prevent this knowledge from the wrong hands, and this must be one."

"Are you sure mine are the right hands then?" Oria joked.

It fell flat, however, because her mother didn't immediately reply. Finally she said, "I'll be honest with you—I don't know. That's another reason I hadn't yet shown you this path.

I hoped you'd find *hwil* first and then I could have been more certain you'd survive this. That's why we do this now, brutal though it may be."

"Do…what?"

"Face the test. If you survive, you'll understand."

"What do I do?"

Her mother softened, took her hands. "Oh, my brilliant daughter, if I could tell you, I would. But I am not ponen. I honestly do not know what you'll have to do to pass."

"Oh." Had she ever felt so small and afraid?

"But I do know that if you're not brave enough now, you won't have another chance. You're out of time, Oria. *We* are out of time. I wish it wasn't so, but it is what it is. You don't have to do this, but if you want to gain your mask in time, this is the path. Just…follow your instincts."

She wasn't brave enough. It made her angry that the cowardice sabotaged her.

"And if I fail, I'll die?" she asked.

"Yes." Her mother's voice echoed hollow in the dark. "Or you might as well be, as when you broke, sleeping the rest of your life away. Don't do this if it's not important to you. You can find another life, a quiet one, perhaps in one of our sister cities."

It sounded possible. Grim, and unlikely to last long, with Yar taking them back to war, and the Trom promising visits.

"Oria…" Her mother sounded hesitant. "I don't say this to sway your decision, but I believe you can do this. The magic is in you, powerful and consuming. You used it to repel Yar when he attacked you, and to bring me out of the pits of grief. This is your birthright, if you're strong enough to claim it."

She took a steadying breath. She might not be strong enough, but she wanted to be.

"You can be. Look how much you've done these last days."

"Thank you." She scratched his scaled breast.

"Chuffta must stay here, however."

"What—why? You said he helps me with the ponen."

"Exactly. And this you must do alone or not at all."

Chuffta had promised never to leave her.

"And I won't. I'll be with you, in your thoughts, in your heart."

With care, she unwound Chuffta's tail from its loops around her arm. He leaned his head against her temple. "If I don't survive sane, promise me you'll return to your family."

"No promises, other than that I'll wait for you always."

"All right," she said, her voice barely audible. "I'm ready."

Her mother's magic built again, like water filling a tub, and a faint blue glow glimmered ahead. Growing stronger, it outlined yet another doorway.

With an indigo blaze it opened, searing Oria's eyes and mind. She felt suddenly supremely unable to rise to the task. Was that a shape within?

It was one thing to face her own death in the abstract, to offer surrender to the Destrye prince, knowing she might be struck down. Oddly, the memory of Lonen's granite gaze steadied her. He wouldn't be afraid. Or rather, he might feel fear—she'd sensed plenty of it in him—but he hadn't let that stop him. She could do no less.

She stepped over the threshold.

Freezing blue seized her with agonizing brilliance, and she flailed, without reason or purchase. A bony hand caressed her cheek as the Trom had done, another rising to join it on the other side, framing her face. Something stared into her. Black, unwinking eyes, full of intelligence and entirely lacking in compassion.

She writhed mentally, her body no longer her own.

"Who?"

A mind-voice like Chuffta's, yet entirely unlike. Unforgiving, uncaring. It asked the question she couldn't answer.

And yet she did give an answer, her deepest heart opening like a night-blooming blossom to the fruit bats that plundered their nectar. It all poured out of her, the jealousy of her proficient brothers, all the bitter restlessness, the shame of failure and inadequacy, the rancor of her thoughts echoing in the walls of her tower, the bitterness of breaking her word to Lonen—and the eroding fear that he'd blame her if Yar sent the Trom after the Destrye.

It shouldn't be so important, but the possibility of losing his good opinion festered in her heart and poured out to this alien consciousness's indifferent scrutiny. All those princesses before her, also trapped by their own inability to rise above, to live up to their vows.

She wanted out with fierce ambition. Not to be forever subject to her little brother, to forswear herself because she didn't have the strength to back up her promises. She wanted to live. To live and burn brightly. *She* would find a way to save Bára.

The determination rose in her, strong and vital, much like the frustrated impatience that had always plagued her. It wanted to burst free, to release and whip about, as it had when she faced off with Yar. And yes, as she'd felt trying to reach her mother. Not only absorbing and calming, but also pushing out, striking and hooking.

This is who I am.

"Ponen," the being whispered. *"Ponen Trom. You are of us and we of you. Welcome."*

<h1 style="text-align:center">~ 25 ~</h1>

"WHAT WE NEED," Arnon said, sitting down with a rolled-up parchment and an excited mien, "is a better, faster way of getting water to the crops, if we have any hope of one more harvest before winter."

"The king is still eating his supper," Natly informed him, grabbing the wooden wine carafe before Arnon could and pouring more for Lonen, and then for herself.

A measly meal it had been, too. Lonen almost wished for Bára's odd array of plants and grains over the stringy meat from an aged animal he didn't want to try to identify. He even had a yen for that cheese of Oria's, with that tangy-sweet honey complementing the smoky rancid flavor—a contrary combination that shouldn't appeal but somehow lingered in his mind. Much as the woman did.

"The king is done eating," he said, schooling his face not to return Arnon's amused grin. Natly had a short temper for such teasing and Arnon seemed to be entertained by poking at her. One would think they'd have other things to worry about, with all the problems on their plates—besides sparse and unappealing food—but apparently not. "Better and faster water to the crops would be excellent, but how?"

Arnon pushed aside the plates, Natly protesting at his lack of manners, and spread out the parchment. "Aqueducts," he proclaimed.

Lonen studied the neat drawing. There was Arill's temple in the center, the squares of residences surrounding it and the palace, then the rings of moats—all circumnavigated by lines that reminded him of the old network of paths that had once connected the cabins and compounds. Indeed, several followed along historic roadways that led to the settlements farther down the valley, where the forests had been cleared to make fields for farming.

For the past weeks since he'd returned to Dru, Lonen had thought about food night and day—how much they needed, how little they had, even with the greatly reduced population, how they could grow, barter, or buy more. Livestock needed grain to eat, too. Slaughtering them all for meat instead of feeding them apparently wouldn't work because then they wouldn't have enough to make calves, kids, and what-have-yous in the spring. Even chickens needed grain to lay eggs—both for eating and hatching to grow into more chickens. The formerly abundant game in the forests had moved with the water sources, so the hunters came back empty-handed or with squirrels and rabbits that made for watery stews. The fisheries had dried up with the drained lakes. They were exploring harvesting fish from the sea, though the tides made that a daunting and dangerous effort.

Lonen had learned more than he'd ever wanted to about animal husbandry and population dynamics, not to mention farming practices which turned out to be far more complicated than planting seeds and cutting down the plants when they were ready. It made him weary to contemplate the mountain of obstacles facing them. By contrast, mowing down golems with his axe seemed far simpler.

Perhaps one reason why men turned to war when farming

failed. A sobering thought.

"What am I looking at?"

"See, with Lake Scandamalion more than half empty"—Arnon indicated on the map the closest remaining body of fresh water a day's journey away—"we need to access the more distant lakes or we'll just be facing the same problem again before we know it. But that would take a lot of bodies and time, hauling water from that far—bodies we need in the fields or here in the city, patching up the treasure boxes for winter."

He and Arnon had taken to referring to the ramshackle collection of falling-down construction that made up the refugee houses clustered around the temple—and now outside the moats, too—as *treasure boxes*, for their own lackluster creations when they'd been boys. With cold weather looming and what little resources the Destrye still possessed concentrated around the city, people stayed, throwing up whatever shelter they could manage. Or fighting with their neighbors to take theirs.

"So we dig…ditches?"

"No—this is better. Jordan brought this idea to me, from Arill's teachings. We build big troughs, essentially, on stilts and let the water roll downhill from, say, the Seven Lakes here, all the way to where we need it." He traced his finger along the lines to the farmlands, then another to the city.

A rill of excitement burned through Lonen's fatigue. "We build them out of wood?"

"Exactly! A good thing that the sun here doesn't scorch as it does in Bára, or we'd have to put a cover on it." Arnon frowned at the plans. "Otherwise there'd be none left by the time it reached its destination."

"And good that we have no golems or fire-breathing dragons to combat," Lonen added, meaning it as a joke, though it fell flat, Arnon wincing at the reminder.

"You and those tales of magic and dragons," Natly teased, slipping her arm through his. "I never know what to believe anymore. Warrior's stories, where the battles grow bolder and more glorious with each telling."

Out of habit, Lonen covered her hand with his, smiling down at her as she expected. She'd begun to look more like her old self, before the Trail of New Hope. No longer careworn, her nails once again sparkled with jewels, her hair elaborately coiled and gleaming with oil rather than hanging down her back in tangles. The people needed hope and to look up to them, she insisted, so they used water to bathe at least weekly. She wanted to look the part of Queen of the Destrye, to make him proud, though they'd made no plans to marry. She'd mentioned the midwinter celebration as the perfect time. As that would be well after any further efforts could be made to supplement the late harvest, Lonen hadn't objected outright.

Actually, he hadn't said anything either way. He'd teased her about marrying him long before the Battle of Bára, and she'd always put him off. Now she behaved as if they'd been engaged all along.

It wasn't that he didn't want to marry Natly, but it felt like a moot point if they were all bound to starve. She didn't understand his reticence to make plans, though, and to press the issue she'd stopped warming his bed after the first few nights. She claimed his nightmares kept her awake, with his thrashing about and yelling, but she'd made it clear that a wedding date would be sufficient to entice her back. Lonen, however, was frankly relieved to sleep alone, and not only because so many of those dreams that drove Natly away involved Oria.

Guilt and a level of mortification chewed at him, that his fascination with the sorceress continued to plague him, making him imagine the scent of night-blooming lilies even with Natly's qinn filling his head, with her supple body pleasuring his. It made him irritable, which Natly put down to the pressures of kingship. But her pride in him, and the delighted plans she made to become queen, rankled more than the sand dunes of decisions that piled up daily. She hadn't been so enthusiastic to wed him before he was king.

Something that proved as impossible as Oria to forget.

"How long to build it?" he asked Arnon.

"That depends. There's a number of options and decisions to make on prioritizing."

Of course there were. "All right, walk me through it."

"You're not staying up all night talking again," Natly protested. When Arnon made a choking noise and Lonen raised a brow at her, she folded her arms, pushing up her luscious bosom. "You need your rest. And I thought perhaps we could…spend some time together."

She looked so disappointed that Lonen regretted his uncharitable thoughts. Of course the nightmares bothered her. She needed her sleep, too. He cupped her cheek and kissed her, inhaling the qinn to remind himself that Natly was the woman he craved. Was supposed to crave. "Perhaps tomorrow night. If we're to build these aqueducts to irrigate the late-season harvest in time to keep our plantings from dying, Arnon is right that we need to start right away. You go to bed."

"All right." She pushed out that lower lip and gazed at him through lush black lashes. "But you know where to find me. Don't keep him up all night." She pointed a jeweled nail at Arnon and flounced off.

Lonen watched the sway of her hips that once so beguiled

him, missing that feeling and disliking the creeping realization that Natly would make a terrible queen. She was nothing like Oria, who would have wanted to learn about the aqueducts. Which he needed to focus on, as thoughts of Oria being his queen instead of Natly were not only impossibly distracting, but impossible, full stop. He studied the aqueduct lines that went to the farmlands. A longer distance, but more critical than getting more water to a people already accustomed to rationing. "So, if we build these first, then would—"

"Lonen." Arnon put a hand over the map, covering the lines and forcing Lonen to look at him. "You can't marry her."

Lonen blinked at him, dragging his eager thoughts from the logistics of building aqueducts. Had Arnon somehow read his thoughts? "Who—Natly?"

Arnon gusted out an impatient breath. "Of course Natly! Who else would I be talking about?"

Who indeed? "I'm not marrying Natly. Not anytime soon, anyway," he amended.

"That's not what she thinks. Nor what she tells everyone."

"I don't control what she thinks and does."

"Exactly the problem. Natly does as she pleases, always has and always will. She would have made a decent princess, but she won't make a good queen. Don't do it, brother of mine."

"She's strong as a horse, can bear many children, understands and loves Dru and the Destrye—what's the problem?"

"The problem is that being queen means *not* doing as she pleases. It's more than wearing pretty dresses and sucking your cock, Lonen! These are dire times. Better for you to lead our people alone than be distracted by her."

The words prickled and Lonen burned to lob back a few of his own. But Arnon had that much right—being king meant not doing as he pleased, either. "I thought we were discussing aqueducts and building schedules."

Arnon held his gaze, then nodded, accepting the truce. "Good. I've made a timetable."

<h1 style="text-align:center">~ 26 ~</h1>

"YOU COME BEFORE the temple as a supplicant," High Priestess Febe intoned, "sponsored by our daughter, former priestess Rhianna. Do you, Princess Oria of Bára, plead to be granted the mask of priestess yourself?"

"I do, High Priestess. You have tested my *hwil* and see that I am ready to wear the mask," Oria replied, her face serenely composed.

"Indeed, remarkable as it may seem, none can find fault with your *hwil*." Febe sounded sour, a bitter complement to the irritated—and suspicious—energy she emanated.

As well she should, as Oria no more had achieved *hwil*, whatever it truly felt like, than ever. But she faked it perfectly well. Nothing the priests and priestesses had attempted to shake her composure had rattled her. At least, not that she showed. It rankled deeply that, for all their pride in their personal magic, the masked ones could not truly see into her heart. As her mother had predicted, once Oria came out the other side of the harrowing test of scrutiny in the heart of magic, nothing less could frighten or upset her.

After that, passing the simple tests of *hwil* proved quite simple. In fact, those challenges had been easy enough, after the horrors of the Destrye Wars, that she could have passed them before, had it ever occurred to her to lie about achieving *hwil.*

How many priests and priestesses of Bára and her sister cities had hit upon that solution? In her most cynical moments, Oria suspected most of them, perhaps all. She hadn't met anyone who didn't leak emotional energy. Over the past weeks, practicing with her mother and Chuffta, she'd refined her ability to sort through what she sensed—and to release it again.

Both sgath and grien flowed in her. Ponen. Not something for anyone else to know, however.

"But the final test resides in the mask itself." The High Priestess took up a golden mask, newly minted, from a stand on the altar. She anointed it with oils, holding it up to the assembled priests and priestesses, who took up a low chant. "Rhianna."

Her mother moved behind Oria where she knelt on the hard stone before the altar. She kept calm and unmoving as Febe pressed the metal mask to her face. It burned her skin, hot from the candle flames and warmed oils it had rested in, but Oria didn't allow herself to flinch. Her mother took up the first of the three sets of ribbons, weaving them through Oria's elaborate braids and tying them tightly.

"Show us you possess the second sight," Febe demanded, her hope that Oria would fail coming through quite clearly. The chanting rose in volume, climbing to deafening levels, to prevent an aspirant from using sound to navigate. Oria stood, walked around the altar, opened the door behind it and stepped inside.

The others followed her, their chanting a drumbeat that accelerated her heart rate. To unsettle her also, then. It would take more than that to distract her.

"Because you are more powerful than all of them," Chuffta said,

sounding both smug and proud.

"*Shh. You'll make me fall.*" She enjoyed focusing the thought at him, though—something else that had become easier with the thick walls of resistance removed.

Men and women saw the obstacle course differently, her mother had explained, though she only knew how she perceived it. Using sgath, the narrow beams stood out to a magic user from the background. Apparently her father had confided to Rhianna that the men used grien much the way bats did, bouncing the magic off surfaces to detect the edges and pitfalls. It went against temple law for him to have told her that, or for her mother to have told her any of it, but it seemed any number of rules had fallen by the wayside in her mother's—and other allies'—determination to see Oria on the throne of Bára.

Careful to use no grien those present might detect, Oria let the sgath flow and walked confidently along the narrow path, careful not to shuffle or appear to feel her way. Though the room was brightly lit enough for the shine to leak around the edges of her mask, the way the metal curved close to her skull kept her from seeing the beams she walked along. The route— which changed for each supplicant—twisted and turned, changing angles, but still fell short of the ones her mother and Juli, the junior priestess assigned to Oria, had designed with diabolical mischief for her to practice on.

She still had bruises from falling. But they'd been worth it, for this moment.

At last, she stepped off the end that narrowed to a needle-thin point, showing her mastery by not breaking it. And that was all. To advance to higher levels in the temple, she'd need to demonstrate sgath, but that would be for the future.

The priests and priestesses surrounded her, kissing their

masks to hers in ritual congratulation, the clinks like the chiming of wineglasses. Chuffta landed on her shoulder. His physical presence still worked to bolster and balance her, though she managed more of that on her own, through understanding the interplay of sgath and grien through her being. He tapped her mask with his nose.

"I bet I could melt it if I tried," he remarked.

She tweaked his tail. *"You'd be sad when I blasted you with my amazing magical abilities."*

He snorted mentally, with which she ruefully had to agree. So far she hadn't been able to do much with the grien besides use it as a release valve. No thunder, no fireballs, no earth-moving. Of course, as her mother wryly noted, most men learned their affinities from other wielders of grien. Oria wouldn't be asking for lessons in that, so she'd have to figure it out on her own.

The story of her life, it seemed.

She felt her mother's aura before Rhianna's soothing embrace surrounded her. With a sigh, she leaned her masked face against her mother's shoulder. "It seems odd for me to have the mask and you to be barefaced," she said.

"I don't mind," her mother murmured. "Those things get cursed hot."

Oria huffed a laugh at that, though she already believed it. She'd look forward to those cool, herbed face cloths now.

"Now," her mother said, releasing her, "to deal with the council. And Yar."

"I don't like that we have no idea what he—and the rest of them—have been up to these last weeks. If only I could have gotten my mask sooner."

Yar had walled her out of all discussions. Neither she nor her mother had been able to find out many details about the city's water reserves or communications with their sister cities—and without masks to allow them entrance as representatives of the temple, they were banned from the council meetings. Folcwita Lapo had turned Oria down with ill-concealed glee when she'd asked to be admitted as a citizen. She hadn't sensed the Trom, but the giant derkesthai glided in lazy circles in the thermals high above Bára, from time to time.

"At least we'll know soon." Her mother patted her arm. "You've done all you could."

Perhaps so. But that still might not be enough.

~ 27 ~

"HOW LONG UNTIL we have the final sections in place?" Lonen shaded his eyes against the angled autumn sun, to better see the lay of the aqueducts through the distance.

"We'll do the stretch to connect to Dru itself last." Arnon pointed at the direction it would take. "It might mean hauling water all winter, but you wanted to prioritize crop irrigation, and the sections to the farthest fields will be done in the next few days. Even manually carrying water from the finished aqueducts to those, the time savings has allowed us to grow a respectable harvest, enough to last through the winter. You've done it, King Lonen."

"We did it. All the Destrye. And thank Arill for the unseasonably warm weather."

Arnon cast a judicious eye at the landscape. "Except for the danger of fire. Everything we haven't watered is tinder dry."

"Perhaps we should be watering more things then," Natly spoke up. "There's plenty of it now, after all." She pointed at the staged aqueduct platforms, painstakingly built into the foothills, funneling water in a series of manmade waterfalls to the ripening crops of fast-growing alfalfa.

Arnon didn't glance at Natly but his shoulder muscles bunched. Lonen suppressed the absurd urge to apologize for her, especially knowing how much Arnon disapproved of their engagement. He also—more ruthlessly—cut off the disloyal thought that Oria wouldn't have said something so foolish. Not only unfair to Natly but probably untrue. He'd known Natly for years and Oria for two conversations. If Natly could still surprise him, Oria would likely obliterate his idealism.

"It looks good," he told Arnon, putting a hand on his brother's shoulder, belatedly aware it was his father's gesture.

Arnon, however, didn't seem to notice. He folded his arms, surveying the construction with a faint smile of pride. "It should work."

With his gaze on the scaffolding of waterfalls, Lonen frowned at what he'd thought were clouds gathering over the peaks, as they did most afternoons in the heat of autumn, though they rarely produced rain as they had in years past.

Not clouds, perhaps but…smoke? He traced the line of it behind low hills, where the harvested grains were stored. Fear crawled down his spine. As if called, a messenger came sprinting up.

"King Lonen!" The messenger barely gasped the words on the last of his breath as he ran up, then dropped to his knees. The scent of char wafted from him and instant dread curdled Lonen's gut.

All these days and weeks of working, he'd anticipated this moment. Much as he'd tried to focus on the positive, to count the blessings rather than the curses, a vague foreboding had plagued him. Not unlike the nearly nightly dreams of Oria casting black magic spells, ripping him asunder—obvious metaphors for his fears of what the Bárans might yet do to the Destrye.

Without hearing the words, Lonen knew.

"Dragons…searing…eating the dead…" The messenger heaved out the news in toxic clumps. "The grain silos, everything, burning."

Beside him, Arnon cursed viciously. "It's not possible!"

But it was. Worse, it had been inevitable, if the nightmares were to be believed.

Now none of that mattered. A greasy chill rolled over him, as if the mummified thing had already dissolved his bones.

"How long ago and are they still there?" Lonen demanded, willing the man to breathe.

"Just past noon. Sire, I—" The man broke off on a strangled scream as the shadow of a dragon passed across the platform where they stood, Natly's cry of unmitigated horror as chill as the shadow. Without thinking, Lonen thrust her behind him. In the same movement, he drew the iron axe he'd never quite lost the habit of carrying. She'd teased him about that, too, that he kept the ugly thing ever with him, when he should be wearing his father's shining sword of Destrye kingship. Call it superstition, but he'd felt better with his battle-axe at hand. Besides that, he couldn't face the finality of his father's passing by taking up the sword of office.

The dragon swooped past again, low enough for the creature on its neck to look them over, raising a hand as it had in the council chambers at Bára. A strange greeting from a soulless creature. Arnon stood at his shoulder, iron sword in hand, and it comforted Lonen that his brother shared his preference for the ugly weapons.

The dragon wheeled away again, followed by a phalanx of others, smoke drifting in their wake.

Like locusts settling on a verdant farm, they set down and the Trom riders began filling those endlessly thirsty barrels of water from the freely flowing aqueducts.

"YOU CAN'T GO alone." Arnon sounded very reasonable, but his face showed the strain of worry. "It's suicide."

"If it is, taking more Destrye with me will only get more warriors killed. This way I risk only myself."

"I don't want to be king," Arnon ground out, jaw tight, as he paced. "Don't make me have to be king."

Lonen waited until his brother made the circuit of the room and had to stop before him or dodge around. When Arnon seemed about to do just that, Lonen grasped him by the shoulders. "The treaty was between me and Princess Oria. If she violated the terms, then she owes me a follow up on her promises."

"*If* she violated the terms?" Arnon threw up his hands, breaking his brother's grip. "Of course she did! The Bárans are without honor of any kind. How many times must she break her word to you before you see her for the evil, greedy sorceress she is?"

"I don't like it either," Natly put in. She sat at the table, hands clasped around a hammered metal goblet of wine. If Lonen were a thoughtful lover, he would have brought her one of those delicate transparent vessels Oria used. A pretty gift for the faithful woman who'd waited for him at home. Natly had finally stopped crying, but her face showed the ravages of her hysterical tears. "Have I won you back from the Hall of Warriors only to lose you again? This Báran sorceress could take your love for me and twist it backwards."

Perhaps that had happened already, and that was why

Lonen no longer felt as he once had for Natly. Why it was Oria who prowled through his dreams. Why he looked forward to seeing her again with an almost savage glee that gnawed at his heart—though that came from hatred. All through the counting of the dead, the damage to the precious crops, the senseless destruction, he'd fumed over Oria's betrayal and relished the moment he'd confront her.

In his saner moments, he told himself that he desired answers. Or revenge. That the fiery longing to wrap his hands around her throat came from the need to choke the pretty lies from her, not the burning need to feel her skin under his hands.

In his less sane moments, he knew only that he had no choice.

He would journey back to Bára alone and do what he could to save the Destrye.

"You'll be a good king," he told Arnon, handing him their father's sword, hilt first, aware of the relief of giving it up unworn. He started to lift the wreath from his head, but his brother stopped him.

"No," he said, with a firm shake of his head. "Wear it. Make those cursed Bárans see you for the king you are, not they barbarian they name us."

"You'll need it, if I don't return."

"If you don't return," Arnon replied with grim conviction, "none of us will need anything ever again."

~ 28 ~

"ORIA?" JULI BOWED her head in unusually somber grace, grave concern wafting off her—though the red curls springing out from behind her mask added a note of irreverence. Seeing with sgath instead of one's eyes changed the way colors appeared. The mask forced Oria into seeing more of the resonance of light on objects, with the wavelengths of the sun very different from the rays reflected by Sgatha or Grienon. But Juli's hair was a particularly impudent shade of orange, which matched her unruly character, so Oria always saw it that way in her mind.

"Come sit, Juli. Give me your news." Focusing on her task, Oria finished working seed oil into Chuffta's hide while Juli crossed the rooftop terrace. Simple tasks like that, ones she'd done so often that she could accomplish them with her eyes closed, made for good practice. She had to consciously concentrate on "seeing" her work, looking for the spots she'd missed, rather than feeling them. Working on Chuffta added an extra layer of difficulty, as he radiated magic on another spectrum entirely.

Amazing how much she hadn't seen before.

"Captain Ercole wishes to speak with you." Juli didn't sit, instead gesturing to the inner chambers. "He waits at your door. I wasn't sure of your equanimity today."

In all truth, she felt amazingly good. Tired, yes, from all the practicing and studying, but the morning sun soothed and relaxed her, so that she felt as oiled and supple as Chuffta. "Send him in. It must be important news for him to bring it himself." Or secret news.

"I hope not. We've had enough grave news to last several lifetimes," Juli tossed over her shoulder, already on her way to admit the Captain of the City Guard.

Oria watched him approach while seeming not to. Another aspect of the mask she'd never understood, that it allowed her perception to move out in every direction. Where her eyes pointed wasn't necessarily where she looked, at all. Ercole had survived the Siege of the Destrye, as the poets had come to call it, where so many had not, and she gave him credit for giving her the backing of the city guard, though he'd never admit to it. His usually vital energy thrummed with nerves. Oh yes, something had him gravely concerned.

He crossed the terrace and knelt, removing his helm and bowing his head. "Your Highness."

She managed to restrain the impulse to correct him. She wasn't queen, not yet, despite all her progress. But, finally masked, she at least stood in the way of Yar taking the throne of Bára—an effective obstacle despite the machinations of Lapo and Febe. Though she and Yar raced each other in a bizarre competition to acquire ideal mates, neither of them had yet located such a person. Having gone through the priestesses of Bára—even testing those not yet masked—Yar had departed for the sister cities to search for a bride. So far Oria had not found a priest whose touch she could abide, but as Yar's senior, she outranked him, barely. Not queen, but as close as anyone in Bára came to the status, so she allowed the fiction.

"What people believe becomes real." Chuffta's mind-voice

hummed in relaxed tones.

"Captain Ercole," she acknowledged. "What a pleasant surprise."

"Not so much, I'm afraid, Your Highness. I bring unwelcome news."

Oria allowed the sudden tension to flow through and out, keeping her attention on the task of oiling Chuffta inch by inch. Needlework, sitting still, and meditating—none of that worked for her yet, but she continued to find for herself the things that did.

"Oh?" she asked.

"A man at the gates claiming to be the King of the Destrye seeks an audience with you."

That took her aback. "Claiming? You should recall King Lonen's face well enough, Captain Ercole. Unless they have a new king?" The thought stabbed at her with surprising force. Lonen's fate shouldn't matter to her, though it seemed to. An emotion to set aside and examine later. Another trick she'd learned—to delay her emotional responses for private venting.

"I should say that the man appears to be Lonen, but he shows no sign of being the Destrye king," Ercole allowed. "He is entirely alone and without any badge of office. I'm afraid he has demanded an audience with you, formal or informal, and said to remind you that you made him a promise."

Aha.

"I advise against receiving him, Your Highness," Ercole continued. "The man seems angry to the point of derangement. He has no forces to back his demands. If you shut the gates against him, he'll have no recourse."

"Except that I did make a promise," she said gently, working her way down the soft membrane of Chuffta's wing. "I will receive him. Make certain he's given safe passage through

Bára. Does anyone else know of this visit?"

Ercole glanced up at her and away. Those who didn't wear masks were discomfited by them. Sometimes that worked to her advantage. Other times…she wasn't sure. "No, my men brought the news directly to me and have kept him out of sight in the guardroom."

"Thank you. Commend them for me."

"His arrival will become common knowledge once he enters the audience chambers."

"Which is why I won't receive him there."

"Not the old council chambers?" Ercole sounded aghast, uneasy concern rippling off him. Though she'd never made it an official edict, she'd avoided using that room since the day of the Trom's arrival. Showing his bravado, Yar used it on occasion, for his "private meetings," but she discerned from his chaotic energy afterwards that he liked it no more than she did. Clearly the rest of the council felt the same way, because they'd started using a different room, never once complaining, though it was smaller and tended to swelter in the afternoon sun.

"I'll see him here. And if you would personally escort him, I would appreciate that." Which meant that he would keep Lonen out of sight of curious eyes.

Ercole hesitated. "Your Highness—I don't mean to question you, but—"

"If you don't wish to make the climb a second time, I understand." She deliberately misunderstood him. "I trust whoever you send as escort."

"I'll do it, Your Highness," he grumbled, knees creaking as he stood.

She smiled to herself, letting the amusement mingle with the piercing sorrow of missing her father, and setting to oiling

Chuffta's other wing, working at seeing each fine tarsal bone while also observing the garden. The jewelbirds zipped about in the waxing heat, visiting the heavy-headed lilies. Soon the blossoms would be gone and then where would the birds go?

"They can fly away, to find other sources of nectar."

"If only the Bárans could do the same."

Slowly, carefully, like easing herself into an overly hot bath, she let her thoughts move to the anticipation of seeing Lonen. Emotions tumbled up, ready to swamp her thoughts with dread, terror, a curious tingle of excitement, and that sexual heat he'd evoked. Mostly, however, she braced herself to make good decisions.

Because Lonen could only be in Bára for one reason.

"What will you do?"

"Keep my promise," she replied absently, spreading the delicate membrane between the final two tarsals, so thin light shone through, the blood vessels hot within the skin and bone, flowing with native magic.

"That may require much of you."

"I have no choice." She wryly acknowledged to herself the irony of saying the very thing she'd chided Lonen for. As another exercise in concentration, Oria extended her perception beyond the tower. Because she expected Lonen, and via the stairs to the tower, she allowed herself the cheat of sensing in that direction only. Soon enough he impinged on her awareness, a seething sun of virulent anger, fantasies of revenge, and determination. The exuberance of his masculine energy momentarily overwhelmed her, and Chuffta wrapped the slim tip of his tail around her wrist, which felt something like a failure.

"It's not wrong to need my help. That's why I'm your Familiar."

"And I'm grateful."

The impact of Lonen's forceful personality diminished, as she allowed it to filter away, venting it through Chuffta and back into the magic below Bára. It would be a good day when she could figure out something useful to do with it, but at least by the time the King of the Destrye stepped onto her terrace, she'd regained much of her calm.

"Your Highness," Ercole intoned with more than his usual gravity, "as you requested, King Lonen of the Destrye."

"Thank you, Captain. You may go."

His rebellious need to refuse, to stay and protect her, punched out and was snuffed just as quickly. With a bow, Ercole withdrew, and Oria indulged in transferring the bulk of her attention to examining Lonen.

He felt different than before, though that burning vitality hadn't changed. If anything, he waxed brighter and stronger, vivid with frustrated impatience, threaded through with dark desire. It was like a complex bubble surrounding him, ever-shifting, confusing her newly won perceptions. To give her sgath a rest, she backed off her focus, to observe more of his surface. He'd traded his furs and cloak for lighter leathers, anticipating the climate of Bára this time, she imagined, and wore the dust of the journey.

Oddly, she wanted to pull off the mask, to look on him again with her eyes, to compare that visual with what she recalled from weeks before, when she'd been an entirely different person.

Lonen cleared his throat and she realized he thought she hadn't noticed him. Out of courtesy, she turned her mask in his direction. "King Lonen. I did not expect to meet with you on my terrace ever again."

The bubble of energy surrounding him popped, spewing entirely rage and betrayed grief. "Then you shouldn't have sent your creatures after us."

Giving Chuffta a last pat, she asked him to go to the balustrade to observe from a distance more comfortable for the Destrye. She wiped the oil off her hands, then poured juice for him into the crystal goblet she'd used when they'd met before. "I didn't."

He swore, something vile-sounding in a dialect not their common trade tongue. She needed no translation, however, given the feeling behind it. "So you deny that—"

She cut him off. "Come and sit. Take refreshment after your long journey. You can tell me what happened, so that I may confirm or deny from knowledge rather than ignorance."

He paused at that, shifting his weight, the blankness of surprise canceling out the stronger emotions for the moment. Then his decision clicked into place and he moved forward—nothing shocking there, as Lonen always seemed to surge ahead once he decided on a course of action—and he closed the distance between them in several strides. Oria steeled herself not to flinch away from the force of his physical proximity.

He stopped short of actually touching her, reeling back the impulse with palpable force of will, then sat on the bench cornered to her, with a huff of breath that sounded very like a laugh, though his face remained stony.

"You're wearing one of those masks," he said, not at all what she expected.

She handed him the glass of juice. "Yes. A mark of my new rank."

"As queen?"

"Very nearly." She didn't elaborate more, knowing he wouldn't like hearing that she'd advanced as a sorceress. And the Báran legalities that intertwined marriage, magic, and the throne would be too difficult to explain to an outsider. "As we discussed before, such things are more complicated in Bára."

"Isn't everything?"

She sighed for the truth of that, though those complications at least kept the current power struggle between her and Yar at a détente.

Lonen drank deeply of the cooled juice, a ripple of pleasure in him further dampening the sharper emotions, then held up the glass to the sun. "I have thought about these goblets, made of such a strange substance."

"We call it glass. Made from sand."

"Surely that's not so. It looks nothing like sand."

She waved a hand at the surrounding desert. "One resource we have in ample supply. It changes when melted. The golems were made in a similar way, with some changes."

The Destrye barked out a laugh. "*Some* changes indeed. Only foul magic such as you have here could create a something so obscene."

Oria sorted through the revulsion rolling off him, complicated with a black sense of betrayal and despair. He reminded her of the glass forges, seething with molten heat so fierce nothing could cool it. "Surely the golems have not attacked? There shouldn't be any outside the walls."

"Don't pretend you don't know." As Lonen's forced calm snapped, so did the glass in his hand. With an oath, he hurled himself to his feet and flung the broken goblet against the stone balustrade, sending Chuffta into startled flight.

"Oria, the Destrye is crazed," he warned.

"No." For she saw it in Lonen's mind as clearly as the sgath showed her the life signatures of everything around her, the images congealing with horror. "The Trom attacked Dru."

She collapsed back against the cushions, cold horror making chill sweat run down her back. The mask chafed and she longed to pull it off, toss it aside, and weep freely. Too late. Yar had outmaneuvered her. Her worst fears had come true.

She was forsworn again—her promises broken and scattered to the winds—and the price would be giving up her happiness forever.

~ 29 ~

THE IMPULSE TO roar his fury, to breathe fire like those fearsome dragons, battled to break free of Lonen's control. He'd been a fool three times over. All along, through the endless journey accompanied by nothing but his thoughts, he'd nursed the hope that Oria hadn't known about the Trom attack, that she hadn't broken her word and betrayed their truce yet again.

Don't let a bit of foreign pussy make you think with the little head instead of the big one. The words of Ion's ghost rattled in his heart.

All this time he'd been feeling this nostalgic sentimentality over those brief encounters with Oria. To the point of fantasizing about having her in his bed instead of Natly. And here the object of his prurient dreams and more disturbing nightmares reclined on her plush cushions, clad in crimson robes and wearing that cursed gold mask, cloaked in offensive calm. He should wrench it from her, break those delicate ribbons, so he could look into those haunting copper eyes and learn the truth.

"You made me a promise." Instead of a roar, the words came out harsh as her fragile glass breaking on stone.

"Yes," she returned with an equanimity she hadn't shown before. "And to my knowledge I kept it."

"Then how did you know the Trom attacked Dru?"

With a heavy sigh, she stood, scrubbing her palms on her thighs, leaving a smear of damp on the silk robe. He hated the thing on her—too like her sorcerous brethren who'd hurled magics at them, and those who'd died so easily under his hand. Oria walked the low wall that bordered her terrace, looking out over the city with every appearance of seeing, which made his skin prickle with unease. The white dragonlet landed beside her, mantling its wings and snaking its neck to fix him with that accusing green stare.

"I see it in your mind."

It took a moment for Lonen to catch up to what "it" she meant. When he did, he didn't much like the implication. "You *can* read my thoughts." His voice came out flat. From behind, she looked more familiar, though her glorious copper hair was all caught up and braided with ribbons as gold as the mask they held. He missed the metallic fall of it that had so bewitched him from the beginning. Then kicked himself for falling so rapidly under her spell again.

"An overly simple way of putting it, but let's agree to that." The mask made her voice strangely hollow. "I see the giant derkesthai flying overhead, a Trom greeting you. There's..." She faltered. "Char in the air. More dead."

"Worse than that." He strode up to her at the railing, intent on forcing her to deal with him honestly. "Our crops burnt to the ground. Much-needed food for the winter, gone. Yes, more Destrye dead, but more deaths to come, from slow starvation and the diseases cold and malnutrition bring. And the water—they're taking it again, in greater volumes than ever before. Foul magic."

"They took the water, too?" She sounded faint but with an edge of anger.

"Why did you do it, Oria? Why?" He stopped himself from asking a third time, from begging her not to be what he most abhorred.

The uncannily smooth mask turned to face him. "I didn't," she repeated. "I don't control the Trom."

"I'm supposed to believe that?" This time the question came out as harsh as he felt. Oria didn't flinch, exactly, but a shiver ran through her, despite the heat. "I was there the day it touched you, and you didn't die like the others. When it spoke to you and you refused to tell me what it said."

"You decide what you believe, King Lonen of the Destrye," she replied, as soft as he'd been hard. "I can only give you the truth as I know it."

"You've changed," he said, before he knew he intended to. But the tentative belief that perhaps she wasn't behind the attack gave him an absurd rush of relief.

"Yes." Not a smile in her voice, but some wry amusement. "So have you."

"Would you take off the mask so we can talk?" He sounded plaintive to himself, involuntarily raising a hand, as if to remove it.

She stepped back, deliberately out of reach. "Don't touch me." No ragged plea this time, but the cool command of a queen. "And no, I cannot show my face to anyone but close family—and then only should I choose to do so. Which, these days, I don't."

"Then how do you eat and drink?" He flung a hand at the pitcher of cool juice, belatedly realizing that she hadn't shared it and thus could have poisoned him.

"Alone," she said, and turned her mask towards the vista again, for all the world as if she saw it.

"Your ways are very strange and unnatural," he growled at

her in his frustration.

She actually laughed, the sound like raindrops on tin shingles. "Oh, Lonen—you have no idea."

Absurdly, he found a smile breaking the aching stern tension of his jaw, and he rubbed it, feeling the sweat-stiffened hair of his beard, realizing suddenly how bad he must look. He should have taken the time to bathe. Or asked to visit Bára's baths before meeting with their queen. Or very nearly queen, whatever that meant. He scrubbed both hands through his hair, wishing he could at least tie it back off his neck.

"Here," Oria said, moving gracefully to the table. It had held a violet fire the night they'd talked but now appeared to be only a smooth white surface, though the glass animals still pranced along the edge. More magic. She picked something up and held it out to him. Bemused, he took it. The leather hair tie he'd worn that night. "You left it behind," she added, as if that explained anything.

Wordlessly, he took it from her and tied back his hair, happy to have the mess of it off his neck. Though he'd been on the terrace before at night, he'd remembered it as more shaded. Looking about, he noted the bareness of the overhanging branches, the crisp brown of the vines. "Your garden is dying, Oria."

She tilted her head to the side. "I'm no longer wasting water on it."

He choked back the protest that it wasn't a waste. That was the idealist in him again, picturing her in the fantasy of the impossible garden, beautiful and outside the world. The visible evidence helped reassure him about her, though. If the Bárans were behind the latest attack and water raid, at least Oria wasn't using their ill-gotten resources. Perhaps he could trust her to uphold her promise in good faith then. The hope felt fragile, too full of idealistic wonder, but without her help, the Destrye would surely perish.

"How will you aid Dru then?"

"I've been pondering this since you arrived." Seeming restless, she paced along the balustrade. "I promised you everything in my power and I intend to keep that vow. However, while greater than it was, my power remains constricted in certain ways. I can think of one solution that is rather simple to execute, but vastly complicated in its ramifications. You won't like it."

"I don't like my people dying either."

"All right." She returned to her couch, under the gently flapping silk awning that provided the only shade. "Why don't you join me, Lonen."

He did, if only to get out of the sun.

~ 30 ~

THE MOMENT OF truth. Oria centered herself as best she could, breathing out the unexpected nerves. Being around Lonen again did strange things to her. As if he triggered the rise of different energy in herself, ones she wasn't accustomed to grappling with. If he accepted her proposed plan, that would be yet another challenge to face.

"I'm not sure this is a good plan at all."

"Nor am I, but we're in a corner."

Chuffta ruefully sighed for the truth of that. The Trom attacking Dru, taking their water, Yar haring off to the sister cities, looking for a bride with bribes in hand: It all added up to him outmaneuvering her. She couldn't possibly find an ideal mate before he did. He was at least three steps ahead of her. But the law didn't require that she have a temple-blessed husband. Just that she have a husband. A bit of a loophole in Báran law—one that existed mainly because so few would contemplate the step she planned.

Subjecting themselves to a mind-dead, magicless, and sexless marriage as well as a loveless one—a high price, even for the throne. Some sacrifices were too steep for most.

Except for her.

"Tell me," she said, pouring him another glass of juice, pleased that her hand remained steady. "Are you married?"

He sputtered on the mouthful. "Engaged. Why?"

Unfortunate but not surprising. "Why haven't you married her yet?" She sorted through the sudden gamut of his emotions—defensiveness and guilt uppermost among them. A very beautiful woman, with masses of curling black hair and luminous dark eyes. Voluptuous and sensual, doing things to Lonen that—Oria cut off the scene, grateful for the mask that hid her flush.

"I've been a little busy keeping my people alive," Lonen growled.

"You're fond of her, but you don't love her." It shouldn't matter, but it did. Oria didn't expect love for herself, but it would be difficult to watch him wish for another.

"Reading my thoughts again?"

"My apologies. Her image rose up quite clearly to me." Along with strong feelings—conflicted ones she didn't care to examine, even if looking too closely hadn't felt overly intrusive. That he didn't love that beautiful woman would be enough. "It doesn't matter, truly, but it would make things even more difficult if it would disappoint you greatly to break your heart or hers by marrying me."

Lonen set the glass down, very carefully. He laced his fingers together and leaned forearms on his knees. Then looked at her. "Excuse me?"

She should have planned what to say better. "It would be a marriage in name only, consecrated by the temple here in Bára, but otherwise non-binding for you in most ways. You would not be required to be faithful to me, so you could continue to be lovers with that dark-haired woman, if your customs allow it." The idea gave her a surge of bitter jealousy. Still, that was only fair to him. She would never be able to be his lover—nor anyone's, as temple law would bind *her* to fidelity—but Lonen should not have to give up intimacy for the rest of his life, too. He didn't carry the burden of expiating Bára's crimes.

Lonen studied her, his dislike of her mask palpable, his astonishment grown stronger. "You want me to marry you, according to your temple laws, and keep Natly as my lover."

"I did say you wouldn't like it." Natly. It had been better before this shadow fiancée had a name.

He laughed, dropping his forehead to his knuckles, then wiping the sweat from his brow. "Nothing with you ever goes as I expect."

"I'm explaining this badly." She held up her arm, and Chuffta came to her, offering his affection and support. She scratched his breast and he leaned into her. That helped calm the strange spike of jealousy, the grief at giving up the dream of finding an ideal mate. Always a fantasy anyway. "This isn't about what I want. It has to do with…well, magic and the way that it works. I've learned a great deal about wielding magic to help Bára, and will continue to learn more. One thing I'm certain of is that I cannot extend my abilities to assist Dru without the Destrye becoming my people, too. Through you."

At least she knew that much now, after spending hours every day studying the texts available only to priestesses in the temple. She loved her rooftop terrace, drying up as it was, even more for leaving it and returning in the cooling evenings.

"Why me?" Lonen asked. He was still watching her with unnerving intensity, that male vitality pricking at her. Though she'd deliberately closed the channel, sensual energy still leaked through, warming her, despite knowing he was thinking of his fiancée. "Arnon isn't married either."

Oria shook her head, partly to dispel disappointment that he was so eager to foist her off on his brother. Of course he would be, but it still wounded her pride. "You are the king. It might have been an easy ritual that made you so, but such responsibilities are binding on planes the Destrye might not perceive."

"But the Bárans do." He sounded accusing. Something darker ate at him, some profound tension.

"Some of us. I do. And the knowledge was hard-won." He wouldn't be able to understand what it had cost her. Even if they remained married the rest of their lives, he would never know her on a profound level the way an ideal husband would. She had to resign herself to that.

"I can't marry you, Oria." Desperation filled his voice, paining her. She hadn't intended to trap him, but the way he thrashed internally confirmed that she had done so. She'd thought—well, she'd hoped—that he wouldn't hate the idea of marrying her so much. They'd had something of a tentative friendship, but apparently not enough to make even a marriage-in-name-only to her palatable. She steeled herself to persuade him.

"You can't afford not to. I can't help you any other way."

"What about heirs? I can't have a queen who won't bear me children."

"What about your brother—can his children be your heirs?"

"Possibly," he admitted. "My older brother left two sons behind when he ascended to the Hall of Warriors. By Destrye law, the crown passes to my father's children first, before going to the next generation. But if I have no sons and Arnon persists in his refusal to be my heir, then Ion's sons would be next in line." He shrugged off the musings and focused on her with renewed intensity. The image broke through her still-clumsy screening, of her beneath him, naked and writhing, her husky voice gasping his name in pleasure. "But why couldn't we be husband and wife in truth?"

"Lonen." Inadvertently she echoed her fantasy self. She knotted her fingers together, face hot under the mask. "Because I simply can't. It's not possible for me."

He was quiet a moment. "I don't understand."

"I'm not surprised, but I'm asking you to trust that I'm telling you the truth. When I ask you not to touch me, it's not because I find you unwholesome. It has to do with who I am. Not who you are. But it's so much part of who I am that it won't change. No matter how long we're married, we will never lie together as husband and wife."

"You speak as if I've agreed to this wild plan."

"Neither of us has a choice in this. You, like me, are bound to act in the best interests of your people. You can't save the Destrye from the Trom without me, and I can't defend them unless I'm their queen."

"And you'd do this, simply to keep your promise."

"Yes. And because this will also make me Queen of Bára, which will let me protect my people here, too." She didn't tell him about Yar. Time enough to judiciously admit him to Báran secrets in the days ahead. Most of the politics wouldn't be his to deal with anyway, so no need for Lonen to know. He didn't say anything, however, the silence stretching out while dark emotions rolled in waves beneath the surface, like the lethal rip currents of the sea.

"I'm sorry," Oria said finally. "Perhaps I was wrong and marriage to me will break your heart, after all." She wished the words back, because she sounded entirely too sorry for herself.

"And you—are you giving up someone or would you have never married otherwise?" he asked, surprising her. The question took her emotional breath away. Impossible to explain to him what she'd be giving up—and also placing a burden of guilt on him he didn't deserve.

Proud of herself for sounding cool and remote, she told him, "You once pointed out that my life is a strange one, to live in this tower alone. I shall simply continue to do so."

"Because of this thing where you can't touch anyone."

"Yes." Better for him to believe that than to know the truth.

"All right then," he said abruptly, standing and scrubbing his palm on his pants, then sticking out a hand. "It's a bargain."

She stood also. Folded her hands together and tried to ignore the spike of hurt and annoyance from him that she refused his hand. "Agreed."

LONEN LEFT HER to go bathe, eat, and rest, and Oria finally cut the ribbons on her mask, welcoming the breezes that cooled her skin.

"*A fine time for you to ignore my advice,*" Chuffta said, but compassionately, without rancor.

"What else could I do?" Oria wiped the sweat from under her eyes, telling herself she couldn't possibly be weeping over the loss of a girlish dream. "I made a promise. And Bára owes the Destrye far more than the price of one woman's happiness."

"*Your mother won't be pleased.*"

"No." Oria dreaded breaking the news to her mother. There would never be a temple-blessed marriage for her, no babies to carry on the maternal line. Though if she could prevent a daughter of hers from facing the thing in the blue light… Even the memory made her a little ill. "But this marriage will put me one step closer to the throne, and that *will* make her happy. I need to arrange to see her and make the argument. Having her support with the temple and the council could make all the difference."

"*Was it worth it?*" Chuffta asked, the first time he'd mentioned her ordeal in the heart of Bára's magic.

"To be able to wield sgath, instead of being at the mercy of it? Maybe. But to have the potential to keep the Trom from consuming everyone and everything, then yes. Absolutely so."

"*You couldn't know Yar would send the Trom to Dru. That he'd even be able to, and so soon.*"

"But I might have predicted it and I missed it. Still, he also failed to predict me."

"*What do you mean, Oria?*" Chuffta's mind-voice bristled with suspicion.

"I won't have a temple-blessed marriage, but as queen I'll have full access to the temple knowledge—the information High Priestess Febe gave Yar to summon the Trom."

"*You can't mean to do the same.*" Chuffta's mind-voice held a panicked edge.

"I can and I will." Oria settled into the resolve. "How else can I control what they do, what Yar attempts? I must fight his Trom with mine."

Chuffta was quiet, his tail winding around her wrist. "*You know the danger in this. Without true* hwil *you'll be subject to corruption from those dark magics. It could be your undoing.*"

"But for the right reasons."

"*I'm not sure that matters.*"

"I understand if this breaks our contract," she managed, no longer fighting the tears. "I'll release you if you feel you can't be part of this."

She felt his slight hesitation as he considered. But then he replied.

"You're not alone. I'm always with you."

"Thank you. That means more than I can say."

She would need all of Chuffta's support in the days ahead—and his company. Something told her that taking the Destrye as a husband would create as many problems as it would solve. It seemed impossible that she should feel lonelier than ever.

As the dry desert wind dried the tears on her cheeks to salt, she turned her thoughts away from the sand trap of self pity.

She had more important things to think about.

Thank you for reading! I hope you loved meeting Oria and Lonen—and Chuffta! The next book in the Sorcerous Moons series is *Oria's Gambit*. Find out how Lonen and Oria consummate their desperate bargain, and how Oria wrestles the dark magic threatening to consume her…

"This series is like crack. It has everything. Complex magic, political skullduggery, epic battle sequences, horrible monsters and a love story that looks like it is going to be one for the ages."

~ReadingReality

I appreciate your help in spreading the word about my books, including telling a friend or leaving a review. Reviews help readers find books! I'd love it if you'd leave a review on your favorite site.

SIGN UP FOR JEFFE KENNEDY'S NEWSLETTER for fun giveaways from Jeffe and other authors.
landing.mailerlite.com/webforms/landing/r2y4b9

Turn the page for a short excerpt from Oria's Gambit.

~ 1 ~

THE GOLEM'S GLASSY claws flashed, arcing through the rosy light of the moon, and sliced open his throat. Blood poured down his naked body, steaming in the chill desert air. Out it flowed, sweeping around him like the bore tides of Bára. So much of it pooled around him that he began to drown in it. He strained to lift his battle axe, to cut the golem down with cold iron, but found a flower in his hands instead.

A white lily, luminescent and fragile, somehow escaping the blood that drained his life away.

The golem struck again and he shouted at it, no sound escaping. Because he had no throat left. Because he was dead.

How could he still be standing?

The golem's claws dripped crimson and its black maw yawned, glistening with glasslike fangs. It wouldn't ever die, forever coming after the Destrye until every last one of his people were dead, unless he managed to cut it down. Out of its mouth, sickly green fire blew, a lethal wind of flame that burned the crops and aqueducts. Not a golem then, but one of the Trom. Skin over bones, a humanoid spider, it grinned, lips red as the claws, hand reaching to turn him into skin without bones, nothing but pulped flesh. No, they were fingernails, enameled and jeweled. Natly's elegant hands slicing across his throat again, lips curving in a lascivious smile. With that third swipe, his head tumbled to the ground, and as she reached for his cock with those scarlet daggers of her nails, he finally managed to shout his anguish and fury.

"Your Highness?"

Lonen jerked in the hot water, the nightmare shredding around him with the spray of droplets. The servant boy gave him a wide-eyed look. Bero. The Báran lad had attended him his last time at baths, too. He was in Bára, again, cleaning up after the journey. No Trom or golems here.

Except in his tortured brain.

"Did you need something, Your Highness? You called out, but I didn't understand the words." Bero carried a stack of the much lighter colorful clothes that men of Bára wore. *Silk*, Oria had called the fabric, another thing apparently made by insects. Despite its disturbing origins, and like the addictive and tangy sweet honey she'd also introduced him to, the cloth had an exotic loveliness, more refined than anything produced in his homeland.

Like the sorceress herself, both unsettling and compelling.

"No, I'm fine." He cupped his hands and splashed water on his face. Sloppy of him, to have fallen asleep in the city of his enemy—and then failing to awaken at Bero's footfalls as he approached. Too comfortable in the soothing waters. Too many months of short sleep. Ion would have slapped him upside the head hard enough to have his brain ringing for the carelessness. But his brother was dead and gone these many weeks, reduced to boneless pulp at the simple touch of the Trom's evil hand.

"Would you care for wine or food now, King Lonen?" Bero asked in the trade tongue, setting out the soaps and oils. "Princess Oria said you're to have anything you ask for."

Luxurious baths, booze, and fine food—an excellent strategy to lull him into meekly doing the sorceress's bidding. The nightmare had served as a timely reminder of his purpose here—to save his people from destruction, not to indulge in Oria's gifts or seductive presence. He might have agreed to her startling proposal of marriage, but he'd proceed on his terms, not hers. For the sake of the Destrye and his sanity both.

"What are the chances of a decent steak?"

FANTASY ROMANCES

BONDS OF MAGIC
Dark Wizard
Bright Familiar
Grey Magic
Familiar Winter Magic (In Fire of the Frost)

HEIRS OF MAGIC
The Long Night of the Crystalline Moon
(also available in *Under a Winter Sky*)
The Golden Gryphon and the Bear Prince
The Sorceress Queen and the Pirate Rogue
The Dragon's Daughter and the Winter Mage
The Storm Princess and the Raven King (May 2022)

THE FORGOTTEN EMPIRES
The Orchid Throne
The Fiery Crown
The Promised Queen

THE TWELVE KINGDOMS
Negotiation

The Mark of the Tala
The Tears of the Rose
The Talon of the Hawk
Heart's Blood
The Crown of the Queen

THE UNCHARTED REALMS
The Pages of the Mind
The Edge of the Blade
The Snows of Windroven
The Shift of the Tide
The Arrows of the Heart
The Dragons of Summer
The Fate of the Tala
The Lost Princess Returns

THE CHRONICLES OF DASNARIA
Prisoner of the Crown
Exile of the Seas
Warrior of the World

SORCEROUS MOONS
Lonen's War
Oria's Gambit
The Tides of Bára
The Forests of Dru
Oria's Enchantment
Lonen's Reign

A COVENANT OF THORNS
Rogue's Pawn
Rogue's Possession
Rogue's Paradise

<u>**CONTEMPORARY ROMANCES**</u>

Shooting Star

MISSED CONNECTIONS
Last Dance
With a Prince
Since Last Christmas

<u>**CONTEMPORARY EROTIC ROMANCES**</u>

Exact Warm Unholy
The Devil's Doorbell

FACETS OF PASSION
Sapphire
Platinum
Ruby
Five Golden Rings

FALLING UNDER
Going Under
Under His Touch
Under Contract

<u>**EROTIC PARANORMAL**</u>

MASTER OF THE OPERA E-SERIAL
Master of the Opera, Act 1: Passionate Overture
Master of the Opera, Act 2: Ghost Aria
Master of the Opera, Act 3: Phantom Serenade
Master of the Opera, Act 4: Dark Interlude
Master of the Opera, Act 5: A Haunting Duet
Master of the Opera, Act 6: Crescendo
Master of the Opera

BLOOD CURRENCY
Blood Currency

<u>BDSM FAIRYTALE ROMANCE</u>
Petals and Thorns

Thank you for reading!

About Jeffe Kennedy

Jeffe Kennedy is a multi-award-winning and best-selling author of romantic fantasy. She is the current President of the Science Fiction and Fantasy Writers of America (SFWA) and is a member of Romance Writers of America (RWA), and Novelists, Inc. (NINC). She is best known for her RITA® Award-winning novel, *The Pages of the Mind*, the recent trilogy, *The Forgotten Empires*, and the wildly popular, *Dark Wizard*. Jeffe lives in Santa Fe, New Mexico.

Jeffe can be found online at her website: JeffeKennedy.com, on her podcast First Cup of Coffee, every Sunday at the popular SFF Seven blog, on Facebook, on Goodreads, on BookBub, and pretty much constantly on Twitter @jeffekennedy. She is represented by Sarah Younger of Nancy Yost Literary Agency.

jeffekennedy.com
facebook.com/Author.Jeffe.Kennedy
twitter.com/jeffekennedy
goodreads.com/author/show/1014374.Jeffe_Kennedy
bookbub.com/profile/jeffe-kennedy

Sign up for her newsletter here.
jeffekennedy.com/sign-up-for-my-newsletter